ABOUT THE AUTHOR

When Chris Behrsin isn't out exploring the world, he's behind a keyboard writing tales of dragons and magical lands. Born into the genre through a steady diet of Terry Pratchett, his fiction fuses a love for fantasy and whimsical plots with philosophy and voyages into the worlds of dreams.

You can learn more about his fiction and download two free books at his website, chrisbehrsin.com.

facebook.com/chrisbehrsin

x.com/chrisbehrsin

goodreads.com/cbehrsin

bookbub.com/authors/chris-behrsin

BOOKS BY CHRIS BEHRSIN

DRAGONCAT SERIES

A Cat's Guide to Bonding with Dragons

A Cat's Guide to Meddling with Magic

A Cat's Guide to Saving the Kingdom

A Cat's Guide to Questing for Treasure

A Cat's Guide to Travelling through Portals

A Cat's Guide to Vanquishing Evil

A Cat's Guide to Dreaming of Fairies

A Cat's Guide to Dealing with Destiny

A Cat's Guide to Preventing Oblivion

A Cat's Guide to Serving a Warlock (Prequel Novella)

SECICAO BLIGHT SERIES

Sukina's Story (Prequel Novel)

Dragonseer

Dragonseers and Bloodlines

Dragonseers and Automatons

Dragonseers and Evolution

Dragonseers and Immortality

More works available at: https://chrisbehrsin.com

DRAGONSEERS AND IMMORTALITY

SECICAO BLIGHT BOOK FIVE

CHRIS BEHRSIN

Cover Design Layout by Chris Behrsin
Copyediting by Tarryn Thomas

ISBN: 978-1-915886-33-0 (paperback)
ISBN: 978-1-915886-42-2 (hardcover)
ISBN: 978-1-915886-28-6 (e-book)

Published by Worldwalkers Publishing

To dragons, in every size and form

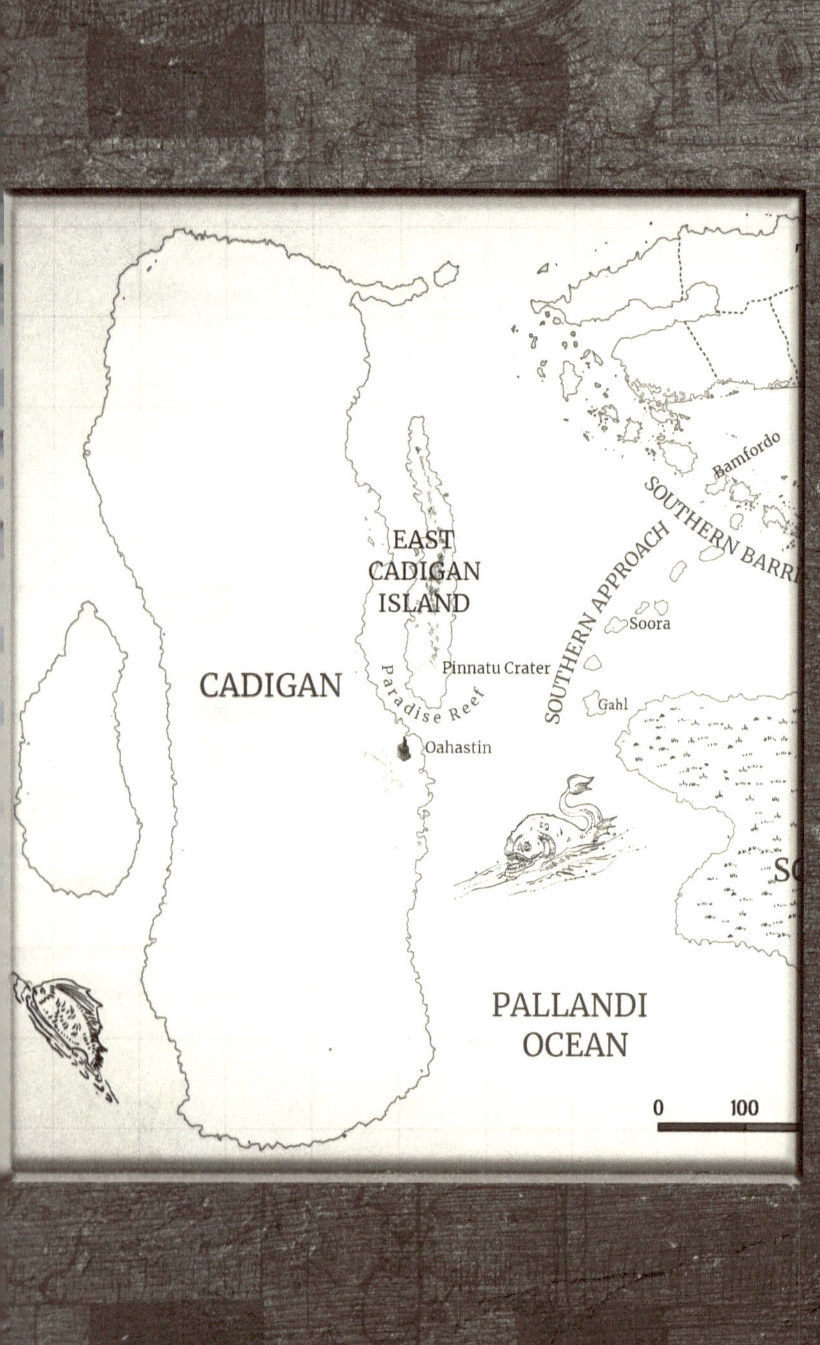

EAST
CADIGAN
ISLAND
CADIGAN
Paradise Reef
Pinnatu Crater
Oahastin
Bamfordo
SOUTHERN APPROACH
SOUTHERN BARRI
Soora
Gahl
S
PALLANDI
OCEAN
0   100

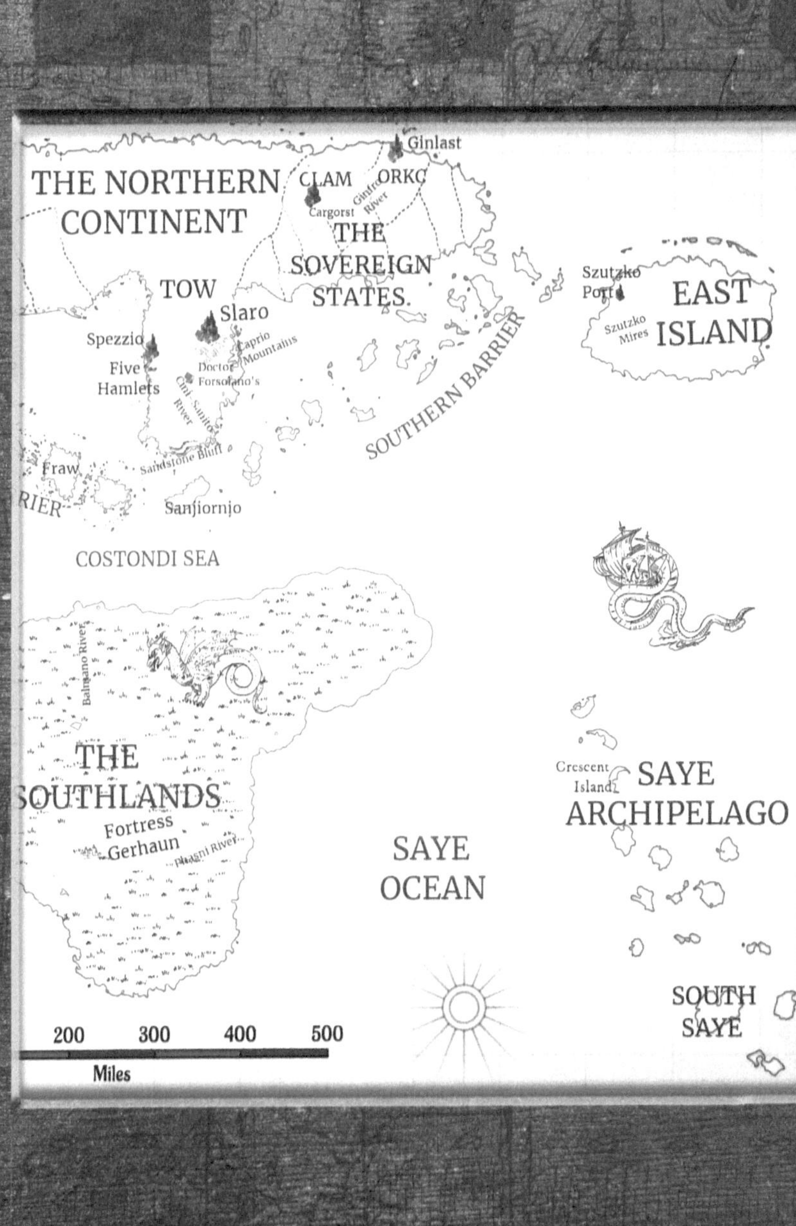

THE NORTHERN CONTINENT
Ginlast
CLAM
ORKO
Cargorst
Ginfro River
THE SOVEREIGN STATES.
TOW
Slaro
Spezzio
Caprio Mountains
Five Hamlets
Doctor Forsolano's
Cini Santo River
SOUTHERN BARRIER
Szutzko Port
Szutzko Mires
EAST ISLAND
Fraw
Sandstone Bluff
RIER
Sanjiornjo
COSTONDI SEA
Balmano River
THE SOUTHLANDS
Fortress Gerhaun
Phasni River
Crescent Island
SAYE ARCHIPELAGO
SAYE OCEAN
SOUTH SAYE
200   300   400   500
Miles

PART I

It's an immutable law of the universe that those who face seemingly persistent darkness, through perseverance, will eventually find light.

– Yol Corinas, Dragon Queen

Secicao stretched out over the landscape below.

Brown toxic clouds from the virulent plant smothered the plains and sucked all freshness out of the air, while the plants leached essential nutrients out of the soil. From expanse to expanse, the thorny branches stained the earth.

To the east, flying black shapes cut faint swathes through the secicao clouds. To the ignorant, these might have looked like birds flocking towards a distant plane. But I knew them for what they really were – black dragons. Once human, until the goddess Finesia stole their lives away and transformed them in both shape and will.

We had all thought Finesia to be a myth, but she now lived out east, behind a wall of her black dragon protectors. She inhabited a land we had known as the Sovereign States, which had once harboured life.

That had always been the ultimate goal of secicao – to suffocate all life out of our world until nothing remained except the creatures that served its mistress.

Now it had achieved that goal, and our planet was almost dead.

I took a breath, inhaling some of the fresh, cold mountain

air. A mass of my blonde curly hair, that I'd not cut for months, kept my head warm. Still, the chill settled in under my scarf, cutting to the nape of my neck and carrying upon it a scent of the secicao oil that ironically powered the automatons which bore supplies up from Slaro far below us.

The Masked Regent Valpeonia, my biological mother and our temporary monarch, had ordered our country of Tow to move to the plateaus and valleys high up in the mountains. The secicao plants at least couldn't reach up here, nor it seemed could their clouds of sulphuric, toxic vapours. Mind you, nothing else could grow up here either, in amongst the glacial snowfalls and craggy limestone. We were simply too high up.

"Pontopa," there came a deep voice behind me. "Auntie Pontopa, Hastina's been looking for you."

I turned to see a teenage boy loping up the slope towards me, his ash blonde hair waving slightly in the breeze. Taka Gordoni's mop had once been sandier, but now it was getting darker – more like his mother's. The hardened edges of his face certainly made him look like her.

But Sukina had been short, and he was a good couple of heads taller than me. Dragonheats, he'd even outgrown his father.

Taka had been born a girl, but he'd had his gender changed at a very young age by experimentation in Slaro palace, where he'd been raised. That made him the only male dragonseer who had ever lived.

Taka strode up to me. "Auntie Pontopa, Hastina says it's urgent. There's some sort of commotion down in the village square and she says she can't handle it on her own."

I raised an eyebrow; Hastina had never been one for diplomacy.

"Is your father involved?" I asked him.

He nodded, giving me a sheepish grin. I didn't ask if the problem had been caused by his father – I just assumed it had. Taka Gordoni was fifteen now, which made me twenty-eight, but I felt as if I had aged a lot more. It had been a good seven years since that terrible night in the palace when Taka's mother, Sukina, had died.

How things had changed since then – in spite of Sukina's sacrifice, I had thought we could still win the war against the secicao and Finesia. But now it felt as if humanity was hanging on by its last threads. We might die fighting, but at the end of the day we would all still die.

"Fine," I said. "I'll be right down."

I turned once more to look out over the landscape, trying to remember how the country I'd grown up in had looked. But that too had been destroyed by secicao, replaced by this cold reality.

I took one last deep breath and followed Taka down towards the campsite on the plateau below, from where green secicao smoke rose to meet us. Though it had destroyed our planet, we still couldn't stop using it. Honestly, we didn't have any other choice.

THE AUTOMATONS FORMED a train that led down the mountain from the campsite towards the city of Slaro below. Before the recent catastrophes that had overturned our civilisation, it would have been impossible to see Slaro from high up in the Caprio Mountains. It used to be covered by a perpetual blanket of smog – at first choked with coal, and later secicao residue.

My biological mother and the protector of this country, the Regent Valpeonia, had ordered the pollution to be cleaned up, reasoning that we needed to be able to see everything that took place in Slaro from strategic points in the Caprio Mountains. Now, those who chose to live in the city consumed less and were less cozy in their apartments – but then, everyone knew we had to conserve resources in these trying times.

I passed Velos and Bellroot on the way down to the city

square, snugly housed in their stables. We'd set up a complex large enough to contain twenty dragons just south of the village, and this allowed troops and dragonseers to get up and down to and from the city very quickly. It was a set of twenty tin-roofed structures, with archways at the front through which the dragons could pass in and out freely.

Velos turned his blue scaly head over towards us as we passed. When he saw me, he loped over and pushed out his muzzle, crooning. I stopped a moment to reach up and stroke his chin.

He still wore his shiny brass armour, the Gatling guns mounted on it facing down for safety reasons. It had all been created by Faso. At the time, I'd hated the inventor for it, yet it had saved my and Velos' life many times. The citrine dragon, Bellroot, wore armour of a similar design. Velos was my dragon, and I'd grown up with him since his birth. Bellroot was Hastina's, and she often said he was bright as a sun – a hyperbole of course.

Atop both dragons' armour were three neat brass seats, though still I missed the old days when I used to fly on Velos bareback. The rest of the armour was a mess of cogs, gears, and wires welded to the metal. Veins running beneath the surface of the plate pumped the secicao oil from soft tanks at the back to the contraption, feeding the mechanisms inside. When the armour was active, the veins glowed green.

Our resident inventor, Faso Gordoni, had also stationed his dragon automaton in the stables, next to Bellroot. Faso was Taka's father, a genius who was both brilliant and frustratingly arrogant. He and his wife, Asinal Winda, had masterminded the dragon automaton and many of the others of its kind that we fought alongside these days.

Faso often modelled his designs on living creatures, with the view that nature had evolved brilliant creations that science could copy outright. Hence he'd created this hulking mechanical beast, with sharp teeth and masses of guns. His dragon automaton had come to our rescue numerous times when we were on the brink of defeat in battle.

Faso had programmed the great brass beast to stay always awake, and always on guard. I guess we'd all grown used to having it living amongst us, although it could never replace a real dragon. Both Velos and Bellroot were unique in their own special way.

The warm breath rushing out of Velos' nostrils washed over me as he pushed his head further forwards. That's the thing about dragons – the dragonfire that constantly burns within their bellies permanently keeps them warm. As long as they eat enough secicao to fuel that fire, that is. Our world was full of ironies ...

"Sorry, can't stay," I said to him in my mind. *"But I'll take you out for a flight later. I promise."*

Velos grunted, as if to say he'd rather stay here. Honestly, I understood – since the world had fallen into ugliness, flying had lost much of its appeal.

I knew I'd have to go down to Slaro later anyway. Even though I felt Hastina and I should be busy fighting our enemies, we instead spent our days managing the migration of the country's population up into the mountains.

Velos scampered back towards his stable as Taka and I carried on down the path and pushed our way past the wheeled automatons designed to carry supplies. They were converted war automatons, faintly humanoid with faceplates over their heads, but their guns had been replaced by powerful cranes. Their destination was another village a little further into the range; Valpeonia's goal was to turn every available plateau above two thousand metres into a human habitation.

I trailed after Taka, intending to discover what the commotion down on the plateau was all about.

WE'D NAMED the village *Meltwater*, because it was situated in a basin housing a lake, albeit currently without much water in it. It stayed that way for around nine months of the year – and then the snow melted, replenishing it for those remaining few months.

Faso had promised everyone forced to live here that he could divert the rush of water in time through a complex network of dams and aqueducts. The problem with Faso was that he wasn't especially convincing while he was making promises, even though he usually lived up to them.

The path led around a mountain peak before we came to the village square. This time it seemed Faso and Hastina were working together – although not very effectively. A mob of around twenty villagers faced off against them, an elderly woman at the front acting as impromptu chairperson.

Faso wore his pinstripe suit, looking as neatly turned out as the day I'd first met him. He was pretty much the only person nowadays who still thought it necessary to keep up appearances.

Hastina's wavy red hair ballooned in the breeze. I caught the glint of the sun off her prosthetic leg as I scrambled down the mountainside. She'd lost her real one to wolves a long time ago in Oahastin; it seems she hadn't been such an aggressive character before that, but the pain had since fuelled her internal rage. If Finesia hadn't 'gifted' her with the ability to transform into a black dragon, thus making her nearly immortal, she wouldn't have survived the attack.

Soon I was standing between Faso and Hastina. Taka kept his distance behind us, clearly not wanting to get involved in this conflict. Another invention of Faso's was his ferret automaton, Ratter, which sat perched upon his shoulder, its beady red eyes glaring at the old woman.

The elderly speaker now turned her angry gaze upon me. "Dragonseer Wells, would you please knock some sense into your two comrades?"

I turned to Faso, who shrugged, then to Hastina who had

her jaw clenched as tightly as the hand she had gripped around her spear.

"If Mr Gordoni tells you that this basin can't accommodate any children, then you should believe him," Hastina said.

"So why can't we all just move somewhere else?" the old woman asked, displaying teeth stained yellow from a lifetime of drinking secicao.

"Because," Faso said through gritted teeth, "the other settlements have already been established."

The speaker looked at the crowd gathered around her. She placed her hands on her hips and laughed from deep in her belly.

"The other settlements are already established, he says. We need to address the needs of our parents." She looked back at the children in the crowd.

"You should be grateful that you have air to breathe," Hastina snapped. "Provided by a dragon queen who is hanging on to her last threads of power to protect you."

"You see, that's the thing," the elderly woman said. "The other cities have young dragon queens who will supposedly last thousands of years. What's to happen when the old dragon dies, I ask you?"

"I've created something," Faso said, looking down his nose at the speaker. "A device that can power a bubble of the collective unconscious. You know, for years we've not understood how to do it, but it's all just science at the end of the day."

I turned to Faso and raised my eyebrows. This was the first I'd heard of it, and by the expression on Hastina's face it clearly wasn't something she'd known about either.

"And does it work?" the elderly woman said in a slightly higher pitch.

"Well, for now it's just a prototype. But we hope to have it up and running in the next couple of months."

The speaker looked around again and cackled out a laugh. "A prototype! A prototype – we're moving our livelihoods, being separated from our children and grandchildren, and the only guarantee we'll have that we'll be safe is a prototype."

I wanted to defend Faso, but a flash of light caught my attention in the corner of my eye. It had come from the sharply angled towers of Slaro Palace. I squinted at it, as the realisation registered.

"Pontopa?" Faso asked.

But his voice seemed distant as I watched the horror unfold. The explosion blossomed in the valley below, looking like a tiny flower from up here, but that didn't matter. My parents – both the two adoptive parents who had raised me and my biological mother – were stationed down there.

As if a part of me was down there in the centre of it, I could almost feel the heat pricking at my skin. I could hear the dismay in the silence of everyone's voices as they turned their heads. Five dark shapes rose up from the enveloping smoke – black dragons.

I clenched my fist tightly, anger surging in my chest. My jaw had dropped in shock.

"Winda," Faso muttered.

"We need to get to Slaro at once," I said.

But I hadn't even needed to say it, because black smoke was already enshrouding Hastina. The air shimmered, and out of the smoke arose a massive black dragon.

The ground shook as, in her dragon form, Hastina shot up into the sky.

2

THE WIND ROARED OVER VELOS' armour and boxed at my ears. It whipped back my hair and stung my eyes as we hurtled down towards Slaro. It bit through me to the bone, my trench coat doing little to block its passage. Still, the warmth coming from my seat on Velos' armoured back at least stopped my blood from freezing.

Meanwhile, I tried to block out my fears of what might have happened to my parents. All I could remember was the time the late King Cini III had ordered his automatons to scorch my parents' vineyard, and for a while everyone had presumed them dead. If something had happened to them, I didn't think I could survive it.

It felt selfish in a way. The world had taken such a beating, but my parents ... I just couldn't lose anyone else.

Sukina's voice came unbidden to my mind: *"Let your worries drift by, and focus only on what you can control."*

I sighed; I didn't know if she was really there in the collective unconscious or just a figment of my imagination. But either way, she always seemed to be there for me, watching from beyond the grave, keeping me safe from own my thoughts.

Velos flew at the centre of our small formation, while Taka

had taken Bellroot to our left and Faso flew on his dragon automaton to our right. Together, we followed Hastina in her black dragon form, as she rushed towards the other black dragons. She still had the ability to transform into one of these nearly invulnerable beasts, a gift that Finesia had stripped away from Taka and me when she and Alsie Fioreletta had abandoned us beneath the Tree Immortal, following her rebirth.

Ahead, an army of grey dragons – more colloquially known as 'greys' – launched out of the stables that had been built over the purposely demolished ruins of Slaro's industrial Northern Quarter. Their roars rumbled across the sky, like distant thunder rolling closer.

Another black dragon launched out of Slaro Palace. I didn't need to see it up close to know it was Valpeonia, my biological mother. Bile rose in my throat.

"*Keep on target,*" Hastina said in the collective unconscious in my mind. "*Remember that you don't have your abilities anymore, so don't get cocky.*"

She had opened up the channel for both Taka and me, but I didn't know who she'd been addressing with that comment.

"*We still have the dragon armour,*" Taka replied in the channel.

"*Dragon armour won't protect you from black dragons,*" Hastina said.

I knew what she meant, yet what she'd said wasn't completely accurate. Black dragons were impervious to damage except for one vulnerability – their unprotected throat.

"*Father tells me that he's modified the Gatlings on the dragon armour to have superior accuracy,*" Taka said. "*He spoke of some sort of special tracking system.*"

"*It isn't worth the risk, Taka Gordoni. Remember who your commander is. Keep your distance, provide covering fire, and do exactly what I say.*"

Admittedly, I had to agree with Hastina that Taka shouldn't risk his life – he was after all the rightful heir to the throne. But that didn't mean Velos and I would willingly miss out on the action. There came another voice, this time not in our heads, but from the speaker system installed on Velos' armour.

"I didn't see the 'either of you' augment," Faso said. "And I have developed new blends especially to protect you."

He flew past on his dragon automaton, wearing his special brass helmet that showed him what the automaton saw through a bulletproof glass visor at the front. Admittedly, Taka and I weren't wearing the helmets Faso had developed for us; we both preferred to see through our own eyes, rather than those of a machine.

I reached down for my hip flask. It contained secicao oil, with enough punch in it to make me able to slow time, see in the dark, and act with remarkable precision. Without the powers of a black dragon, I now had to rely on the stuff again.

"We should augment when we get closer," I said. "When we know we might need it."

"Dragonheats, I'm not going to listen to this," Faso said. "Augment, for wellies' sake."

I screwed up my eyes. He was right; I couldn't let fear get in my way.

Just as I started to lift the hip flask to my lips, Hastina collided with another, enemy black dragon. She wrapped her forelegs and tail around her assailant, and together they tumbled to the ground.

From the direction of the palace, Valpeonia cut through the sky towards another of our opponents. As the enemy turned, she opened her maw and her lips wrapped around the black dragon's throat. The enemy dragon went limp; Valpeonia opened her mouth and the other beast fell towards the ground. At the same time, Hastina released her quarry from her grasp, also letting it drop.

Both my biological mother and Hastina were stronger than they'd ever been. Seeing their immense power sent a shiver down my spine, because I knew that it came at a cost. They had borrowed it from Finesia, and she would enter their minds to try and take it back. If the goddess caught either of them off guard then that would be the end of it, and they would lose their souls.

Alas, I'd been so enthralled watching my birth mother and Hastina in battle, that I'd failed to see how we'd closed the gap separating us from the other black dragons.

They were charging headlong towards us. The greys coming from Slaro were chasing them, but they couldn't match the black dragons' speed. Valpeonia and Hastina also were moving towards them but weren't going anywhere near fast enough. Faso, Taka, and I would have to fight them alone.

"I said augment!" Faso shouted over the speaker system. "They're coming our way."

"*I wish we could still turn into black dragons,*" Taka said in the collective unconscious.

"*Trust me, so do I,*" I said, and raised my hip flask the rest of the way to my lips.

The liquid first cooled then warmed as it trickled down my throat.

Immediately, my vision ghosted into speckled green, and I saw the white outlines of anything that was warmer than its surroundings. Time slowed right down, and my sense of hearing became so attuned that I could hear heartbeats from yards away. My mind also calmed and I gained an intense ability to focus.

The three enemy black dragons were even closer now. The two on either side of their formation had their jaws wide open and their long talons extended, ready to strike. The one at the centre was much larger than the other two, and recognition dawned on me. An image that had been imprinted on my neural circuits that would stay there until my death.

Alsie Fioreletta. Her raven hair. Her wicked grin. Her incredibly graceful form. She was Finesia's right hand and my nemesis – and she was here, except she wasn't in human but in dragon form.

"Still, you recognise me," she said in the collective unconscious, her voice as sharp as a newly forged sword.

"Why are you here, Alsie?" I asked.

"To finish my task, of course. You were meant to die at the Tree Immortal – you and the boy."

"Then we shall have the pleasure of seeing you die today instead."

Alsie's jaws opened, and a peal of high-pitched laughter echoed through the collective unconscious. This soon developed into a wailing scream, as powerful as the legendary banshee's. It only worked in the collective unconscious, but it was strong enough to disrupt any of a dragonseer's abilities.

A sharp spike of pain stabbed into the centre of my forehead. In less than a second, it spread throughout the rest of my skull. Nausea rushed from my stomach to the base of my throat. I clutched my hands to my temples.

Then through blurry eyes I saw Alsie charge.

I only saw her coming because of my slowed sense of time and the increased acuity granted by the secicao. I ducked to the right just as Velos – his abilities also honed by the secicao pumping through his armour – entered a fast dive.

"Auntie Pontopa!" Taka screamed from behind me.

Gravity rushed up at me. Velos' armour rumbled under my thighs as its Gatling guns turned towards Alsie and ejected their bullets.

I turned my head. Bellroot and Taka had dived away from another black dragon, who was in close pursuit. Faso had managed to find the time to turn the dragon automaton side on, and bullets sputtered out of the side-mounted Gatling guns, their shells falling towards the cobblestones below.

I followed the trail of a bullet in slow motion as it travelled right into the third black dragon's throat.

"It worked," Faso screamed. "My VPTT works!"

"VPTT?" I asked.

"Vulnerable Point Tracking Technology," he said. "Remember that."

Bellroot had already turned, and he used the momentum to sweep upwards and behind the dragon automaton, which turned its Gatling guns upon the pursuing black dragon.

Taka screamed and jerked Bellroot to a halt just as the dragon automaton released its mechanical fury on the second black dragon. My senses homed onto the one bullet that I knew was heading straight towards the black dragon's throat.

Its roar became a weak hissing sound and it plummeted towards the city below.

I turned to see Alsie, her wings outstretched, her form blocking the sunlight. She hovered there, assessing us. She was keeping her distance – wisely, knowing the danger. But her green eyes were focused precisely on me.

"You cannot possibly hope to storm the palace by yourself," I said to her.

"I merely needed to confirm that the rumours are true. Somehow, it seems, you have survived being left for dead beneath the Tree Immortal. But now, Dragonseer Wells, your days are numbered. You and the boy must die, and then the world will finally be ours."

She turned and sped off in the other direction, soon vanishing beneath the curve of the horizon. None of us dared follow; too many times we'd been lured into chasing a black dragon only to find a larger ambush lying in wait. But still, Alsie Fioreletta's warning had set my heart pounding.

She was Finesia's right hand, and had remained utterly loyal to her – ever since I had known her, at least. Since Finesia's rebirth, her forces had largely left us alone, although that hadn't stopped secicao spreading across the Northern Continent and enveloping every single inch of the land save the iciest plains to the north.

Thing is, I didn't quite believe that Alsie had only now emerged to confirm the rumours of my and Taka's survival.

She'd been scouting the terrain, calculating the best path for an attack. Which meant that Finesia was preparing to strike.

And when she did, I honestly didn't think we could win.

I swallowed my fears, once again trying to focus on Sukina's words.

"*Come on, Taka,*" I said. "*Let's get inside.*"

I pushed down on Velos' steering fin to lower him towards the palace, and Taka followed us.

"*What was that all about?*" he asked.

"*I don't know,*" I said, but I would do whatever it took to find out. I had vouched to Sukina a long time ago that I would protect Taka, and I was never going to break that promise, even if it meant sacrificing my own life.

BOTH HASTINA AND I – along with Taka and in some respects Valpeonia – were dragonseers, with the ability to sing songs that all dragons understood.

We had other special talents that came with the job as well. For one, we could talk telepathically through a medium known as the collective unconscious, which allowed us to communicate with true dragons, and command legions of them in battle. But we could only speak using language to the several remaining massive golden-scaled dragon queens, who had relocated to our country of Tow in order to protect the people.

The queens had such a strong connection to the collective unconscious that they had become a source of it; and the force they generated repelled secicao, meaning a massive protective bubble surrounded each dragon queen over a sizeable area. This pushed the secicao clouds away, creating an environment in which humans could breathe normal air.

The aging dragon queen Cralanein lived under Slaro Palace, and it was she who kept the air in the city clean. She'd been unable to use her powers during Cini II's and his son Cini III's reigns, since the kings had drained her of her silver blood in order to create a drug called Exalmpora. This had allowed them to subjugate dragonseers like Alsie Fioreletta, turning them over to their side, leading to the birth of the black dragons and ultimately causing Finesia's rebirth.

Now their rule had been overthrown, Cralanein's blood flowed as normal through her veins, enabling her to generate the protective bubble again. This had made the city of Slaro one of the remaining safe places left in the country, as the air outside of the bubble had been so filled with the noxious secicao gas that it had made it unbreathable.

Yet our capital was overpopulated, and we all knew Cralanein didn't have much life left in her, hence our contingency plan up in the Caprio Mountains.

A thick blanket of dust hung in the air above the courtyard of Slaro Palace when we touched down, and the ground was strewn with rubble. The sky held a bleakness that reminded me of how Slaro used to look, back when it was covered with smog. My eyes stung and the chill hung upon me like a blanket.

The angular towers of the palace loomed up above us through the shroud of dust. The building's original architect had constructed the place to look like a clock, to communicate the value of each second spent working towards industry. Now the towers just seemed to remind us of how little time we had left.

Velos lowered himself to the ground, allowing me to scramble off the side of the armour and onto the polished cobblestones. Taka was already on the jumbled earth; he stood between Valpeonia and Hastina, who had now transformed back into their human forms.

I'd inherited my blonde curly hair from my biological mother, Valpeonia. She looked at me with her cold blue eyes, then nodded – her way of telling me she was glad I was safe. She wore the same black outfit and cloak she had worn as the

Masked Regent, but not the dragon-shaped vizard that had given her the title.

Before she'd revealed her identity to me in the last year, I'd thought she'd been killed during the late King Cini II's brutal regime, known as the Dragonheats.

"Pontopa—" A voice came from behind me, the most familiar in the world.

I turned to see the woman I considered my mother, Versalina Wells, running towards me. I knew her as Mamo. She was partly my biological mother as well, for during the Dragonheats, Valpeonia had turned up nearly dead at my parents' doorstep, pregnant with me, and I never would have been born if the venerable Doctor Forsolano hadn't transplanted me into the womb of the woman I would eventually call Mamo.

Inside that womb, as the story went, I had gestated while Valpeonia had almost died. But I'd recently discovered that my biological mother had already started the transformation into a dragonwoman, and it was that which had saved her life. She was one of the few black dragons who had managed to resist being mentally reprogrammed to become a servant of Finesia – and Hastina was another.

Before I knew it, Mamo's arms were wrapping around me in a warm, tight hug.

"Wellies, I know you have to do it, but every time I see you fighting up there, I think it's going to be your last."

I pulled back a little and looked at her. She had straight strawberry blonde hair, and her freckled cheeks glistened, wet from tears.

"I've survived a lot worse than that, Mamo," I said.

"But they were black dragons," Mamo said, shaking her head. "Why attack here after so many months of silence, and why so few?"

"I don't know, but Alsie was there." I hesitated – I wanted to tell her about Alsie's death threat, but I knew it would only worry her more.

"We're just glad that you're with us," my father Cipao said, hovering nearby. He limped forward, hobbling from an injury he'd gained in his days as a jockey. "I know we haven't got many days left ahead of us, at least according to the *Observer*. Still, we need to make our last days special ..."

I stared at Papo in disbelief. He had a magazine in his hand, fresh off the press I suppose, and he'd probably just read those words. Valpeonia had reinstated the magazine just a couple of months ago. The *Tow Observer* had been Papo's favourite publication for a long time.

He'd even managed to acquire copies during our stay in the Southlands. There we'd stayed in Fortress Gerhaun, under a bubble of the collective unconscious generated by its late dragon queen, Gerhaun Forsi. Just like the one in Slaro, her bubble had pushed away the noxious secicao clouds and allowed anyone inside to breathe the fresh air.

Now we were back here in my home country of Tow, where it all had all started, but alas, this place had certainly changed.

Papo ran his hand through his greying hair and smiled, displaying the hard lines on his face. Mamo broke the embrace and allowed me to give him a hug in turn.

I buried my head in his shoulder. I didn't cry – I hadn't for a long time. But I felt myself shaking as the emotions surged out of me, buried under years of torment. My father's embrace held that kind of power.

"I know it's hard," Papo said. "But your mother and I, we're so proud of what you've become."

"Thank you," I said, breaking the hug and turning to Valpeonia. "But the fight isn't over yet."

"It says in the *Tow Observer* that ..."

"I don't care what the *Tow Observer* says," I snapped. Then, as Papo's eyebrows shot up, "I'm sorry. Please, if you'll excuse me."

I walked back over to the others, Alsie's threat echoing in my mind. *You and the boy must die, and then the world will finally be ours.*

Regent Valpeonia cocked her head as I approached. She wore the same black attire that she used to when she had been the Masked Regent, but with the addition of a red silk scarf wrapped around her neck like a stole.

"I think they're planning something," I said. "A mass scale assault – and Taka and I, we're in danger."

Valpeonia nodded slowly. "Taka told me ... he said that was Alsie Fioreletta up there. I didn't get close enough to recognise her."

I glanced up at Taka. "Did Alsie tell you anything?"

He shook his head.

I turned back to Valpeonia. "She told me that our days are numbered – that she must first destroy Taka and me, and then she will destroy everyone else."

Valpeonia's face fell. "But why would she go after you like that? Finesia's not fickle enough to seek revenge. And no offense, but she sucked your powers dry. You can't be any threat to her."

She was talking about when we'd last encountered Finesia in the Tree Immortal and been defeated, causing the ancient tree to crumble apart. Taka and I had lost the ability to transform into black dragons then, but in many ways it was a blessing in disguise, as we could no longer hear the voice of Finesia, the goddess of legend, inside our minds.

Finesia had used the tree to leach power out of our bodies and into hers, rebirthing her and leaving us to die. She and her loyal servant Alise Fioreletta – another dragonwoman – had watched all this taking place, until Hastina flew in to save us. That day, the Tree Immortal had died, we'd lived, and the world had taken an even darker turn.

"I don't know what Finesia's up to," I said. "I need to see the academics. Are they in the palace?"

"They went to Spezzio," Valpeonia said. "There's a vein

under the earth there that they wish to study; I'm not sure what it's about, but it sounds important."

"Then I must go there at once and talk to them."

"No." Valpeonia put up her hand. "Alsie Fioreletta has already come looking for you. She could have set up an ambush."

"I can handle myself," I said. "Besides, something tells me that my life isn't as important as Taka's – Finesia captured him, not me, when she imprisoned him in the Tree Immortal. For some reason she's worried that he survived."

"That doesn't mean you should be putting your life in danger," Valpeonia said.

"Alsie couldn't have sneaked many dragonmen past General Sako's defences at the Eastern Front."

"Still, we don't know how many she has brought through, and we don't know how many Gordoni's technology can handle."

I took a deep breath. I just wasn't getting through to them.

"We don't have any other choice," I said patiently. "We have to do something. We can't just sit here waiting for them to attack."

Hastina nodded and stepped forwards. "I'll go with Dragonseer Wells," she said. "But Taka should stay here."

Taka sucked in a breath through his teeth.

"If this is about me," he said, "I should come with you too. Finesia didn't destroy everything inside me. Something is still there, if I could just work out how to tap into it."

"It's too dangerous," I said.

"But I'm fifteen, now."

"You're also still in many people's minds the heir to throne," Valpeonia pointed out.

"What does it matter?" Taka said. "Dragonseer Wells said it herself – if we do nothing, there won't be any throne left to sit on, there won't be any city to rule. We'll all be dead."

He paused a moment, leaving the silence hanging. I saw hesitation uncertainty in both Valpeonia's and Hastina's eyes, and neither was usually the type to let her emotions show. I felt it myself too. I'd promised Sukina – Taka's mother – all those years ago that I'd protect Taka with my life, but every time he voluntarily put himself in danger like this, my promise to her grew more strained.

Valpeonia sighed, then gave Hastina a curt nod. My biological mother knew as well as we did that Taka had reached an age that he could make decisions for himself.

"Take an escort of a hundred greys," she said. "I have a feeling you'll need them."

Hastina nodded in reply, saying nothing. Taka and I remained silent also; we simply turned and followed Hastina out of the room.

3

THE THREE ACADEMIC elders had never revealed their true names to me. Instead, they referred to themselves as the anthropologist, the biologist, and the historian. I had first encountered them in the lava tube system beneath the Pinnatu Crater before it had erupted, suffocating the island and all its residents beneath a curtain of pyroclastic ash and birthing an army of shapeshifting and immortal black dragons.

It hadn't been a natural eruption, but rather caused by an elderly mad scientist named Colas Lamford – the same man responsible for turning all the dragonseers of Valpeonia's generation into black dragons. Out of the bubbling lava and through the clouds of volcanic ash an army of dragonmen and dragonwomen had arisen – the first of Finesia's minions, who would go on to eventually conquer this planet.

I'd learned from the three academic elders that Taka possessed a special quality never before seen in history. Through the ages, dragonseers had been typically female, but there were two exceptions. The first was Taka, his gender changed when he was a child due to experiments performed on him by Colas. The second was one of Taka's and Faso's distant ancestors, who had also used Exalmpora to change her gender. She – or indeed he –

had then fathered children, and all of them had turned out to be male.

Most dragonseers could only have one child, and they were always female. The drug-modified ancestor had produced a purely male line of humans who weren't quite dragonseers, but still males with remarkable intellects, like Faso Gordoni and Colas Lamford.

Taka was the first time that the male and female lines had reunited, which had given him the ability to become more powerful than any of us could have imagined. Alas, Finesia had robbed him of that ability when she'd drained him of his blood and used it for her own rebirth.

I had a hunch that these three academics, whom we all thought had perished during the eruption of the Pinnatu Crater, might have some additional information on Taka. That's why I wanted to meet them so badly. They had recently remerged mysteriously underneath Slaro Palace in Cralanein's chamber, after Finesia's rebirth.

In all honesty, I still knew very little about them; somehow, whenever I encountered them I always seemed to forget the questions I wanted to ask. Instead, a completely new set of questions would come to mind as if I'd been meaning to ask them all along.

At the time I hadn't seen this as strange or enigmatic. Instead, it seemed to be just a natural part of the world, like the rise and fall of the sun by day and the moon at night. I therefore didn't know how they'd survived the eruption of the crater, nor did I even consider that I might not end up getting the information that I needed. Indeed, the mission made perfect sense.

Of course, we couldn't take Taka to Spezzio without Faso insisting on joining us. So as before, Taka mounted Bellroot, I rode Velos, and Faso flew on the dragon automaton in the centre.

Hastina again led the way in her black dragon form. She kept turning her triangular head from side to side, scouting for any danger. But Faso also wore his helmet; he claimed its technology would detect any black dragons within a range of a few miles.

As Valpeonia had ordered, a flock of a hundred grey dragons surrounded us as escort, their wide wings slicing through the air. The greys were smaller than Velos and Bellroot, and sadly completely infertile.

For a long time, we had thought that this would mean the extinction of dragonkind. But then Velos and the late dragon queen Gerhaun Forsi had mated and she had eventually laid a dragon queen's egg, which was now hatched and safe in the caverns underneath Slaro Palace.

We all hoped that when the young queen came of age, her offspring would be fertile once again. But first we had to completely eliminate the secicao – a battle we seemed to be losing.

Taka and I took turns singing the dragonsongs that kept the greys in formation – songs more of harmonies than of melodies, which didn't tend to stick in the head but still sounded pleasant to the human ear. They were the vocal equivalent of wind chimes tinkling in a breeze.

It seemed that Taka wasn't the only reason Faso was tagging along this time. His wife, Asinal Winda, hadn't been in the palace as Faso had feared when the black dragons had attacked, but had instead joined the expedition to Spezzio. She was an accomplished engineer, and I often thought she was even smarter than Faso, though neither of the two would admit it for different reasons.

Seventy miles wasn't far on dragonback, especially with the propulsion at the back of the dragon armour driving us along. Admittedly we weren't travelling at full speed, since the grey dragons didn't have the same technology as Bellroot, Velos, and the dragon automaton, could take full advantage of our tail-wind. In the end, we made the journey in a good two hours – and that was going at a leisurely pace.

I guess we all just wanted to enjoy the weather ... the sun on our faces was one of the few pleasures we had left. It wasn't as cold as it had been back at Slaro. We flew above the brown secicao clouds that covered the country in swathes, the sun reflecting slightly off them, sending some warmth upwards. Above the murk, only a few normal clouds hung high in the sky.

It wasn't long until we saw Spezzio ahead of us, its five funnelled towers stretching upwards. They lay near the port and were part of a massive automaton factory which King Cini III had built to create the war automatons. The towers billowed out sooty coal smoke as the workers within the building assembled the mechanical Rocs, Hummingbirds, and other war automatons that supplied the front lines in the fight against Finesia.

I'd visited the city many times during my childhood, as I used to live in the Five Hamlets – a town that lay just south of here.

But, while I longed to be under Yol's bubble of the collective unconscious that protected Spezzio, I now had no incentive to go home. I didn't want to see the secicao creeping across Papo's vineyards that had once been so fertile with fruit, nor did I want to see how the thorny branches had torn apart the stones of our two cottages that Papo had built with his own hands. I didn't want to see Velos' stable, where we'd spent a large part of my life roasting secicao beans for King Cini III, reduced to rot and rubble.

"Gas masks on," Faso said over the speaker system.

"We have to go through the secicao clouds?" I asked.

"I'm afraid so," Faso replied. "You can either descend voluntarily, or drop right into them on that strong air current we're about to fly into."

I sighed. I suppose I'd become kind of fearful of secicao. So much so, in fact, that I'd abandoned the bit-and-clip breathing tube and nose peg – a bit like what divers used – for a fully-fledged gas mask. I reached down under the compartment in the seat beneath me and produced the mask. It made a sucking sound as it tightened around my face.

I pushed down on Velos' steering fin and he descended. A dull brown colour replaced the blue of the sky, and the world darkened, as if we had dived a few hundred metres into a gloomy lake. Acid scratched at my skin, and trickles of sweat developed on my forehead.

If I took off my mask inside these clouds, they would kill me in seconds. Just a year ago, when I'd still had the abilities granted by Finesia, I could have breathed this stuff. But now I had to rely on the oxygen from the tank on my back. For a while, Taka and I had thought that Finesia had still left us with immortality, but now it seemed even that had been taken away.

Return to us, Fallen, said a sudden voice in my head. *Maybe then I will forgive.*

My heart skipped a beat. It was Finesia's voice – the same voice that had convinced me to murder the dragon queen, Bassalhan, after it had taken control of my mind.

The voice couldn't have been hers, surely? Just a fragment of memory from those times when she'd been able to control me. But those days were long gone.

Beneath us, the twisting branches of the virulent plant whizzed past. Their tips reached up into the clouds like tendrils feeling in the dark, as if they could somehow sense our passage.

"Bank right," Faso said. "We're almost there."

His voice lifted me away from my worries and brought me back to the present moment. I pushed on Velos' steering fin and he turned sharply, sweeping alongside our escorts.

Soon enough, we emerged into blue sky just above Spezzio's port. I pulled off my mask and took a deep breath of fresh air. How I longed for the day where we'd never have to wear these wretched gas masks again.

THE MINES YAWNED up at us from the shadow of the rolling hills below. The Specian Hills that ran to the north of the port of

Spezzio were nowhere near as high as the Caprio Mountains, but even so, they were rich in minerals and supplied much of the coal to our country of Tow.

Night had already fallen, and torchlight flickered out from the gaping mouth of the mines. A smokiness drifted over to us from the automaton factory to the west, and I could smell coal fumes.

Above, the stars shone through an inky dark sky, fighting to be seen between the wisps of smoke and the few strands of secicao clouds that had managed to creep over Yol the dragon queen's protective bubble. In the distance and in all directions, the secicao clouds emitted a faint green luminescence. But they remained distant. So long as the dragon queen lived in Spezzio, they couldn't enter the city perimeter.

Now the Spezzio mines didn't just supply coal to the nation, they also housed Yol and her covey of greys. Yol had only one job here – to protect us all.

"*So you finally came,*" Yol said, her voice reaching out across the collective unconscious. She had opened a channel to Taka, Hastina, and me.

"*Queen Yol,*" I said, "*the Masked Regent sends her greetings.*"

"*As I'm sure you all do too, and I send my own. The three elders are waiting inside to greet you.*"

"*What are they doing here?*" I asked.

"*They found something,*" Yol said. "*While you've been up last week in the Caprio Mountains, Asinal Winda has been investigating a strange presence that has emerged in one of the caverns.*"

"*What do you mean, a presence?*" Hastina asked.

"*A light ... and something in the collective unconscious. I've never seen anything like it before.*"

"*And the elders?*" I asked.

"*They arrived only a couple days ago,*" Yol said. "*They remain just as mysterious to me as they do to you. Now they tell me that they want to meet you in person – all three of you.*"

Yol was the dragon queen who reminded me the most of

Gerhaun Forsi; her voice was laced with compassion, while still retaining that sense of leadership and knowing.

After Gerhaun's death, the remaining dragon queens had taken over Fortress Gerhaun while I'd been stationed there. Their presence had ensured that a protective bubble of the collective unconscious would remain to shield the thousands of soldiers within. Problem was, they hadn't appreciated me being there so much, particularly after I'd transformed into a dragonwoman.

Yol had shown sympathy for my situation as a dragonseer – and as a woman for that matter – who was losing her mind to Finesia. And she had demonstrated a level head when I was due to be executed after I – not in control of my senses and in black dragon form – had murdered the head dragon queen, Bassalhan. She had saved me from my inevitable execution, and she'd listened to me all the way. If I'd had to deal with any of the other dragon queens at the time, they would have ordered the grey dragons to rip the very skin from my bones.

A rush of warm air rose to greet us as we entered the mine. Grey dragons loomed in the cavern within, their shadows flickering against the walls in the dull torchlight. From the passageways beyond them came the clink, clink, of the automatons mining. A cargo automaton, with a big bundle of coal in a basin on its back, trundled below us back out of the cavern mouth on caterpillar tracks.

Our escort of greys left us at the mine entrance, dispersing to land next to their own kin. I could hear their emotions in the collective unconscious, as they too seemed anxious about the future, and I sang a dragonsong to at least soothe them a little.

That left us with Velos, Bellroot and the dragon automaton alone as we flew into a huge passageway, pitch darkness reaching out to cut us off in our tracks. I was tempted either to augment or to rummage for my helmet in the compartment underneath my seat, as either action would give me the ability to see in the dark.

But I might need the secicao oil if we unexpectedly encountered one of Finesia's minions, and it was stuffy enough in these caverns without me ramming my head inside a metal cage.

"*I don't like this, Auntie Pontopa,*" Taka said in the collective unconscious.

I didn't either, but Taka had seemed particularly spooked by our experience in the roots of the Tree Immortal. There I had battled Alsie Fioreletta and lost. It was meant to have been our final battle, but I had a feeling I would have to fight her once more.

"*Just listen out for the dragons inside the collective uncon-scious,*" I said. "*Let them be your beacon.*"

"*Yes, Auntie,*" he said, and even though I couldn't see Taka in the darkness, I felt him relax.

Velos veered off to the right, and then amber light shone out from a wide opening ahead of us. It wasn't coming from torches, this time, but from a campfire burning in the chamber's centre. Around it sat the three old men I'd first met inside the volcano. They had known much of my destiny back then, and even now there was a sense there was a lot more to them than meets the eye.

A great dragon queen lay on the floor behind them, shining like true gold, not merely a yellow colour like Bellroot. Yol didn't seem to mind the fire in front of her, though the smoke wasn't drifting in her direction, but towards us.

A pot stood over the fire, and a familiar smell drifted up from it, carried upon the currents that led outside. There was porridge in the pot, the same that they'd served me above the lava lake all that time ago. I'd kissed Lieutenant Wiggea above that lava lake – I shuddered as I remembered – not at the kiss, but how Wiggea had later fallen into the boiling magma to be reborn in black dragon form.

Wiggea was gone for good, now. Hastina had killed him for the second time, ripping out his throat coldly and without remorse. He had been her husband, and I'd often wondered if I harboured more sadness for his loss than she ever did.

Faso's wife, Asinal Winda, sat closer to the entrance, stooped over some great brass contraption. It looked like some kind of gigantic millepede, as thick as a human head, no doubt intended for the exploration of these caverns.

When they saw us come in, the three elders stood up from the fireplace and beckoned us over. That was when I saw a strange passageway behind them, narrowing to a hole only large enough to fit a cat.

It had an eerie light emanating from it – the same light that Yol had just mentioned. The ceiling and upper walls of the passageway appeared to be green, whilst the lower space was red. I didn't like the look of that light, and I couldn't imagine what evils might lurk behind it.

You could never truly appreciate the scale of a dragon queen until you stood directly at her feet. Yol wasn't as massive as Gerhaun had been, and neither was anything like the size of Bassalhan when she was alive. But still, she was a good nine times the height of our dragons, who were at least three times the mere human height of Hastina and me.

I wondered how she'd managed to get down into this chamber in the first place. I guessed there was a passageway in the gaping darkness that extended above us; perhaps she'd employed the greys to dig a way in for her. But no draught came from that direction and the smoke didn't drift that way either.

Only Hastina, Taka and I stood before Yol. Velos and Bell-root had touched down near Yol's tail, while Faso had landed his dragon automaton near Winda. He hadn't dismounted yet, instead staying hunched over his seat on the back of the mechanical beast, looking for something in the compartment underneath.

Meanwhile, the food over the fire smelled so good that it set my mouth watering. I'd been so busy that I'd not eaten for a good twenty-four hours. Yol lowered her head, as if to give us permission to eat.

She could not only communicate with us in our heads, but she could also read our emotions as well. She was after all a source of the collective unconscious – every dragon queen was.

My nose led me to the pot, and Hastina, Taka, and I sat down with the three elders, forming a circle. For a while I let myself bask in the heat coming off the fire, which felt as if it could find the cracks in my skin and seal them up.

Faso, from the other side of the cavern, looked at the pot and shook his head, then walked over to say something to Winda in an admonishing tone. I'd not had a chance to ask him if he knew that his wife was here. More and more, they'd been working on separate projects lately, but their work never seemed to keep them apart.

Faso's six-legged ferret automaton, Ratter, emerged from his flared-out sleeve and scurried down his arm. The sidekick ferret sat on the millepede automaton and glared at Winda with its glowing red eyes.

"She's a resourceful young woman, that Asinal Winda," the anthropologist said.

I turned back to him as he reached out towards the pot and ladled some porridge into a bowl. The three elders were in fact nearly identical triplets, and they'd retained their similarity into old age. But they did each have a feature that allowed me to tell them apart. The anthropologist, for example, had a mole that protruded from the wiry beard at his chin.

"Resourceful ..." I said, considering the word. "Much more so than Faso, I guess." The anthropologist lowered his head and smiled.

"Faso does have his remarkable qualities," the biologist said, "but Winda is the one who truly leads him, albeit from the shadows. She's exactly the wife a man like Faso needs."

I shook my head. Though Asinal was Winda's first name, we all called her Winda – her childhood nickname. She always seemed so subdued that it was hard to think of her as a leader. But then, I had seen her put her foot down at some of the most opportune moments.

There were so many questions I wanted to ask the elders – for example, how had they survived the eruption of the Pinnatu Crater? Also, why had they stayed hidden under the radar for a good four years while the world was deteriorating, when we truly could have used their skills? Why, for that matter, had they chosen suddenly to reappear once the world had been reborn?

But again, these questions remained mysteriously unasked. I also knew there was a question somewhere that I was meant to ask, something about Taka – the whole reason I'd come here in the first place. But it had hidden itself in the recesses of my mind. Instead, my attention had now turned to the much more pressing matter.

"You called us here," I said as I took the bowl of porridge that the anthropologist offered to me, "presumably for a reason?"

I nodded towards the passageway.

"I believe Regent Valpeonia has already told you something about that," the biologist said. His distinguishing feature was a birthmark that crossed his right cheek diagonally, eventually vanishing into his beard.

I glanced towards the strange light that was emanating from behind the fire. It kept drawing my gaze as I raised a spoon of porridge to my mouth.

"She told us that you've discovered a vein of something," Hastina said. "But she hasn't yet told us what."

She didn't sound at all happy about being kept in the dark like this. But then Hastina was never happy about anything.

"That's because the Regent Valpeonia doesn't know," the anthropologist said.

"Nor do you need to know, for now," said the biologist.

"The knowledge is not for you, but for those Finesia calls her Fallen," said the historian. His top lip was slightly cleft.

The three elders lifted their heads all at once, and their gazes roved between Taka and me.

When Finesia had been running rampant inside my head, she'd called me that multiple times. Before that, I'd been her Acolyte – but after I'd failed multiple times to succumb to her overt wishes, she'd stopped gracing me with that title.

"What makes us so special?" Taka said.

"You will learn that in due time," the biologist said, and he stood up and clicked his fingers. The historian and anthropologist both stood and did exactly the same.

There came a scratching sound from behind me, followed by a hiss. Ratter leapt off the millipede, just as the larger automaton's thousands of legs – or however many it had, to be fair – pinwheeled into action. Those legs propelled it straight towards the strange light. It moved much faster than I'd expected, trailing green secicao gas behind it. Then it disappeared from view.

We waited a few minutes with no one saying much. The elders remained standing, and even Faso was silent.

Rather, we peered into the passageway and the eerie light coming from it. I felt an urge to move towards the cavern, but a much more primal part of me told me that what lay within would not be good for me. I could sense a presence there – an eldritch one – as if Finesia were watching us from the recesses within. The light brightened a bit, and I felt a slight burning at the back of my mind.

Something was probing, searching for my soul. Looking for a weakness – a way in.

"*Can you feel that too?*" Taka asked me in the collective unconscious.

I certainly was feeling some kind of presence. It was as if a source of the collective unconscious had emerged that was even stronger than Yol, or worse than that ... something even stronger than a source. Something that could nullify a source. But what?

"*Be careful,*" Hastina said, "*this doesn't feel good.*"

Dragonheats, she could say that again.

There came a whistling sound from within the cavern, like steam passing through a kettle.

"No, not now," said the anthropologist.

"It is not yet ours to control," said the biologist.

"She has a stronger grasp on it even than we previously thought," said the historian.

"Yet she cannot keep it," the anthropologist said. "Not forever."

"It's too early to reveal ourselves," the biologist interposed. "She cannot know we survived."

The historian sucked a breath of air in through his teeth. He turned towards me and Taka.

"Get out of here – all of you. You must evacuate now."

"What?" Hastina said.

"The dragon queen, the dragons, anyone you can save," the three elders said together, as if they were three people melded into one.

Suddenly there was a gust of wind, so strong that it snuffed out the fire. A sudden chill descended, and then the earth shook violently, throwing us all to the floor. And when I looked up, the elders were nowhere to be seen.

Only three strands of faint black mist remained in their former locations, which soon dissipated into thin air.

4

FOR A MOMENT I STOOD THERE, exchanging glances with my companions and completely bewildered. The expressions on their faces told me they felt much the same. I had a sense that we hadn't quite got what we came for, but something inside my mind was also masking why. The cavern was continuing to shake, but at the present moment none of us felt any urgency to escape.

Suddenly, a voice spoke into the collective unconscious inside my head.

"You seek a source to restore your powers, and so the world will give you powers for good." It didn't take me long to realise it wasn't one but three voices – the three elders speaking in unison. *"But you need to find a way to the world's source, before Finesia uses its power for herself."*

The cavern shook again. By the shape furrowed upon Taka's brow I realised he had heard it too.

"What do you mean?" I responded in the collective unconscious.

But there was no reply.

Somehow, the elders could speak in the collective unconscious. It was as if—

Dragonheats, it had been so obvious, and I felt such a fool for being so blind. They must have survived the eruption at the Pinnatu Crater because they were dragonmen themselves. Black dragons – Finesia's minions. We couldn't trust them, surely? But they had to be really powerful if they could manipulate my mind like this.

"*Survive another day,*" they said again, and the cavern shook one more time, more violently than before, "*then worry about our identity. You and the boy must live.*"

This time the quake dislodged some rocks from the cavern's ceiling, which crashed into the floor below. A deeper rumble came from the earth, a violent and threatening one.

The strange light flared even brighter from the passageway that the giant mechanical millepede had entered. Both the warm amber and cool green lights were now intensifying into more brilliant whites.

Yol was standing upright, peering up at the ceiling, and greys had entered the cavern from the surrounding corridors to encircle and protect her. Some turned their heads rapidly from side to side as they flew, looking out for other threats. Others drew in close to Yol, hugging the ceiling as if looking for escape routes.

"*That light,*" she said, staring at the mysterious cavern. "*My power—*"

Her voice crackled in the collective unconscious like a dying radio, and I could feel my connection to her breaking.

"Dragonheats, what are we standing around here for, doing nothing?" Faso said. "The old men said to get out of this place. We've got no reason not to listen to them."

"But where did they go?" Hastina asked.

I glanced at Taka. Clearly the elders hadn't included Hastina in the channel when they'd spoken to us. I wondered if I should say something, but then another groan came from the cavern, suggested that such matters could wait.

"Taka, get up on Bellroot now," Faso said. "Hastina, you know the way, so please get us out of here."

"And who put you in charge?" Hastina asked, her hands on her hips.

"I don't care, for wellies' sake. We need to evacuate pronto."

"Not yet," Hastina said, and she focused her harsh glare on Winda. The muscles of her fingers tensed, as if ready to draw her spear from her back. "What was that mechanical beast, and what did it do?"

"It wasn't the millipede automaton that caused this," Winda said, her voice surprisingly calm. "We only designed it to cut through the rock – it's what the elders wanted us to do."

"Then what did it find?" Hastina asked.

She was starting to show her old angry self, but I guess that is what Hastina was in times of crisis. Velos and Bellroot together opened their mouths and let out loud roars to call us over to them. Within the collective unconscious, I could feel the fear in my dragon's pounding heart.

I nodded towards them. "Faso's right," I said. "Hastina, we can discuss this later."

The cavern rumbled again, accompanied by another violent quake. It sent me reeling in the right direction, towards Velos. Faso swore from behind me. Winda helped him up off the ground.

There came a breeze from the glowing passageway, and I caught the sulphuric whiff of secicao fumes. Then the green mist rolled out of the darkness.

The clouds at first were translucent plumes, but they turned a brownish colour as they gained density. *Secicao*. It had somehow burst through Yol's protective bubble. The golden dragon queen craned her head upwards.

"*I can't fight it...*" she said into the collective unconscious. "*It's too strong.*"

It sounded as if she were struggling to put her thoughts into words. Then it dawned on me what Yol was saying, and my gut twisted as the realisation washed over me. She couldn't hold her protective bubble any longer – through this cavern and whatever lay within, Finesia had found a way to break in.

I looked up at Yol. "*The civilians,*" I said.

There were tens of thousands of people sheltering at Spezzio Port, all believing they were protected by the dragon queen's bubble. They believed that if they stayed and worked in the city, then Finesia couldn't get to them. Trusting that Yol's presence would keep them all safe.

And now we had failed them.

"*We can't help them now,*" Hastina said. A black cloud started to rise around her. She bawled out a command in an even louder, inhuman voice. "Everyone evacuate immediately!"

"Finally," Faso shouted. "That's what I've been saying all along!"

Yol bellowed, then she spread her giant golden wings and lifted into the air. She sent down a billowing wind that I had to brace against to keep my feet. The caverns rumbled once again, massive rocks splintering from off the walls.

From my left came a loud crash. I spun around to see a stalactite denting the floor, just metres from Velos. It sent up a cloud of red dust, which was now turning green.

Dragonheats! My legs didn't want to move; something about that green light had paralysed me. A part of me, hidden deep within, desired to stay rooted to the spot.

To let the secicao wash over me, to become one with this new, better world.

Your destiny, my Fallen.

Finesia ... No, that couldn't have been her voice, surely ... just a fragment of memory. Whatever it had been, I had to ignore it. I willed my brain to switch off, and it was as if my legs now took action by themselves. I sprinted towards Velos, who roared to beckon me onwards. In front of me, Taka took off on Bellroot. A whistling sound came from above, and the dragon automaton streaked by overhead, with Faso and Winda on board.

Velos turned his tail towards me, and I clambered up and found my place on top of his armour. I didn't even have a chance to harness myself into the cold metal seat before he took wing.

I craned my neck to look upwards. Wind gusted down from the ceiling, and Yol and Hastina had now disappeared beyond the darkness. Grey dragons spiralled up towards it, flocking to protect their queen, as the toxic secicao gas filled the cavern floor below.

AFTER SEVERAL TWISTS and turns through blackness, we broke out into a cold blue open sky. We launched from a crater leading beneath the peak – not a natural one, but one that had been drilled open by machinery. Yol was already high in the air, Hastina, Bellroot and the dragon automaton hovering not far from her.

Sunlight glinted off the brass spiral heads of the drilling automatons stationed around the crater, before the sun disappeared entirely behind a curtain of dense grey clouds. The air gained a more bitter cold.

Greys continued to swarm out from the crater like bees from a hive. I watched them for a while, before there came a loud crashing sound as the crater collapsed.

I felt the pain as hundreds of dragons were hit by tonnes of falling limestone. Falling rocks clipped against wings. Heads bashed against the cavern walls. Each death punctured a hole in the collective unconscious that tore at my heart. As custom dictated, Hastina, Taka and I sang a dragonsong to thank the dragons for their bravery, for their service to our world.

We finished the final notes of our song, and around us, the remaining greys sang out their own croons. Velos joined in, and so did Yol and Bellroot. At times like this I wasn't sure whether I heard the notes in my ears or in the collective unconscious, but I still took it in. I was a part of it all.

There were still greys alive down in the caverns. They could breathe the secicao gas, and they would find other ways out. They could survive this. That wasn't what we all feared the most as silence descended – all I could hear was the howling wind, as if it wanted lament the change about to occur – the fall of Spezzio Port. Tens of thousands of civilians who had trusted the air to remain clear would suddenly realise they could breathe it no more.

The secicao clouds rolled out of the sides of the mountains, like smoke out of a cauldron. It emerged green at its edges, yet quickly thickened to the normal brown, sickening colour. At first its progress was slow, but it soon sped up as if it were a pyroclastic flow gaining momentum from a volcano. It carried with it the same eerie green glow as in the cavern. This wasn't normal secicao gas; it was filled with something new, something terrifying.

"Is there any way the people can survive it?" I asked Yol in the collective unconscious.

Now we were away from that eldritch source, I could communicate with her again.

But I knew she couldn't penetrate whatever entity I could sense dwelled down there. It was as old as the world itself, and like Finesia, all it wanted was to destroy what we had worked as a civilisation to build – entropy incarnate.

"They will have seconds once the secicao rolls in," Yol said in a channel that was open for we three dragonseers. *"Help me to send down the greys. They can at least provide an escape route."*

I sucked in a breath, for I knew what this meant. We were already struggling to house the population in Slaro and I wasn't sure we could take in any more refugees. But these people had nowhere else to go. Perhaps we could find another place for them, and maybe Yol could relocate her protective bubble somewhere else. But they would lose access to the factory – the one place that supplied the automatons we needed to fight Finesia. This attack had been strategic, and none of us had any idea how the Empress had pulled it off.

Hastina began to sing first, and Taka and I soon joined in. Yol also let out a loud, but nevertheless gentle crooning sound, that caused the greys to turn their heads towards the city. They flew down one by one, fanning out into wide formations.

We instructed them to land on every single street they could find. If each could rescue just one civilian, that could be considered a win in this grave situation.

Meanwhile, the secicao gas continued to roll out of the mountainside, gaining velocity. It ploughed out over the streets and charged towards the factory that still innocently billowed out its own smoke from its five chimneys.

I could all but imagine the horror of the people down there, the expression of shock on their faces as they looked out their windows from their family dinner table and saw that this meal would be their last.

"*That light,*" Taka said into the collective unconscious. "*Can you see?*"

From atop Bellroot's back, the boy pointed towards the crater, from which a thin beam now shot into the sky like a beacon. Green smoke drifted up from it, and I could see something coming out of the base. A winged form, misty and ethereal, and moving fast.

"*That is …*" Yol said. "*No, it can't be.*"

"*What?*" Hastina asked.

"*The God Dragon,*" Yol said.

"*God Dragon?*" I asked.

"*Both our greatest ally and greatest enemy, depending on the tides at the core of the planet. A creation of the Gods Themselves, destined to be sent at the hour of our world's greatest need. Gerhaun Forsi wrote about it, though none of us believed her, and now I realise that was folly …*"

But all this talk of legends, and the Gods Themselves, wasn't what I was most concerned about. Instead, I had eyes only for the creature of which Yol was speaking. An impossible form, created only of gas and light, stretching its wings across the sky. Its skin seemed to shift and warp as if the thing were constantly renewing itself.

"*Can we fight it?*" I asked.

But Yol didn't answer the question, I guess because she didn't have time. The strange beast was already turning towards Yol, seeking her – as a target.

"*My end has come much sooner than I thought it would,*" she said instead. "*Now it is time to say goodbye.*"

"Yol, no!" I screamed aloud.

But my words were meaningless, and there was nothing any of us could do. She was too far away for any of us to fly in and try to protect her. The golden dragon queen already had her wings outstretched, her pale underbelly exposed, ready to accept her fate.

"*Yes, I see it now. The light is bright with visions of the future, and I see your destiny, Dragonseer Wells. I was right to save you.*"

Perhaps if I'd been more conscious of what Yol was saying, I might have asked her what she meant. But instead I was completely transfixed by the dancing form of the dragon made purely of light.

It's strange, but for a moment I felt a connection to it. Its eyes glowed white, and it was difficult to see where it was look-ing, but still I could feel its gaze focused back on me. For an instant I felt it reaching out in the collective unconscious, but fearing Finesia I didn't let it into my head.

Even so, I felt a massive amount of guilt brewing within its soul, as if it didn't want to do any of this. It was as if something had taken control of its mind. I recognised that pain very well – I'd been in the exact same place when Finesia had taken control of me and used my transformed dragon body to kill Bassalhan.

It happened so quickly – the beast of light moved faster than a comet, leaving wisps of green gas in its wake. It flew like a long giant arrow straight into Yol's chest, where it disappeared.

My heart was pounding, and I sat stock still on Velos' armour, wondering if Yol had managed to survive it. But she had seen her own death; she had known of her end.

A faint green glow spread across the dragon queen's chest. Veins of it moved across her body, and then from out of her nostrils came plumes of green gas. Her eyes were now bright white fires. I wanted to scream out something more, but my breath had caught in my throat.

It felt as if the sky had collapsed in on itself. There was no bright explosion, no flashing lights, but something did explode in the collective unconscious. The rift passed all the way across the realm, and every single living creature for miles around would have felt it, even if they didn't know what it meant.

But I knew, and Hastina and Taka would know, as would Valpeonia in Slaro Palace and every single dragon alive ... the death of a dragon queen.

The glow faded from Yol's skin, which all flaked away, glowing softly like dying embers. Soon enough, no dragon queen remained; only an empty space in the sky. The mysterious God Dragon that had killed her was also nowhere to be seen.

PART II

The enlightened never truly suffer.

– Cralanein Iaste, Dragon Queen

5

It's hard to describe my feelings during our journey back to Slaro Palace, but at least I knew my thoughts were my own. I hadn't been as close to Yol as I had to Gerhaun, but still, in many ways her death had felt more significant. At least Gerhaun had died of old age. But Yol, it seemed, had been murdered.

I felt betrayed by the academics, the three old men who had guided me up the Pinnatu Crater. I'd seen that volcano erupt, and the ash that had thundered out of it had almost killed me. It should have killed them.

But they hadn't died, because somehow they'd transformed into black dragons – no doubt servants of Finesia. We'd all seen the black mist, and it had smelled of the same stuff that was produced when agents of Finesia transformed into their dragon bodies. Their presence at both that eruption and the birth of this God Dragon couldn't have been a coincidence. We'd all been duped.

What worried me the most was the fact that Finesia had found an easy way to take down the dragon queens. Valpeonia, through her network of scientists, including Faso and Winda, had developed automatons that could kill black dragons. With those on our side we at least had a chance, albeit a small one.

But that technology required factories to build, which in turn required people. Those people couldn't live without the protective unconscious-bubble generated by a dragon queen. Now, Yol's demise meant only six dragon queens remained, along with Gerhaun's fledgling dragonet whom Cralanein guarded in the caverns underneath Slaro Palace. I had no idea how long we had until she killed them too.

We were flying safely above the secicao clouds, sped on our way back towards Slaro by a cold and strong wind. I was alone aboard Velos, while Taka and Hastina flew on Bellroot – he at the back, she at the front. Faso was mounted upon the dragon automaton with Winda in the rear seat.

As we travelled on in silence, Yol's final words kept echoing around in my head. *You cannot let the God Dragon arise again.* I had so many questions, but I had no idea who would know the answers.

I guess similar thoughts were also milling around in my comrades' heads, because Faso and Winda, whose dragon automaton led our formation, said nothing over the speaker system. Nor, I noticed, did they say a word to each other. Neither Taka nor Hastina spoke in the collective unconscious either.

It was strange – when Gerhaun had died, we'd been able to give her a funeral. But we had no body of Yol's to bury. She had just disappeared into the void.

I shuddered, and then I cleared my mind of these thoughts as my mentors had taught me to do. They would do me no good.

Instead, I focused only on sensation – the thrum of Velos' armour beneath me, the chill in my hands that were clutched around Velos' steering fin, the pertinent odour of secicao in the air coming from below, and my fluttering stomach.

I entered a trance where I knew only myself. I wasn't aware how much time had passed until Slaro Palace came into view, its five angular towers piercing the sky. That was when I thought it was a good time to break the silence.

"So what do we do next?" I asked in the collective unconscious, the channel open for both Taka and Hastina.

"Well, who do you think might be the best person to ask about an entity almost as old as the Gods Themselves?" Hastina replied.

I shrugged. *"Valpeonia?"* I asked.

"No," Taka said. *"Not her … Cralanein."*

Hastina's voice came back laced with approval. *"And so that is who we shall ask."*

CRALANEIN WAS the most securely guarded citizen of the kingdom of Tow, and probably the world, for that matter. There were only two ways into her chambers – through the secret passageway coming from the throne room, and via a large cave mouth opening in Mount Spindle – one of the taller peaks of the Caprio Mountains.

The former was protected by the standard palace defences – Valpeonia's specially trained forces and a host of automatons of the finest calibre – while the latter on Mount Spindle was guarded by another army of automatons. Day by day, hosts of Roc, Mammoth, and war automatons braved the harsh conditions to monitor anything larger than a sparrow that might be moving nearby. A covey of two hundred greys also were posted at that entrance, and a good two-score soldiers. There were also more than two thousand Hummingbird automatons – fist-size response units that could quickly rush to the palace with a report if anything tried to enter the chamber.

If that weren't enough, five of the Roc automatons, and over two hundred Hummingbirds, guarded the spacious cave passageways that led into Cralanein's chamber itself.

Cralanein needed that protection, too. After decades of experiments and torture under Cini's reign, she had become as frail as gossamer. If anything at all managed to get close to her, she would be all too easy to kill. Of course, the would-be murderer would have to get past all our defences first – because admittedly, we weren't just protecting the aging dragon queen, but also Gerhaun and Velos' daughter – the newly hatched dragonet whom we all saw as the future of dragonkind.

Hastina, Taka, Valpeonia, and I entered now through the palace passageway. Faso and Winda had left us in the courtyard, as they wanted to make some modifications to the dragon automaton. I'd decided to leave them be.

A torch sconce cum secret handle opened the stone door that led to a spiral staircase underground. No more sconces had been placed on the walls of the staircase, and so the only light to navigate by came from the corridor at the bottom. The passageway smelled of mildew, but that was soon replaced by a more metallic scent.

In the next room, empty vats lined the corridor leading to Cralanein's expansive chamber. They were ceiling height and surrounded by rock that glowed green and blue with phosphorescence.

King Cini II had once filled those vats with Cralanein's silver blood. Dragon queen blood mixed with secicao and a few drops of dragonseer blood created the famed Exalmpora, a potent drug that eventually converted dragonseers into servants of Finesia. This supply had been responsible for altering Taka's gender from a very young age, and had also turned Valpeonia, Hastina, Taka and me into dragonwomen and a young dragonman.

I stayed as far from those vats as I could as I passed them, remembering the horrors of the days when Finesia had inhabited my mind. Taka did exactly the same, keeping as close to me as possible. Finesia's embrace had been so enticing, and the Exalmpora had linked us closely to her.

Still, I couldn't help remembering the drug's warmth as it trickled down my throat, and with that memory came a sense of longing – the metallic tang at the back of my tongue, the thrill as my muscles tore themselves apart and out of my skin emerged a much stronger and surer beast, albeit one that was the stuff of nightmares.

A part of me still yearned for the Exalmpora. Yet I had no doubt that if I took it, it could turn me right back into that horrifying monster once again. If, that is, Finesia willed it. Ultimately, only the living goddess had control over these things.

Only Valpeonia and Hastina didn't seem to mind the presence of the vats. Both women seemed too engaged in conversation to be affected by their surroundings, but in the meantime, I couldn't help feeling that something was missing. There was an empty space in the collective unconscious within Cralanein's protective bubble. The elder dragon queen was still hanging onto life, protecting all within Slaro, and we had faith she would continue to do so for a very long time.

"So let's run through it again," Valpeonia said. "Where exactly did the creature go to?"

"I don't know," Hastina said. "It was there one moment, then it was inside Yol, and then she just vanished. She died before our eyes."

"But if we didn't see her body, we don't exactly know if she did die."

"We felt it," Hastina said, her eyes moving first to Taka, then to me. "We all did. A rift in the collective unconscious, the same as with Bassalhan."

Like Gerhaun, Bassalhan had been Hastina's mentor. I had to admit, it must have taken a lot of strength on her behalf to forgive me for murdering her – if, that is, she ever had.

Valpeonia lowered her head and stopped walking for a moment. She put her hand to her chin. "This creature ... you said Yol called it a God Dragon?"

Hastina nodded. "Have you ever heard of such a thing?"

Valpeonia shook her head. "No, which makes me wonder if this isn't some kind of trickery."

"How can it be trickery?" Hastina said. "We all saw it with our own eyes."

"You saw it with your *mind*," Valpeonia snapped back. "No one can truly know the exact image that light burns into the back of their retinas. If Finesia has managed to learn something new – some way into our heads – how far can we truly even trust ourselves?"

I'd wrestled with that same dilemma many times in the past, particularly when under Finesia's spell. I'd had no way of telling what was real and what was only a clever trick presented by her to control me.

I looked at Valpeonia, and she turned to me and held my gaze. She was implying that Finesia might still be in my mind. Indeed, Finesia had managed this before – lying dormant until she needed to strike at an opportune moment. How would any of us ever know?

But that kind of thinking had sent me down a dark path before. We needed to believe we had control of our own minds.

I looked again at the vats, and Valpeonia noticed my stare. "I guess it stirs up bad memories."

"Still, sometimes, I long for Exalmpora," I said. "The sweet metallic taste on the tongue. Losing all my inhibitions and embracing my wild side."

Valpeonia lowered her head. "As do we all. Fortunately, I think we'll soon have emptied the last vestiges of Exalmpora from out of these vats. Faso Gordoni and his team have created a generator that runs off the blood of a dragon queen and can create a temporary bubble of the collective unconscious."

I nodded, remembering our conversation with the elderly woman up in the mountains. "He mentioned it – but he said it was still only in prototype."

Valpeonia smiled. "Oh, I believe it's a lot further along than that. But you can understand why we won't provide him with gallons of dragon queen blood just for testing."

I understood all right; Cralanein needed the blood to

generate this bubble of the collective unconscious in the first place.

"So it's true," I said, "you didn't feel Yol's passing at all?"

Valpeonia's lips were pursed as she shook her head slowly. "I did not."

"I didn't feel it either," Hastina said. "It wasn't like with Bassalhan."

"But—" I turned to Taka. His eyes were as wide as I imagined mine were. "Taka, please tell me you felt the rift."

"It was awful," he said. "Even stronger than it was with Gerhaun."

I gave him an approving nod. He hadn't been fully trained as a dragonseer when Gerhaun had died, and his connection to the collective unconscious had grown since then.

"So that means—" I looked at Valpeonia, my biological mother, "—your connection to Finesia – could it be hampering your connection to the collective unconscious? Perhaps she's found a way past your mental defences and can disrupt your minds."

"That's ridiculous," Hastina said. "We're fully in charge of our own senses. Tell her, Regent Valpeonia."

The Regent put out her hand and inhaled deeply. "As I have already said, we have to be vigilant – all four of us. We don't know if we can trust our own minds. But we have to trust ourselves, despite that."

"But our feelings aren't in our minds," Hastina said.

"Look," Valpeonia said, "if you want a lecture in neuro-science, go and talk to Faso Gordoni. We came to talk to Cralanein, did we not?"

All of a sudden, something caused me to shift my attention, and fear spiked in my chest. It wasn't that I didn't feel something in the collective unconscious, but rather that I realised the reason for that empty gap in it.

"The young dragon queen," I said, panic in my voice.

"What?" Hastina demanded.

"Can't you feel it? She's not here!"

Taka sucked in a breath. Hastina and Valpeonia both looked at each other.

"You can't sense it?" I asked. "The absence, the gap in Cralanein's bubble where there should be life."

But neither of them replied. Rather, Valpeonia rushed to the steel door into Cralanein's chamber and pulled at the wrought iron handle. She yanked it open with preternatural strength.

We should have seen light, but instead we were greeted by deep darkness. All the torches had been snuffed out.

WE ENTERED the pitch black chamber, and I kept as still as I possibly could, not daring to move an inch. I could taste bile and fear at the back of my throat.

If any of us stepped too far to the right we'd plummet to the base of the caverns. I reached to my hip flask, wanting to augment so I could at least see something of what lay ahead. But, probably sensing what I was about to do in the collective unconscious, Valpeonia put her hand to my arm and stilled it.

There came the smell of burning phosphorous as Hastina struck a match and lit a torch on the wall. She took this and used it to light a second torch, giving us enough brightness to see our side of the massive chamber. We couldn't yet see Cralanein at the other side of the room but we could hear her breathing and sense her in the collective unconscious. She, at least, was still alive.

A narrow ledge along the lefthand wall led all the way to the much larger niche where Cralanein had been resting all this time. Right now, we couldn't see that niche, as the room was so full of darkness except for a pinprick of blue light in the distance coming from Cralanein's roost.

That light wasn't normal; there was something there with Cralanein, an eldritch presence in the collective unconscious. It felt just like what I'd sensed in Yol's chamber before her death.

"Here, take this," Valpeonia said, and she handed me one of the lit torches from the wall. She took another and handed it to Hastina, then nodded to her.

"Hastina, you lead. Pontopa, you take the rear."

It made perfect sense for one of them to go first. If Hastina slipped, she could turn into a dragonwoman during her fall and fly back up again.

I wanted to reach out into the collective unconscious and speak to Cralanein; to check if she was okay and ask her what had happened. Alas, Cini II's experiments had destroyed her ability to communicate in this way. She might have been a source of the collective unconscious, but she was nearly blind in the medium. She had also lost her physical voice, and the ability to use her body. The only way to communicate with her now was through touch alone.

Hastina slid onto the ledge and navigated expertly along, using one hand to keep her balance. Torchlight reflected off the glowing rocks in the ceiling, and shadows danced upon the red walls. Taka followed her, his footing sure. Valpeonia watched him, clearly anxious that nothing should happen to the heir to Cini's throne.

Valpeonia stepped onto the ledge and I followed, keeping my focus on the wall ahead of me. I had no choice but to keep the torch close, feeling it blazing against the skin of my face. I worried the draught might catch the flame and set my hair on fire. Still, I thought it better to brave the heat than stretch so far out that I lost my balance. I no longer had the ability to turn into a black dragon if I fell.

Keeping my feet as far from the edge as possible, I managed to reach the other side. I was close enough to the blue light now to see that it came from a small hole in the cavern wall, no wider than a mouse. The light wasn't strong enough to illuminate anything else.

Hastina's torchlight spread out across the larger niche. It reflected off something shiny, and I walked over to pick it up. In my hand I held a single spherical automaton with a small protrusion, which it used to shock enemies.

"A Hummingbird," I said.

A single one of these automatons couldn't do much damage in a battle, but they were programmed to swarm in the thousands, thus, like a nest of wasps, creating a formidable airborne force.

Valpeonia approached the automaton and examined it. Then she marched across the cavern, beckoning Hastina to follow. The red-haired dragonseer discarded a disused torch from the wall and set hers in its place.

A faint green smoke was emanating from the hole, glowing slightly. The rotten eggy smell of secicao hung pervasively in the air.

Beneath it, Cralanein lay prone on the floor. She was as gigantic as the other dragon queens, but the way she was curled up made her look only half their size. Three parallel silver scratches ran across the width of her flank. Around her, her guardian Rocs and Hummingbirds lay inert on the floor. There was no sign of the fledgling dragon queen to be seen anywhere.

The smell of sulphur suffused the air, coming from Cralanein's nostrils. Meanwhile, the imagined taste of Exalmpora lingered at the back of my tongue. Green secicao gas still poured out of the glowing blue hole on the cavern wall, for somehow it had managed to find its way inside Cralanein's protective bubble as if to fill into the young dragonet's absence.

Hastina, Taka, Valpeonia and I stood in a circle around Cralanein, who lay breathing shallowly near our feet. The silver scratches on her flank glistened in the torchlight. Some light also reflected off her golden skin, though a green secicao-stained patina masked much of it. Her wings were sprawled across the floor, the membrane stretched across the pinions like the tattered fabric of worn-out curtains.

None of us dared touch Cralanein to try to talk to her. Normally, to wake a dragon queen was bad enough, for when they slept, they slept deeply, and there was a legend that one of my ancestors had tried to wake a dragon queen once, only to have her head bitten off.

I doubted Cralanein would do that to me, though. But still, she was so fragile that I wasn't sure she'd survive being jerked out of a dragon dream. The scratch on her side suggested something might have attacked her, though I had no idea what.

We'd taken the opportunity to light all the torches in the cavern, and so we now had a full view of it again. Other than the inert automatons, and the wounds on Cralanein, there were no signs of any battle. No broken rocks, no debris scattered around, no broken limbs or torn off automaton parts were scattered across the floor. No smell of gunpowder or blood.

Yet still, there was no sign of the young dragonet anywhere. Whatever or whomever had done this had made a clean job of it.

I turned back to look at the blue light coming from the hole in the wall. It flickered off the walls as if a tiny blue flame were burning within, out of sight. Again, I felt that eldritch presence stir within me, as if something was watching me – something evil and almost as old as the world itself. For a moment, I imagined I smelled the putrid, eggy tang of secicao, and a faint tendril of glowing green gas emerged from the hole.

"Who do you think should talk to her?" Hastina asked, referring to Cralanein. In other words, she was asking who should reach out and connect to her in the collective unconscious.

"I can," Taka said. "I can handle it."

But Valpeonia shook her head. "Taka, the horrors that Cralanein has endured are unspeakable. I don't want to put you through that."

"But if I'm to one day become king ... if the people allow it ... I know King Cini did terrible things ... but shouldn't a potential ruler experience the past so that they know not to repeat it?"

He no longer referred to King Cini as his uncle, which was a good thing. Right after Taka's birth, Cini III – the son of the

Cini II who had started the dragonheats – had stolen the baby away. Taka had spent his subsequent childhood indentured in the palace court, the mad king planning to train up the child as a dragonseer who could help him battle the dragons in the Southlands.

"One day you shall learn all these things," Valpeonia said. "But only after we've found a way through these fearful times."

There it was again – Valpeonia's hope. I couldn't help but wonder if she really believed her words or if she was just putting on a brave face.

"So you're saying you'll talk to her," Hastina said.

Her eyes had narrowed. She looked as though she was starting to not trust my biological mother. Dragonheats, I wasn't sure how far I trusted Valpeonia either. I had lived most of my life not knowing she was actually alive, and I was still sure she kept many secrets from me about her past and what she had become.

"She's saying I should," I said. "I've already seen the horrors of Cralanein's past. I know her fragility."

"All four of us have seen more horrors than a normal person can imagine," Hastina snapped back, and she crossed her arms. "But if you so strongly feel it should be you, go ahead. Don't let me stop you."

Valpeonia's eyes displayed a glint of knowing. She smiled at me, then turned to Hastina. "Is that jealousy I'm starting to sense in you, Dragonseer Wiggea?"

"No ... it's just ..." Then her expression changed. "Wait, that's—"

She spun on her heel. "You," she said, and pointed at a spot in thin air between two flickering torches. "What the drag-onheats are you doing down here?"

At first, I thought she must be going mad. I looked at Taka, who was also giving her a confused frown. But then, when I looked at Valpeonia, her expression changed from similar confusion to abject shock.

Then, I felt it too – another presence, filling that emptiness. I turned back towards the empty spot on the wall, and I squinted my eyes. Indeed, my mind must have been playing tricks on me, because beneath the torchlight three old men sat with their backs to the wall. Three puffs of black smoke surrounded them, fading quickly.

It seemed as if the anthropologist, the biologist and the historian had been there all along.

6

Torchlight reflections danced in the whites of the three old men's eyes. The elderly academics sat unmoving on the cavern floor, the crackle of the flames the only sound that breached the powerful yet momentary silence.

"What the wellies?" I said presently. "How is this possible?"

"There's no such thing as magic," Taka said. It was strange thing to say, because we'd seen plenty of magic beneath the Tree Immortal.

"They're evil," Hastina said. "Servants of Finesia. There can be no other explanation."

The three elderly academics looked back at us, not seeming to mind our contemptuous stares. Their eyes were as placid as a frozen lake. Every single muscle on their faces remained completely relaxed. They didn't seem threatened, even though Hastina had already reached behind her back and drawn her spear.

"Dragonseer Wiggea, check yourself before you make any rash accusations," Valpeonia said.

Hastina didn't even look at her, but kept her glare focused on the elders.

"You're not telling me I should trust them, are you?" Hastina asked.

"Have we any rational reason not to?"

"Of course we have. They were there during the appearance of that God Dragon thing, and they disappeared behind a plume of black smoke, just the way black dragons do."

"Yet, perhaps you are jumping to conclusions too quickly. You've still got to work on your hot-headedness, Dragonseer Wiggea. It is your weakness."

"I'm not jumping to conclusions – it is exactly what we all saw. Tell her, Dragonseer Wells."

"I saw it too," I said, "and so did Taka."

"And did any of you see three black dragons?" Valpeonia asked.

"Well, no," Hastina said. "We were too busy avoiding an earthquake."

"If you didn't see exactly what happened, you cannot be reliable witnesses," Valpeonia said.

I clenched my jaw; I really didn't know whose side Valpeonia was on. Inhaling a whiff of camphor from the torches, I looked back at the three elders. Their expressions hadn't budged an inch.

"I saw it all," I said.

"You saw what, exactly?" Valpeonia asked.

"I saw the dark smoke, and then there was nothing. Just the same smoke we all saw around their ankles just now."

"So they just vanished?"

"That's what I saw too, Regent Valpeonia," Taka said. "They were there one moment, and then they just vanished into thin air."

"And the black smoke ..." Valpeonia put her hand to her chin. She turned to the elders without a trace of contempt in her gaze. "Perhaps, sirs, you have a reasonable explanation for this."

The three academics stood up together, their movements completely precise, as if part of one body. They stepped forwards as one, the grey smoke coming off the torches reaching out like tendrils, trying to follow their path. The torchlight danced to the cadence of their step, the shadows flickering rhythmically upon the walls as if part of some synchronised dance.

Hastina kept her spear pointed at the biologist's throat, her hands so tightly wrapped around the shaft that I had no doubt she would kill any one of them at the slightest flinch. Yet I felt no tension from the old men; they weren't afraid of her at all. It was as if they already knew that she wasn't going to strike, and somehow, I knew it too.

It wasn't that she didn't have the will to strike, but rather it was physically impossible to do so. They had too much power over her – and over us all.

"We do have a rational explanation," said the anthropologist.

"Although a rational mind would find it difficult to explain using conventional language alone," said the biologist, "because the answer you seek is rooted in the myths of this world."

"Dragonmen and a goddess of legend who now walks the earth," said the historian. "Twenty years ago, most would have thought this to be nonsense."

"The truth, however," said the anthropologist, "is that our identities needn't concern you for now. For there are more pressing issues at hand."

Then, it happened all over again; the will to question them just floated out of my mind. There was no more reason to ask why they were there. Any suspicions of their treachery had dissolved into nothingness. Rather, there were more important questions to be asked.

As the words floated out of Taka's mouth it felt as if he'd been destined to ask them all this time. There was no anger in his voice, no contempt or distrust. Only necessity.

"What happened to the young dragon queen?" he asked.

"There we go," said the anthropologist.

"A pressing need to solve the problem at hand," said the biologist. "Quite fitting for a future ruler."

"That wasn't so hard, was it?" said the historian.

All three men turned their heads slightly to look directly at Taka. Hastina continued to watch them, her eyes narrowed. But she didn't appear to be as fierce as she had before, almost as if she had started to trust them.

"The truth is that none of us know," said the anthropologist, "where exactly Finesia is holding her."

"But we do know that no one stole her away," said the biologist.

"The fledgling dragonet is not quite herself," said the historian.

"She attacked Cralanein," said the anthropologist.

"The claw marks are the fledgling's own," said the biologist.

"Then the young dragon queen spread her wings and flew away," said the historian. "Out of the caverns and into the open world, to be reborn anew."

A whistling sound came from the darkness far above our heads, and a chilling draught found its way to us, travelling through the cave network all the way from the peaks of the Caprio Mountains. The colour blanched out of Valpeonia's face, and her cheeks sagged as her mouth curled downwards, her eyebrows following the frown in one sweeping motion.

"But dragon queens cannot fly until the time of their naming," she said.

"So history has always said," agreed the anthropologist.

"But history does not always model the future," said the biologist.

"Most years, history repeats – but not every year," said the historian.

Taka nodded. "And now we see the birth of something new."

"Exactly," all three elders said together.

"What are you all gabbling on about?" Hastina asked. "Just get to the point."

She had lowered her spear, the butt of it now resting lightly on the cavern floor.

"Why don't you see for yourselves," the anthropologist said, and he lifted his hand and pointed at Cralanein's head.

I'd failed to notice, but the aging dragon queen had opened her eyelids. Her yellow eyes roved the room as if seeking a target. From deep inside her body came a soft croon.

"Who?" Hastina asked. "Who should talk to Cralanein?"

"She knows who she is," said the biologist.

"For Cralanein has already called her forwards," said the historian.

"And she has been given permission," said the anthropologist.

They were right. Somehow, I knew it was I who needed to talk to her. It just didn't make sense for it to be anyone else.

Cralanein's eyes focused on me and drew me forwards. I reached out and pressed my hand to her brow. The dragon's power surged through my muscles from the collective unconscious; I felt weak, but not in a bad way. Rather, my whole body surrendered, and instinctively I knew I was safe, at least for the moment. Such instincts are one of the less remarked upon talents of a dragonseer.

And so I closed my eyes, and let the truth pour into my mind.

SECICAO STRETCHED out over the landscape below, spreading from expanse to expanse. Above it, green sparks streaked across the brown roiling clouds that boiled like molten lava.

I floated above all this, bodiless, my mind suspended in the web of the collective unconscious. I'd experienced visions like this before, and they were much more real than any dream. They gave the collective unconscious substance, displaying our world's history that had been imprinted on our collective minds and handed down through the generations.

As Valpeonia had pointed out, our memories could play tricks on us about what was real and what wasn't. But there was no trickery in the collective unconscious – or at least when connected to it in its purest form. This vision was a real as it comes.

A green wispy form flew out above the horizon. It was as long as a serpent, but its face had the fierceness of a dragon. Every scale upon its surface emitted an ethereal glow, and its eyes blazed white like diamonds held up against the sun.

The ethereal dragon-creature danced around in spirals, chasing its own tail. As it moved, it lost its lustre, fading into a dull verdigris. But this didn't last for long before it dived into the clouds, moments later to reappear glowing bright green once again.

"*The God Dragon,*" I said, into the collective unconscious, because I had no mouth in this visionary world through which to speak.

Then I heard Cralanein's voice in my head. It no longer sounded like that of an old crone, but young – full of authority and renewed vitality.

"*I told Gerhaun Forsi about this long ago,*" she said, "*and bade her pass the knowledge on to the other dragons.*"

"*And how do you know of it yourself?*" I asked.

"*Because I've known it from a very early age – my mother taught it to me, and likewise her mother taught it to her. Therefore the knowledge has descended through the generations since the Gods Themselves brought the first Ambassadors to this earth.*"

The Ambassadors were protectors of our planet, originally appointed, as legend had it, by the Gods Themselves. I was a direct descendent of the very first Ambassador, Candida, it was said. All dragonseers in fact were descendants from one of the original eight.

"*I guess the other queens wouldn't listen?*" I asked.

"So it seems," Cralanein said. *"Perhaps Yol believed a little bit, she and Gerhaun and Bassalhan. The other dragon queens are too trapped in their own ways. The dragonheats didn't only change the way humans think, but the ways we dragons do too."*

I felt my body, in the real world, sigh from deep within my heart. But I didn't let it pull me back; I needed to stay rooted in this vision. I could sense Cralanein was weak and would need to sleep again very soon. But first, I needed to hear what she had to say.

"What is this God Dragon?" I asked. *"How can something like this possibly exist?"*

"It's a being as old as Finesia, an immortal fashioned by the Gods Themselves."

"Who?"

"None other than Honore," Cralanein said. *"Resurrected from the heart of the world, much as the black dragons were born out of the fires of the Pinnatu Crater."*

My heart skipped a beat, as for all my life I'd known Honore as a character from stories – from our creation myth itself. He'd been an immortal dragon, the ruler of all other dragon immortals. In the true version of the myth Gerhaun had taught me, he had battled his nemesis Finase – the immortal male human leader. Their goal was to drink of the sap of the Tree Immortal, hence permitting either humankind or dragonkind to rule the earth forever.

But they had perished in that battle, their immortality stripped away by the Gods Themselves. In their place, Finase's wife Finesia had drunk of the Tree Immortal, and her loneliness had driven her to madness. As the legend went, this madness had caused her to hack the Tree Immortal into thousands of pieces, which became the first roots of *secicao*. The Gods Themselves, disappointed in what had come to pass, left our world to find other planets to govern. But before they did, they'd fashioned the first mortal humans out of mud and dragons out of the sulphur of the earth. They'd left us here to fend for ourselves.

But Honore had died with the other immortal dragons.

"*How can he possibly still exist?*" I asked Cralanein. "*He died in the age of myths and immortals.*"

"*He exists in the same way that Finesia exists,*" Cralanein said. "*Through magic born in an age of the gods. Now Finesia is too powerful for the likes of man and dragon, and so our planet itself has rebirthed the God Dragon as a defence mechanism to fight her. It is the only way to defeat her.*"

"*But we have all this new technology to fight her,*" I said. "*We've developed automatons powered by secicao itself. Using it, we can defeat any of her minions.*"

"*And yet to Finesia and the God Dragon, that technology is like a candle flame to a gale. Once the goddess is at her fullest power, there will be nothing you can do to destroy her.*"

In the vision before me, the God Dragon curled up around itself, its body forming an upward spiral. It used the momentum to turn back towards me, and for a moment behind its white glowing eyes I thought it saw me.

"*It killed Yol,*" I said, "*so it isn't our ally. It's evil.*"

"*Not evil,*" Cralanein said. "*Like dragons, and the winds, and the storms, this is only a being trying to find its place in nature. Honore doesn't yet know who he is, for he needs to find his soul.*"

"*Storms don't seek out and maliciously kill dragon queens.*"

"*Yet horses, dogs, and even dragons throughout history have been used for evil deeds. That doesn't make the creatures them-selves evil. One might say different things entirely of their enslavers.*"

"*Are you telling me that he's being controlled?*"

"*Alas, I am. Finesia has found a way to get even this ancient creature of legend to do her bidding.*"

The God Dragon Honore was now hurtling right towards me. At first I wanted to duck out of the way, but then I centred myself. I didn't have a body in this vision, and so it couldn't do me any harm.

Instead, I tried to look for some life in those white glowing eyes. Every tameable creature I knew had shown some sign of compassion. That was when I saw—

The face was incredibly familiar. A fair few years ago, I'd seen it every day. I knew so well those curves in the cheekbones, those widened nostrils, the furrowed eyebrows. It was as if no time had passed at all between then and her death, for the face belonged to Gerhaun.

I blinked, to see the face had shifted to now be Bassalhan's, the queen Finesia had coerced me into murdering in cold blood. Another shift and I saw Yol, and then Velos, and Hastina's dragon Bellroot, and a younger version of Cralanein, and all the other dragon queens, and then a succession of faces I'd never seen before. But despite that I knew them anyway – a facsimile of every single dragon who had ever existed throughout history seemed to be embodied by this creature.

"He's beautiful," I said.

"All dragons are, aren't they?"

"Yes, but this – why attack his own kind? I just don't get it."

This time, it was Cralanein's turn to pause. I felt a deep sadness welling within her, a truth of the way of things that she was powerless to undo. *"Honore is a dragon, and lives and only lives for the future of dragons in any form."*

"Including immortals," I guessed. *"But Finesia's black dragons aren't true dragons."*

"Yet they might be the future of the dragon race if no other dragons are allowed to live upon this earth."

As if it could hear Cralanein's warning, the God Dragon in the form of an ancient dragon-serpent displayed a snarl. He turned his body away and retreated towards the horizon.

"But that doesn't explain why Honore would kill the dragon queens."

In front of Honore then, and swimming away from me, Cralanein's head appeared in the sky. Again, I was looking at a much younger version of her, free of the stains and deformities caused by Cini II's atrocities during the dragonheats. She turned her golden head to look at me, her eyes as soft as starlight.

"*What do you know of the other dragon queens?*" she asked. "*Did Gerhaun ever mention what ails them?*"

"*No,*" I said.

"*You know not then that Yol and Gerhaun were the only ones capable of birthing a dragon queen, and even secicao seemed to have been taking that away.*"

I felt my breath catch in my throat in the real world. Gerhaun had told me many times that a dragon queen hadn't been born in a thousand years. "*Are you telling me that Gerhaun's dragonet is the only queen left that is capable of carrying on the dragon line?*"

Cralanein said nothing, but then she didn't have to. I could work it all out for myself.

"*Then Finesia knows that she can use the young dragon as a bargaining chip to get Honore to do as she pleases.*"

"*Because if Honore attacks Finesia,*" Cralanein went on, continuing my train of thought for me, "*she will kill the dragonet, meaning that Honore would have no choice but to protect the black dragons and anyone who threatens them.*"

"*So why doesn't Finesia just kill the dragonet anyway?*"

"*Because not even Honore would tolerate the murder of a young one. Once Finesia does that, Honore will seek vengeance, and Finesia isn't yet powerful enough to win a battle against him.*"

"*So she's just delaying her own demise?*"

Cralanein shook her head. "*Finesia plans to gain enough power to defeat him.*"

"*And how will she do that?*"

Cralanein's voice grew faint. The vision of her I saw in the sky suddenly displayed her aging form. "*Dragonseer Wells,*" she said. "*I'm sorry, but I don't have much time left.*"

The whole vision around me was fading now, and I couldn't see Honore anymore. There was something about Cralanein's state, her frailty, and I knew this was going to be the last conversation any of us had with her.

I brought myself back into the visions. Focusing on the secicao clouds, remembering their smell. Watching the lithe form of the God Dragon as it whizzed through me and started to turn.

"The young dragon queen," I said. *"They stole her away—"*

"She did," Cralanein said.

"But the automatons ... we put them here to protect you. What happened to them?"

"Are they not powered by secicao?" Cralanein asked. *"Originally the sap of the Tree Immortal, which is now her blood that runs through the world."*

I didn't like what I was hearing. How had none of us ever thought about this?

"You mean to say that it was Finesia who disabled the automatons?"

"Just one simple command, and the secicao that ran them refused to provide power anymore."

"But we've used those automatons to actually kill black dragons," I said. *"They were her servants, promised eternal life by her. If she could use the automatons to kill them, she would have to have broken that promise ..."*

"They were just pawns that served her will," Cralanein said.

I thought about that for a moment. All this time we'd relied on secicao, thinking we'd use it against Finesia to win the war. But it was a trap; secicao had always been a trap. That was what Gerhaun had been telling us all along.

Which meant everything that used it – the dragon armour, Faso's automatons, anyone who augmented their abilities by drinking secicao oil – Finesia could turn their power off at any moment, rendering us helpless.

Cralanein was right; we were all so fragile – like candles in a gale. Around me, the light shimmered, and I saw the cavern once again for a moment. Cralanein was weakening, I could feel it. She was dying.

"*Cralanein?*" I asked.

"*I'm still here.*"

Beneath me, I watched the God Dragon dive into the secicao clouds again. He looked so innocent, just from the way he moved. So incapable of doing harm. But then I'd thought the same of Taka once when he'd been just a young boy. Finesia had taken hold of him when he was still a child, turned him into a dragonman, and forced him to kill his surrogate uncle, King Cini III.

All of sudden the sky lurched beneath me, and I felt myself falling. But this time I wasn't leaving the vision.

Instead, I was in Honore's mind, looking upon the world through his blazing eyes. I experienced it all: the green lightning flashing through the secicao clouds, filling the God dragon with abundant energy; the sweet and seductive scent of secicao; the voice of Finesia trilling through his thoughts, whispering her wishes, though I had no idea what she said.

I felt just as afraid as Honore was, but underneath that fear I also felt a will to destroy. I'd felt that very same way when Finesia had inhabited my mind – as if I were both incredibly powerless and the most powerful being upon this world.

Then, I saw her for a moment in my mind's eye – the great black dragon form of the goddess Finesia, and at the same time her giant pale humanoid form, her long hair swaying beneath her shoulders like liquid gold. In both forms, her eyes were the same colour – rich and golden. They swivelled upon me, and I sensed her looking at me.

"*Fallen one,*" she said. "*You do not belong here.*"

I felt a sharp spike of pain in my head, and the vision flickered away as I tumbled through the threads of the collective unconscious back into my own. I wasn't in Cralanein's vision anymore, either, but instead I had been plunged through the cold abyss that separated the collective unconscious from the real world.

"Cralanein?" I asked in the collective unconscious, then out loud, "Cralanein?" The words came out much weaker than I'd intended, as my breath had caught in my throat. *"How does Finesia plan to defeat Honore?"*

No reply came.

I turned to see the alarm on my companions' faces. Valpeonia, Taka, and Hastina were all staring at me, their faces also turning white. I looked down then at the dragon queen. Her yellow eyes had turned pearl white.

"Cralanein," I said again, but this time my voice came out strained and breaking.

Valpeonia stepped towards me and put a hand on my shoulder. I was shaking.

"She's dead," I said. But I hadn't dared remove my hand from Cralanein's forehead yet.

I had been right not to do so, because then it came, surging through my arm and blazing through my mind – the last ember of a dying lump of coal. Cralanein's final command – her dying wish.

"Trust the elders," she said. *"They are your allies, and they are much more than you have ever imagined."*

And that was the last that anyone heard from her. Because momentarily, a rift opened up in the collective unconscious stronger than anything I'd felt before, even with Gerhaun.

Cralanein's passing was like an earthquake, tearing our world in two.

IT WAS as if my heart had decided it no longer belonged in my chest, and instead had suddenly taken a deep dive into the pit of my stomach. Flashes of memories flooded into my mind, familiar faces, as vivid as if I were standing before them in broad daylight.

Sukina. Gerhaun. Wiggea – the dragonelite who had been both mine and Hastina's lovers at different times – all the souls we'd lost during the fight against Finesia. So much sacrifice, and for what?

I immediately felt nauseous, and keeled over to retch. I also heard Taka making some gurgling noises, as his feet shuffled around a bit. But neither Hastina nor Valpeonia had moved an inch.

I looked up to study both women, searching for at least a trace that they'd felt what I had. They were dragonseers. They were meant to feel each passing, not just of the dragon queens, but of the individual dragons. But their expressions registered no sorrow.

Dragonheats, if Finesia could use secicao to disable our automatons and steal away Gerhaun's dragonet from right under our noses, then there was no guessing what she could do to Hastina and Valpeonia.

I shuddered, but then I turned back to the elders. They too had blank expressions on their faces, but underneath it all, deep within the folds between their features, I could sense their compassion.

Yet I only had to blink to find that the elders had once again vanished into thin air. Black smoke surrounded where their ankles had been, and then it just floated away.

Their voices came in unison inside my head.

"Other places to go, other tasks to complete. But once you need us, we shall be present with you again."

I took a deep breath. This time, no one else seemed concerned over their elusiveness. It was as if the old men had hypnotised them to believe they hadn't been there all along. I still hadn't a clue who the elders actually were, but Cralanein had told me we could trust them, and I had trusted Cralanein completely.

That was when Valpeonia sprang into action. The look she gave Cralanein lying supine on the ground wasn't one of mourning but of urgency. She needed to behave, I realised, like a true leader.

"We have between four and five hours," she said. "After that, Slaro will be lost to secicao."

She glanced at Hastina, then gave me a knowing look. I knew precisely what she was suggesting.

"Faso's generator," I said.

"We need to take Cralanein's blood," Valpeonia said. "That's what Mr Gordoni said he needed – more of the silver stuff to power the generator."

"No," Taka said. "You can't do that, Regent Valpeonia. It's just not—"

Valpeonia raised a hand to shut him up. "We have no choice, Taka."

"But my father said it wasn't ready," Taka said.

"His type like to do much more testing than is strictly necessary," Valpeonia said. "Sometimes we just have to take a chance."

I lowered my head. I knew the implications; Taka being here would only slow us down, and I didn't think I could watch them leach blood out of Cralanein's corpse either. That stuff was just a couple of steps removed from Exalmpora, and I knew I was still weak to its lure.

The sparse remains in the vats had been bad enough. I feared that if I caught a whiff of a stronger dose of that stuff, then I'd be lost to Finesia once again.

At the same time, I was concerned regarding what Cralanein had told me. Yet I hadn't discovered exactly how Finesia planned to kill Honore – we didn't even know where Finesia had taken the dragonet, for that matter. If we could rescue her, we could also save the other dragon queens.

But I knew right now that we had to save the citizens of Slaro from the secicao that would inevitably close in as

Cralanein's protective bubble faded. This other matter could wait until Slaro was safe.

"Take Taka and go to talk to Faso," Valpeonia said. "We'll handle things down here."

Hastina already had her head cocked, and was assessing the golden body of the dragon queen. Upon death, the greenish patina of Cralanein's skin had faded, as if she were pushing away the secicao stains so that she could once again display her true form.

"Come on, Taka," I said, and took a step back towards the ledge that led out of here.

Taka took a step towards the door, but then he stopped and turned to take one last look at Cralanein. He took a deep breath and walked forward and then, one eyelid after the other, he closed both of her eyes.

PART III

There isn't a human upon this planet who can be trusted. Every single one of them plays their own games, damaging the natural world they live in, all the while failing to realise that the damage they cause will last an eternity.

– Tarinah Bogodan, Dragon Queen

7

FASO HAD CONVERTED much of the west wing of Slaro palace into a workshop complex for his team of engineers. He claimed that he'd used this space when he worked for King Cini III, long before even Sukina had met him. But back then he'd only used a couple of underground rooms, whereas now he'd ordered walls and columns knocked down to create a space large enough to house a hundred dragons.

He also had many more employees than he'd had at Fortress Gerhaun. His team milled around the lab like drunken ants, but still with a purpose, as if they knew exactly what had to be done. The whole place smelled of cheap cologne, mixed with the eggy scent of the secicao oil that powered the automatons.

In one corner, a few scientists in their white coats were stooped over what looked like a stove. At first I thought that they must be performing some kind of experiment. Faso, for a long time, had been talking about the possibility of mixing secicao with molten brass to create some kind of alloy – a metal stronger than titanium, or so he'd told me. Perhaps he had finally started trying to bring this dream to fruition.

As I got closer, I caught the smell of eggs and bacon, and my stomach started rumbling as I noticed the plates that a tall female scientist was handing out to a line of other researchers. It was already dinner time, it seemed – I hadn't realised how much time had passed since we were in the mountains earlier this morning.

Part of me wanted to go over and grab a plate myself, but I knew time was precious, and so Taka and I set out in search of Faso. Taka pointed him out, working in a cordoned off section, adjusting the rivets on the beak of a gigantic Roc automaton. These eagle-shaped aerial juggernauts had won so many battles for us, launching volleys of missiles and bullets from the guns and launchers on their wings at hundreds of black dragons.

I failed to see that they needed any improvements, but Faso would always find something to keep his team busy. I wasn't complaining, mind – though it had taken me a while to get used to Faso, his genius had saved our necks countless times. But that didn't mean I would go easy on him now.

I strolled over, letting Taka trail behind me. Faso raised his head.

"Pontopa," he said, with a cocky smirk. "Why the sour face?"

I shook my head. "Your son's here, Faso," I said.

He turned to Taka, who folded his arms over his chest.

"Ah yes," Faso said. "You as well. What the dragonheats is the matter?"

"Papo, you need to stop what you're doing and work on the generator at once. We need it up and running pronto."

Faso shook his head, chuckling to himself. He ran his fingers through his oily dark hair. "Always in a hurry, you dragonseers. When are you going to learn that science takes time and patience?"

I huffed. We really didn't have time for this, and Taka looked a little lost.

"Faso, just shut up and listen," I said.

He turned to me, his eyes wide.

"Cralanein has died," I said.

Faso's jaw dropped. "No! You're kidding! How?"

"Old age, but that doesn't really matter. We have no more than an hour, if that, before her spirit fades out of the collective unconscious and the secicao gas closes in. You saw what happened to Spezzio City."

Faso's gaze went distant. He pursed his lips and whistled, and then he looked down at the floor.

"Faso?" I asked.

"Just a moment," he mumbled. He closed his eyes and took a few deep breaths.

After what seemed like a really long moment, he opened his eyes again. "I'm sorry, it's just a lot to process. First Yol, and now this. What the wellies is going on?"

"It's too much to explain right now," I said. I didn't want to tell him about the absent young dragonet, to keep anything extra from slowing him down. "Look, we have to keep fighting, Faso Gordoni. And right now you need to get your team working around the clock."

"I understand that. But you know, I was never made for this management stuff; I just want to be making new things. It's what I've always dreamed of."

"There won't be a world left to build anything from if you don't get it together."

It didn't seem like Faso was listening to me, though. Rather he was shaking his head, his breathing shallow. He glanced over his shoulder at the great hulking oven-like device a few yards away from us. It had a funnel at its top and brass pipes leading over it, which then wrapped around it like two coiled snakes. A long drawer spanned the length of its base, which I presumed was designed to house the coal. I figured the dragon queen blood would go right into the spout at the top.

Faso had already explained how the device worked in layman's terms. Just like a dragon queen's blood would be heated inside her body, the machine gently heated the blood, passing it around in the pipes that wrapped around the device.

Of course, I knew it was much more complex than that – otherwise, it would be up and running already.

"You do know it's only a prototype?" he asked. "I've told Valpeonia a thousand times, this isn't ready to go yet."

"Then you'd better get it working fast," I said. "Because if you don't, we all die here. We can't evacuate now – there's nowhere else to go."

Faso took another deep breath, then he blew out his cheeks and let the air out slowly. His face had gone slightly red.

"Fine," he said. "We'll get to work."

He turned on his heels and walked over to a bell hanging off a pillar in the centre of the room. He pulled on a cord to ring it, three times. The sound pealed out, as loud as church bells. When Faso did things, he liked to do them boldly.

"Change of plans, change of plans," he said. "We have work to do, people, so gather round for a briefing."

I shook my head, then my stomach rumbled again as a whiff of bacon passed my way. The technicians had already absently left the rashers alone in the pot, and so I saw no harm in taking a few on the way out.

Despite the cavernous nature of the workshop, it was blazingly hot in there and admittedly a little stuffy. It had been a long day, and I decided it would be better to get a bit of fresh air. Besides, I could sense Velos waiting in the courtyard. He hadn't even moved to the stables to join the greys.

"Why don't you supervise here, Taka?" I asked him. "Make sure your father keeps everything in order."

He glanced over at Faso, who had his head held high as he watched the technicians in their white coats gathering closer. He didn't seem to be in too much of a hurry, but I guessed this was all part of the show. Asinal Winda had moved right up to him, and was muttering something in his ear, probably wondering what the dragonheats was going on. But Faso didn't seem ready to pass that information on to her yet.

"I think my father's got this," Taka said. "I'll stick close to you, Dragonseer Wells, if you don't mind."

I nodded to him. We'd made a pact since what had happened at the Tree Immortal that we'd look out for each other. That way, if Finesia tried to take over either of our minds, then the other would know it and be able to force cyagora down our throats. The drug had enough power in it to numb our suggestibility to her, but it numbed other emotions too.

"I just want some fresh air," I said. "Sometimes, with everything going on, we need to rest."

Taka laughed. "After telling my father how hard he needs to work, you want to rest?"

I nodded and smiled sheepishly.

"Don't worry," Taka said, "I won't tell him if you don't. Besides, Papo deserved it."

"He works hard, your father does."

Taka shrugged. "Don't we all – it's just that you seem to know how to work on the right things and he ... well, he does whatever takes his fancy."

"He's a good man, underneath it all," I said.

"I know," Taka said. "I know ..."

But from his expression, I wasn't sure how much he believed it. For sure, there was no way that Faso could live up to Taka's mother in any of our estimation.

The central courtyard was emptier than it usually was this time of the afternoon. No one had moved to clean up the rubble, or sweep the dust off the ground, or pull out the charred shrubs. It was as if a ghost had haunted this place so violently that no one dared come near.

Velos was stationed at one corner and Bellroot at the other. Sunlight glinted off the polished brass on both of their armours, the sun having just peeked out from the clouds overhead. I looked up, taking in the sight for a moment, wondering if this would be the last that we saw of the blue Slaro sky before it was permanently covered by secicao clouds. *Not if Faso manages to get the generator working*, I told myself. I had to have hope.

Velos and Bellroot had their heads turned away from each other, keeping as close to their own corners as they possibly could. They'd never quite seen eye to eye, those two dragons, despite having fought on the same team through numerous battles.

I felt sorry for the citrine dragon as I went to spend some time with Velos. I was sure Hastina and Valpeonia were still down in Cralanein's chamber, hopefully by now draining the golden queen of the last dregs of her vital blood. If Bellroot knew anything of what was going on down there, he wouldn't be happy about it, but somehow I doubted he had a clue.

If I was right about Hastina, Bellroot would be slowly losing his connection with her. That was what had happened to me when Finesia had taken over my mind. I'd almost lost my bond to Velos completely, and I think he'd never quite managed to get over it.

Velos lowered his blue scaly head towards me as I approached. He pushed his snout into my chest, and I rubbed him under the chin, taking a whiff of the two faint plumes of smoke that rose out of his nostrils.

Taka loitered close, and I cocked my head towards Bellroot to indicate that he probably could do with some company. Taka grasped it immediately, and he skipped over to fill the inevitable space left by Hastina's neglect. He didn't say anything – not out loud or in the collective unconscious – but somehow, he knew that I just needed a moment. I guess he needed that time too.

I was worried, admittedly. So many thoughts were spinning around my head, all of them filled with unanswered questions.

Would Faso and his team be able to fix the device in time, and would it work at all, for that matter? What about my mother and Hastina? Was Finesia in their minds as I suspected?

Were we about to lose them as we had lost Wiggea, and our once-loyal ally and Sukina's former lover, Charth?

Then there was the issue of the God Dragon, Honore – could we win him over to our side, to fight for true dragonkind and life upon our world rather than the destructive existence of the black dragon immortals?

What about Finesia? What was she up to, and how did she plan to become strong enough to fight Honore? Where was Alsie for that matter?

Every question I asked myself seemed to lead to the largest of them all – when did Finesia plan to finally destroy us all? No matter how hard I tried, my train of thought always still led to despair.

Velos seemed to sense my anxiety, and he let out a soft croon in an attempt to snap me out of it. He looked at me with his massive yellow eye as his voice continued its low whine. After a moment, I realised he was singing that same dragonsong I always used to sing to calm him.

"I'm sorry," I said. "I just feel so powerless right now."

Though he wouldn't understand the words, he would understand the emotions behind them. The look he gave me said that the only power I could gain in this situation was to refuse to give up the fight. That brought me some comfort.

I must have lost track of time, because I didn't know how long I'd sat there before I heard footsteps within the courtyard – two pairs of them, one softer than the other.

"Pontopa," Mamo said, "we wondered where you'd got to. Where have you been all this time? Rumour had it that you suddenly departed towards Spezzio, but no one could tell me for what reason."

I looked up and shook my head. I hadn't heard her approaching, or Papo for that matter, who stood only slightly behind her.

"There are things going on here," I said. "I just can't explain it to you yet, Mamo. I don't want to cause any panic."

She stepped forward and put her hand on my shoulder. Papo sidled around me and placed his hand on the other one.

"All this coming and going," Mamo said, "all this secrecy. I know why you do it, but it feels strange to be kept in the dark like this."

The blood had completely blanched out of Mamo's face, and just by looking at her I could tell she was worried sick. I looked at Papo, and he nodded his head as if in agreement with my mother. But he said nothing.

"Just tell me this," Mamo said. "Has something terrible happened? Because everyone felt it, you know? There was this sadness that washed over us. Before you'd explained to me about how the collective unconscious works, I'd have thought nothing of it. But now, people are talking."

My heart skipped a beat. "What are they saying?"

"They all feel that we're in grave danger, that Alsie is about to return, and she's bringing her armies. No one has any rational reason to think that way – but that doesn't stop the rumours, mind."

I nodded, taking it in. As I'd said, I really didn't want to cause any panic, and the less the people knew about Cralanein's death, the better. At the same time, I couldn't help thinking about that altercation we'd had with the old lady up in the Caprio Mountains. She'd wanted to be close to her grandchildren, so they could all prepare for the end. Keeping information from the citizens of Slaro would really do the opposite. If the worst happened, then keeping quiet would strip away the people's chance to prepare and spend their valuable final moments with their loved ones. In many ways, maybe it was better that way.

"There's no impending attack," I said. "At least not to our knowledge."

"If you don't want to talk about it," Papo said, "or if you can't for whatever reason, we will understand. We've never asked

Doctor Forsolano to betray his doctor-patient confidentiality, and we'd never ask the same of you."

I sucked in a breath through my teeth – I really didn't like keeping this from my parents in this way.

Taka solved the dilemma for me because he had already drifted over to join in the conversation. He cut straight to it as well, without even looking to me for permission.

"Cralanein has died," he said, "and so has Yol."

And before my parents had a chance to ask any further questions, he filled them in on everything that had taken place. Never once during his explanation or afterwards did I chide Taka for his decision, because deep in my heart, I knew it was the right thing to do.

All the time, my parents remained silent. Tears welled in my mother's eyes, but she didn't move her hand to wipe them away. Neither of them showed any panic. It was as if they had accepted that we were going to lose, sooner or later.

I thought I'd have some time to ask for some advice, but there came a swishing of wings from the south, and I peered through the murk to see three grey dragons approaching, a rider mounted upon each. All three riders wore olive-coloured uniforms. The leading rider looked stout and strong, and I recognised her immediately.

She was my former dragonelite bodyguard, the humble Lieutenant Talato. From the urgency evident in her posture, it was clear she wasn't bringing good news.

8

As protocol dictated, Lieutenant Gereve Talato's grey dragon mount didn't land in the courtyard, but on the dragon landing pad just south of Slaro Palace. Taka and I left my parents with the two dragons, and immediately strolled over to meet her.

Neither of us had seen her in months, but I guessed she'd preferred it that way. After her lover, Lieutenant Candiornio, had perished during the Battle of the Tree Immortal, she'd opted to retire as a dragonelite. In a way, I wondered if she partly blamed me for Candiornio's death.

Whatever her reasons, I'd put her through so much, and I didn't blame her for wanting to distance herself. Somehow it seemed safer for her to serve General Sako on the front lines, rather than to stick close to me.

As we climbed the stairs to the landing platform, Talato quickly dismounted from the back of the grey. She gave Taka and me a brief salute, and then didn't waste another moment on proprietaries, cutting straight to the chase.

"Urgent news from the front lines," she said, "courtesy of General Sako."

I nodded, my face tight with anticipation. "Go on," I said.

"We've been attacked, ma'am. And taken great casualties on the eastern front."

"Black dragons?" I asked.

"No ma'am," Talato said. "Our own. Our automatons turned on us."

"Dragonheats!" I clenched my fists. "The secicao—"

I'd been so caught up in the issues surrounding Cralanein's death, I'd completely forgotten about her warnings regarding secicao. The very substance we were using to power our technology was likely to turn on us at any moment, catching us unawares. Now, it seemed, Finesia had seemingly decided it was an opportune time.

Talato raised her eyebrows. "Do you know what's going on, ma'am?"

I had my fists clenched so tight that my nails dug into my palms. How much should I tell? But when Talato was my bodyguard, I had trusted her with my innermost secrets. I had no reason not to do so again.

I took a deep breath. "Secicao – it's not ours to control, even as much as we think it is. Finesia has complete control of it."

"You know I've never believed in that stuff," she said. "Myths and magic. It's all been designed to make us fear the future."

"But you've seen it with your own eyes – the rebirth of Finesia, the black dragons, what happened at the Tree Immortal ..."

I stopped myself before I could go any further. Candiornio had been killed by a projectile lobbed from the Tree Immortal during that terrible battle – an event I was sure Talato wanted to forget.

But she didn't seem perturbed by my blunder. "Things might have happened, but I refuse to believe Finesia has more control than we do. The sacrifice of our comrades can't have been for naught."

I looked into her dark eyes then. In her pupils, I first saw sadness, but I only needed to look a little further to detect wisdom gained through months of endured grief.

"You're a good soldier, Talato," I said.

"Thank you, ma'am ... but I didn't come here to discuss personal issues."

"Tell me: How many casualties?"

"Not severe. Fortunately, we only had a few Rocs and several Mammoths deployed at the time, and a good two hundred war automatons. General Sako had been keeping them on standby until we absolutely needed them. Thank the dragons he did."

I nodded and my lips formed a faint smile. Like myself, General Sako had never been keen on the new secicao technology, though he was a little more enthusiastic than I was about the use of it.

That smile soon melted away when I remembered the grave expression on Talato's face.

"We still needed to retreat, ma'am," she said. "We fell back to the Cini-Sanito river, where Admiral Sandao was holding the First Regent Fleet. We lost a good thousand greys and several thousand men during that perilous march."

"But you say you defeated the automatons?" Taka interrupted. For a moment I'd forgotten he was there. "Is everything now under control?"

I'm sure Taka hoped, as I did, that Talato had only come to deliver the message. We had enough going on here in Slaro that we couldn't really spare the resources to help.

The slow shake of her head told me more than the subsequent words would. "We need as much help as you can spare over there. The black dragons are on the move, Dragonseer Wells, and we fear that this time they aim to wipe us out for good."

IN THE END, we decided that I had to travel alone. Valpeonia and Hastina needed to extract Cralanein's blood for the generator, to save everyone in Slaro. We still had Faso's workshop here, and his automatons were our best chance of surviving – with or without secicao.

Fortunately, he'd told me at one point that his Vulnerable Point Tracking Technology system that we'd used to take down the automatons didn't need secicao at all. So we still had a chance, as long as he could get the generator working.

I sent Taka to tell his father what had happened, and to try to convince him to put a team aside to shut down any active automatons in the city and then drain every single automaton of secicao. Coal and steam alone could power them, though I knew they would be nowhere near as powerful as they had been when they were powered by secicao fuel. Admittedly, Faso had a lot on his plate right now, but he was the best person to get this done as quickly as it needed to be.

I also sent Valpeonia a quick note in the collective unconscious, to tell her what had happened. She told me to be careful, although I could hear the strain in her voice. I was sure she knew the battle I was about to face could end me, but then, a woman like Valpeonia would understand the necessity of such sacrifice, even if I had once inhabited her womb. She might have also had Finesia in her mind, numbing her emotions a little – in truth, I had no way of knowing.

I didn't stop to say goodbye to my true parents, because I didn't want to believe that this would be my final battle. It was just one more day in the job. No harm would come to me and no harm would come to them. I had to believe that.

I would help General Sako repel Finesia's attack, Faso would fix the generator, and then we would gather our forces and find a way to save this planet. Talato was right – we had to have hope.

Talato mounted Bellroot, being familiar with the controls from having used the ones on Velos' armour many times before. One of her soldiers took the rear seat on the citrine dragon's armour. The other took the rear on Velos' back. Both Talato and the soldier had their Pattersoni rifles drawn, ready to fire at any threats that emerged.

A control panel in front of them also allowed them to operate the Gatling guns on each side of their dragon's armour. Fortunately, these could also work on automatic, as I doubted either rear-seated soldier knew how to work the controls.

The voice came into my head just as Velos lifted into the air.

"You are not alone in this quest. We will protect you."

It took me a moment to realise it wasn't one voice that had spoken, but three in unison – all of them thin and reedy and old. It sounded just like the elderly academics. Or was it my imagination, Finesia playing mind-tricks on me once again?

"Who are you?" I asked. *"What do you want from me?"*

A picture of one of the elders, the anthropologist, emerged in my mind. As it did, the clouds wheeled by below me, and it was as if his head were floating in front of me, his wiry beard dangling beneath the mole on his chin. Dragonheats, it was so vivid, I could have sworn I was actually looking at a floating head.

I thought Finesia had to be playing tricks on me for sure. But then I remembered what Cralanein had told me before she died – I could trust these old men. I guessed, or at least I hoped, that meant I could trust this weird vision too.

"Did Cralanein not tell you of our allegiance?" he asked.

"She did, but—"

But I'm still not sure, I wanted to say. Doubt once again started to cloud my mind.

The head of the second old man, the biologist, appeared in the sky, and the image of his peer dissipated before my very eyes. The birthmark across his left cheek seeming to waver slightly as his lips moved. *"You know that you can trust us,"* he said.

"Trust ..." I said, almost in a trance. His words seemed mesmerising. I had no reason not to listen to them. I had no reason not to believe.

I turned back towards the soldier stationed on the back of Velos. The man saluted, and his expression told me he wasn't seeing any of this. It was an illusion within my own mind, just like it had been when Finesia had taken control.

Dragonheats, I wondered if Lieutenant Talato had brought some cyagora with her – a drug powerful enough to numb my senses from this. She was steering Bellroot to the right just below me, and nodded at me when she saw me looking at her.

In front of me, the third academic materialised out of the clouds, and the second vanished. His voice came out from beneath that slightly cleft top lip. *"You have no need for drugs, Dragonseer Wells. No need to use anything to alter your mind."*

Then the other two heads appeared once more, forming a triangle in the air in front of me. They began to spin in a circle, and the clouds seemed to swirl around them. It was almost as if they had control of the clouds. But this was an illusion, I reminded myself. None of this was real.

The elders spoke next in unison.

"You have no need for distrust, no need for agony. You are at one with the collective unconscious, and so is the boy, destined to become more powerful than you could ever imagine."

I clutched my hands to my temples; I wanted to scream. I turned to see if Talato had noticed me, but her gaze was now focused dead ahead. Even the soldier behind me seemed not to be watching me. It was as if they had been programmed to turn a blind eye to my moment of desolation.

"No need for despair," the three old men said. *"Just trust what you see before you, and in doing so trust yourself. A battle is ahead, but so are we to guide you. We have managed to reach you beyond your doubts, so now use your powers to help us reach Honore."*

Velos swerved downwards, and I gripped his steering fin to steady him. Beneath us the secicao clouds boiled and roiled, and I imagined the deathly branches underneath them reaching out to wrap us in their embrace.

This had to be another of Finesia's tricks, surely – but

Cralanein had told me to trust these old men. Could she possibly have been wrong?

"*What is this?*" I said in the collective unconscious. "*And who exactly are you?*"

But when I looked up, the faces of the three old men were nowhere to be seen, and only a bright sun was searing down from the clear sky.

9

IT WAS AROUND HALF an hour's flight to the Cini-Sanito river, travelling at full speed. On one of the several dragon-carriers they had brought upriver, they had knocked out the bulkheads between the compartments so that the ship could house a dragon queen.

Therefore, all we had to do was look for a hole in the secicao clouds created by the protective bubble. What with the pellucid sky above us, and the sun guiding our way, they really weren't hard to find.

The *Saye Explorer* – a frigate I'd seen far more of than any other ship – was the fleet's flagship. Two funnels towered up from its deck and into the sky, spewing out plumes of coal smoke and not secicao from its two thick funnels, thank the wellies. I had to guess they'd already worked out that secicao was the problem, and no longer trusted it as fuel.

I sensed Tarinah on board her dedicated dragon carrier as we approached. I'd always considered her the grumpiest and least forgiving of the dragon queens, and hence had avoided her wher-ever possible. She'd given me a hard time after Gerhaun's death, when the remaining dragon queens had arrived to occupy the fortress in the Southlands. She had accused me of being a servant of Finesia, knowing I'd turned into a dragonwoman and massacred thousands of civilians under the goddess' thrall. She hadn't been wrong, but while Gerhaun had trusted that I could win over Finesia in the end, Tarinah and a few of the other dragon queens had wanted me executed. Perhaps if I had been, Finesia would never have been reborn.

But at this moment, Tarinah was asleep. Green sparks emitted by the secicao clouds plucked away at the protective bubble of the collective unconscious, creating a shimmering effect around its perimeter.

A tinny voice came from the side of Velos' armour, startling me. "*Saye Explorer* gives Dragon Velos and Dragon Bellroot permission to land. Please follow the path of the Hummingbirds, and do not deviate from your current path."

I turned to Talato, who had Bellroot flying only a few yards away from me, my eyebrows raised.

"He knows we're all on the same side, right?" I shouted to her over the roar of the wind.

"It's just protocol, ma'am," Talato replied. "No one's sure who to trust nowadays."

I clenched my teeth as I watched the two spherical Hummingbird drones rise out from the destroyer, their reedy propellor blades whirring above them. The automatons weren't glowing green, so I knew they were no longer augmented by secicao. Still, apart from that and despite their size, these automatons could still prove formidable foes – particularly when they swarmed en masse.

"Please don't deviate from your current course," the voice said over the speaker again.

"Oh for wellies' sake," I said. "Can you hear what I'm saying down there? Has Faso installed that capability on my armour at least?"

"Affirmative, ma'am. Loud and clear."

"Then what's all this stay on your current course stuff about? Why the distrust?"

"We do trust you as a dragonseer, ma'am, but we need to keep a close eye on the armour. Anything mechanical we need to deem a risk – I'm sure you understand, ma'am."

"You don't have to worry about that," I said. "We drained our armours of secicao just before we took off."

I reached out and touched the secicao flash on my hip. I might have drained Velos, but I'd forgotten to empty this out. I guess I'd thought I still might use it at the last minute, even if it could take over my mind.

"I'm sorry ma'am, but orders are orders," the soldier replied. "They came directly from Admiral Sandao himself."

I shook my head. Whoever this chump of a sailor was, he'd clearly forgotten that I was at the top of the chain of command here, even higher than Admiral Sandao. But I thought it better to just leave things be. Some of these men had seen me transform into a black dragon and attack their own, so I guessed it was perfectly rational of them not to trust me.

The two Hummingbirds tilted forwards, and their little rotors let out a high-pitched buzzing sound due to the speed of their blades. They stopped right in front of Velos, turning and adjusting their speed to match Velos' and Bellroot's own. Then they split up and traced a path down to the Saye Explorer. All the way, two protrusions from the back of the little spheres watched us – their lenses no doubt attached to one of Faso's proprietary monitoring screens down on deck.

The Hummingbirds led us over to the landing deck, situated aft the fore funnel. I couldn't see any sailors on deck, just a couple of war automatons with their brass faceplates and machine-gun appendages tracking Bellroot and Velos as they approached the carrier. Again, they didn't have the green secicao tint running through their circuits, so I guessed they were safe.

I saluted the war automatons, not that they would have noticed. Then Velos scuffed his claws against the ridged deck plating. I felt a slight pain in my fingernails, the same twinge that he felt whenever he landed on something hard.

"Admiral Sandao and General Sako await you in the operations room, ma'am," that same voice said over the speaker system again.

"On my way," I said and climbed down the ladder into the bridge.

THE UPPER BRIDGE of the *Saye Explorer* was an elongated room that spanned nearly the entire length and breadth of the ship, wrapping itself neatly around the fore and aft funnels.

The main command centre, or CIC as the military types liked to call it, lay in front of the foremost funnel. The officers of the First Regent Fleet used the space between the two funnels for strategy briefings, conducting their business around a long oval table. That left the space at the back for the rest rooms and secicao dispensers.

I emerged from the spiral staircase that led down to this section and into the musty yet homely scent of South Saye tea. Secicao had taken over the entire Saye Archipelago to the southeast, making this an incredibly limited resource. But I guessed the officers now believed they wanted to savour the best in their final days.

It was stuffier on deck than I remembered. I guessed, now that the sailors were back to burning coal, they had to deal again with a lot of heat from the boiler room. I took my handkerchief from my pocket at the bottom of the stairwell and wiped some sweat off my brow.

Many enlisted officers, as well as General Sako and Admiral Sandao, sat at the table.

"Blunders and dragonheats," General Sako said, as he glanced at his pocket watch. "I expected you half an hour ago, Dragonseer Wells. What's the reason for this delay?"

General Sako was Sukina's father and Taka's grandfather. He was a short, barrel-chested man. His thick moustache ran down either side of his face and curled up at the sides. He had a short temper, but I'd always known him to be a good man.

I shook my head and glanced at Talato, who had now seated herself beside Admiral Sandao at the opposite side of the table. The old admiral, unlike the general, was thin and mild-mannered.

"Sir, the delays were entirely on our side," Talato said. "We got held up on the way to the palace."

General Sako's moustache twitched. "Held up by what, may I ask? I thought we ordered you to take a direct route."

"You did, sir. But we thought we saw black dragons on the way over to Slaro Palace, so we had to take the long way around them."

"Black dragons in our territory?" I asked, my eyebrows raised. "How did they manage to get past our defences unnoticed?"

Talato looked abashed. "It turns out they weren't black dragons at all, but just a regular flock of greys on patrol. It took us a while to realise—"

"And how did you manage to mistake—" General Sako began.

I put up a hand to silence the general. After everything Talato had been through, I didn't want to see her take an unnecessary grilling. General Sako harumphed but let me speak.

"Talato, did you take secicao oil to speed you on your journey?"

She nodded, her head down. "Yes, ma'am."

"Then that would have been the problem," I said. "It wasn't the machines that turned on you here, but the secicao."

Talato's eyes went wide. "You mean to say we were hallucinating?"

"Well, what else do you think it could have been?"

"We're all tired, ma'am. Everyone here has been losing sleep, wondering when Alsie Fioreletta will finally muster her forces and attack."

I nodded, then turned back to General Sako. "You must order your soldiers to dispose of all secicao they have in reserve. It's dangerous, and Finesia can get into the minds of anyone who uses it. That's what has happened to Talato, I fear."

"Blunders and dragonheats," General Sako said. "The men too!"

I nodded and delivered a brief report. This was the military after all. They already knew what had happened to Yol, but they hadn't yet heard about Cralanein's passing. I turned my head between each astonished face as I delivered my report, watching the blood drain slowly out of their faces. No one said a word – no one even coughed.

"The situation is grave," Admiral Sandao said after I'd finished. "I trust Talato told you about the automatons who turned on us."

I nodded. "She said your losses were substantial."

"Unfortunately, yes." I could never get over how soft spoken the admiral was. "Fortunately, we didn't have many of the automatons in deployment. We've always been prepared for contingencies, and we've never wanted to fully rely on secicao power, despite Mr Gordoni's advice to the contrary. After the ambush by our own forces, I sent some of my marines and twenty greys out to investigate what had happened. They flew back after seeing a mass of what they described as a thousand black dragons gathering through the clouds."

"A thousand black dragons?" I asked. "How the wellies did they get away?"

"Our marines," Sandao said. "They managed to fly out and come back without being spotted. Now we're standing at the ready, waiting for them to attack. But the remaining Rocs we had in our arsenal were shot down while fighting the rogue Rocs. We don't have anything to fight back with."

My ears perked up at this, and the hair rose on the back of my neck. I reached out, probing the collective unconscious for any sign of enemies approaching. There was nothing, only the faint murmurs of Velos and Bellroot above deck, the soft snores of Tarinah sleeping, and the heartbeats of thousands of greys stationed within the surrounding dragon carriers.

"Something doesn't sit right, here," I said.

"What do you mean?" Admiral Sandao asked.

"Just … did your men augment on their little reconnaissance mission? Could this massive army have been an illusion they saw, just like Talato and the other envoys did? A hallucination, perhaps?"

It was as if everyone in the room had decided to hold their breaths at once. Finally, Admiral Sandao leaned forward and opened his mouth to say something. But he didn't get a chance, because the boat suddenly rocked, and klaxons sounded outside.

10

"BLACK DRAGONS SIGHTED AT SIX O'CLOCK." The same voice that spoke had been the one to order me to follow the Hummingbirds onto the deck. "Black dragons sighted at six o'clock. Everyone take defensive positions."

Dragonheats, Sandao had been right. The enemy had been holding off their attack until my arrival.

General Sako and Admiral Sandao were immediately on their feet, strolling over to the bridge. I heard General Sako bawling out orders to his men. Soldiers rushed up from the lower deck, and from outside came the buzz of deploying Hummingbirds – hopefully not powered by secicao. Then there came the clanking and creaking of brass joints shifting – war automatons shifting into position.

From outside there came a crash that quickly evolved into a hiss. The boat rocked once more, and I smelled a spray of salt in the gust of wind that howled down the staircase. The momentum sent me reeling towards the wall. I planted a foot behind me and turned to steady myself.

Talato had moved closer as if she wanted to protect me, to resume her previous role.

"With me," I said. "We need to get Velos and Bellroot up into the air, pronto. I need support commanding the greys."

"Ma'am—" Talato looked towards the bridge. She wasn't under my command any longer, and General Sako might have expected her here. But right now, he was probably too busy to care.

"We haven't time to deliberate, Lieutenant. Come on."

I climbed the steep winding staircase, not looking behind as I moved. That tinny voice came out from the loudspeaker again.

"Queen's Carrier is under attack. All units defend the Queen's Carrier."

Dragonheats, now I knew what was happening. Finesia was going for Tarinah. She wanted to take another dragon queen down – three losses in one day. I couldn't stomach the thought.

A thick spray of brackish water greeted me as I emerged from the hatch. The river seemed ablaze with green fire as geysers shot up out of the water. It was as though a volcano had emerged beneath the *Saye Explorer*. I stumbled out towards the deck railing, the boat swaying violently as the river tossed us around. In the distance, green sparks from the clouds smashed violently against Tarinah's protective barrier. Rumbles of thunder boomed from afar.

In the collective unconscious, I could feel Velos struggling to keep his footing on the swaying boat, and so I quickly rushed over to his location. I gripped on to the ladder at the side of his armour, climbed, and then took position in the front seat. I buckled my harness together and pulled back on Velos' steering fin to launch him into the air. A glance over my shoulder confirmed that Talato had successfully mounted Bellroot.

There came a whirring sound from below. I had steered Velos over to Tarinah's carrier, and I looked over the side to see a massive hatch opening that spanned the width and nearly the length of the flat deck, only stopping at the thick dirty funnel at the back that was spewing its coal smoke into the air. The hatch was opening, sliding out in two halves on rollers, each metal plate folding down into the sides of the ship.

The mechanism moved surprisingly fast, and it wasn't long until I could see the great golden form of Tarinah, the dragon queen. The glowing glare she gave me with her deep yellow eyes told me that she still didn't trust me, yet she did not address me in the collective unconscious.

Once the hatch had completely opened, Tarinah spread her great golden wings. Both her golden skin and the ridged deck plating below her glinted in the sunlight. She launched into the air, letting out a massive roar.

Hundreds of grey dragons swarmed in to protect their dragon queen. Tarinah kept low, fortunately. If she flew too far away from us, she'd take her protective bubble with her. I was sure that the sailors and soldiers on board every ship would have their gas masks, but still, the secicao clouds would hamper visibility and help fuel the black dragons' power.

I turned Velos around, keeping close to Tarinah. I'd still not caught sight of the black dragons, but then I didn't have telescopes and periscopes like the crew on board did. I reached for my hip flask; the secicao oil within would help me see further. But then I remembered myself. Drinking that stuff was a sure way to let Finesia into my mind.

"Ah, Dragonseer Wells," a female voice said in my head. I thought at first it was Finesia, but it didn't have the same power to it. Still, it was laced with danger and spite. I paused a moment, trying to work out who it could belong to.

"I had hoped that I would meet my daughter instead of you," the voice continued, and then I recognised her for who she was. *"I thought I would finally be able to convince Hastina to join my side."*

"Indira," I replied. *"It does me great pleasure to finally be able to put an end to you. This battle is long overdue."*

I'd first met Indira not in this form but under the guise of the mad scientist known as Travast Indorm. She'd been largely responsible for the birth of the black dragons at the Ginlast automaton factory.

"*Oh, how you jest,*" Indira said. "*We have already destroyed your Rocs, and you have only yourself and your dragon now, I believe. This, I'm afraid, shall actually be the end of you.*"

"*We still have enough forces to take you down,*" I said, though I was not sure how much I believed it. I really didn't know how many dragonmen Indira had brought with her.

"*You have always been such a naïve fool, Pontopa Wells. You speak with such confidence, without understanding how much power Finesia wields.*"

"*Oh, I know,*" I said, and then I took a gamble. "*But if you think Honore is going to remain on your side, then you're horribly wrong.*"

Indira laughed, both in the collective unconscious and with a loud roar that resonated from the clouds. "*So you know. And you have already seen your end, because the ancient God Dragon is now completely under Finesia's thrall.*"

"*That is where you are wrong,*" I said. "*And it is your own arrogance that shall be your undoing.*"

I really was taking a leap of faith, here. I'd just seen the three old men in the clouds, who clearly were a great deal more than mere men. They had told me that I could find a way through to Honore, and Cralanein had said it too. I didn't yet know how, but I had to find out. First, I needed to protect Tarinah, the dragon queen who was guarding the First Regent Fleet.

I could see the black dragons at the edge of the secicao clouds. They danced across the cloud line in a circle, not seemingly ready to enter Tarinah's protective bubble.

Green lightning flashed from the west and there came a boom of thunder. An eggy whiff of secicao followed, and I noticed a stream of green gas floating out of the clouds. Panic surged in my chest when I saw how it travelled inwards. Once again, Finesia had found a way to break through the protective barrier of a dragon queen.

Underneath the queen's carrier, the river glowed green, the waves thrashing as if the water belonged to a wild sea. The ships beneath held their positions, but from the way they tossed on the river's surface I was grateful that I was high up on Velos' back and not on one of their decks.

I turned back towards the clouds, trying to work out Indira's location among the distant black dragons.

"*What sorcery is this?*" I asked. "*Explain yourself, Indira.*"

"*All will become apparent very shortly, my dear.*"

From the timbre of the voice, I realised I was no longer talking to the black dragon – it had instead beneath it a richness, of a kind that had lived through hundreds if not thousands of generations. Indira had just become a vessel for something much more powerful than her. The voice of a goddess ...

"*Finesia,*" I said. "*You will never end us.*"

"*Oh, but it's only a matter of time,*" she said. "*After all, we are immortal, and so have plenty more time than you do.*"

Her voice had a certain allure to it. It made me want to open up my mind to her and reveal things that I knew she shouldn't know. But I kept my mind closed to protect any secrets it might contain.

"*No,*" I said. "*Your days are numbered, and the sad thing is that you don't seem to realise it. You've always underestimated the power of human will, Finesia. That is your weakness, and that will be your undoing.*"

"*So you think,*" Finesia said, still using Indira's voice, as there was no way I would let her into my mind. "*Just as I was about to prove you wrong.*"

Her voice seemed to trail off into the depths of the darkness. Or rather, it was swallowed by a loud crash that came below. Out of the water, just beneath the queen's carrier, arose a great tidal wave. And out of that came a lithe and gigantic serpentine form, glowing green.

The God Dragon emerged from the depths of the Cini-Sanito river, more massive than I'd ever seen him before. As in my vision before Cralanein's death, it wore the faces of thousands of dragons, flickering ethereally from one to the other. They weren't what I saw with my eyes, but instead were the dragons I knew from memory and those dredged up from the abyss of myth. In the flying serpent's faces, I only saw the impressions of dragons I'd always known in my own mind.

I looked for traces of kindness in each of those faces, but it wasn't there. All I saw was wanton destruction, the wish to annihilate every living thing. It had instead latched onto the will of another, the wishes of an empress. Evil incarnate.

The God Dragon trailed great glowing plumes of green smoke behind it, and the way its lithe body danced made it look as if it belonged in the realm of the gods. It turned towards Tarinah, its eyes set on its target. I didn't waste a moment, pulling back on Velos' steering fin to lift him. The elders hadn't given me precise instructions, but even so I knew exactly what I had to do.

Tarinah let out a roar and turned towards the God Dragon. She'd have to know exactly what she was facing; dragon queens could communicate telepathically across great distances, and no doubt Yol had told her of the danger.

The air seemed to shimmer around a great ball of fire that emerged from Tarinah's throat. It headed straight towards the God Dragon with a brilliant display of light and heat. The fireball hit the God Dragon, where it exploded, bathing the scene in flame. Then it faded, to display the God Dragon unscathed, still speeding towards its target.

Tarinah managed somehow to manoeuvre out of his way, and the God Dragon passed her, missing by inches. Grey dragons lunged in to attack. As soon as their claws connected, green sparks flashed off the God Dragon, flaring brightly. Together, several grey dragons tumbled towards the ground, their bodies limp.

I sang a dragonsong to order the greys away. This assault wasn't helping things one bit.

"*What are you doing, Dragonseer?*" Tarinah demanded, in my mind. "*Have you turned traitor once again?*"

"*You must not fight it,*" I said. "*That is Honore, and we need to convince him we're on his side.*"

"*Honore died in combat against Finase. Now stand aside.*"

"*Believe what you must, but this God Dragon is invincible,*" I said. "*Your actions are futile either way.*"

But Tarinah remained uncowed, and she let out a roar that caused the grey dragons to turn their heads towards her. I'd never had my song cut off by a dragon queen before, but whatever she had told them drew power away from the notes of my song.

I could feel it in the collective unconscious; they would no longer listen to my commands. Tarinah could order them to attack me right now if she wanted and tear me out of the sky, but she kept her attention on the God Dragon. Honore had now turned around and was speeding towards Tarinah even faster than before. He was coming in for another pass, ignoring the raking claws and streams of fire coming from the grey dragons. They seemed in fact to be filling him with strength.

For a moment I wanted to give up, but I remembered the three floating heads of the old men in the clouds, and what they had told me. *Just trust yourself in the coming battle, and we will do the rest.*

Naturally, though, Tarinah didn't seem to trust me. It seemed she had already realised that to battle this beast was futile. She sang her own song to order the greys to form a wall between her and the God Dragon, which was now almost upon her.

In the distance, Indira's black dragons still circled, keeping a safe distance, ready to take us all down once Honore had eliminated the dragon queen.

"*You cannot win this one, my Fallen,*" Finesia said in my mind. "*All you can do is submit to me, and I will do the rest.*"

And she was right, I did need to submit – but not to her. I

blanked the fear out of my mind, then I turned my attention towards the God Dragon. I observed its path as it almost collided with Tarinah a second time. But instinct told me she still had some fight left in her, and she dived out of the way once again.

This time her motion was slower. The trail of green gas that Honore had spread in his wake seemed to have affected the dragon queen, sapping her strength. Something deep within me, perhaps inherited from my ancestors, told me what to do next. I sang a song and it was unlike any song I'd sung before.

This time, I didn't sing it from my memory, but from another place. In my mind, I could sense the three older men singing with me, and it didn't take me long to realise it wasn't my song but theirs.

The tune had no melody, only a harmony older than the age of mortal man and dragons. It tinkled like wind chimes through the breeze, pushing away any evil, any fear, any will of mal intent. It sourced itself from an ancient and arcane wisdom that was as old as time itself.

The God Dragon had already gained momentum. He barrelled through the wall of grey dragons, and I could see his target was Tarinah's very heart. This time she couldn't escape it. She was too tired, and the God Dragon too fast.

But it couldn't resist the will of the song, the will of the powers within it. It jerked to a halt right at the tip of Tarinah's tail, and then it turned back towards me.

"*No,*" Finesia said. "*It can't be – it's impossible. The Gods Themselves are dead. I killed them myself.*"

But her voice had just become nattering at the back of my mind. Instead, I heard another voice, the elders there, the academics. Except they weren't academics at all. I should have known the first time I'd met them in the lava tube caverns that these three weren't mortal men.

"*Finesia,*" they said, "*leave this young Ambassador's mind. Leave her alone now. She is not yours to command.*"

For the first time I knew who I was speaking to. The myths

were wrong; the Gods Themselves had never left us. They'd been walking our world all along.

In the distance, I heard a roar. Just one at first, but then the cries resounded from every black dragon. They turned and charged inwards. There were so many of them that when they approached, they looked like a swarming flock of crows.

At the same time, the God Dragon was about to pass below me. Talato flew Bellroot just next to me, and I looked over at her.

"Lieutenant, keep in line with Velos," I said. "There's something I have to do."

Her eyes went wide as I unbuckled my harness and stood up on Velos' armour. I gave her one parting glance, and then I toppled backwards as if I were a diver plummeting into water.

Honore's back glowed as I fell through the sky towards it. Tendrils of secicao gas whipped out from his form, as if they yearned to cut me apart. But they couldn't reach me here, as right that moment I was more myself than I'd ever been. I wasn't going to let secicao harm me, and I wasn't going to let Finesia in.

For the first time since I had murdered the dragon queen Bassalhan, I surrendered control of my mind. And in doing so, right at that moment, I found myself under the protection of the three old men – the Gods Themselves.

I DON'T COMPLETELY RECALL the events of the battle that followed, as at that point my mind was not my own. I only recall it in disconnected fragments pieced together afterwards as best I could.

Those that saw the battle from the decks of the steamships, and even Lieutenant Talato on dragonback, recalled how I had fallen through the sky. Many told me later how they'd thought I'd abandoned them.

They had been at the battle for the Tree Immortal at the Saye Archipelago, when, under Finesia's control, the tree had lobbed green projectiles of magic that had forced anyone it hit to surrender themselves to Finesia's thrall.

Every single sailor and soldier at that battle had seen their own comrades throw themselves off both ship and dragon mount into the raging sea. Then they had seen their old friends re-emerge as black dragons, forever immortal and therefore lost to the void.

As I fell towards the God Dragon Honore, some even reported that my skin glowed green, and so they told me later how they'd feared me lost to Finesia. But I hadn't been. This wasn't Finesia's magic thrumming through me, but something even more ancient.

It was the myths that were wrong – the Gods Themselves had never abandoned us. Instead, they'd found their way back to our world, and had brought themselves down to our level. But I wouldn't learn exactly why they had done so until later. For now, I only knew that they had surrendered some of their power to me. They had granted me the courage and faith in myself to ride Honore and sing to him songs that were as ancient as the Ambassadors.

I felt the air burning around me as I dove like a dolphin through the acidic secicao clouds, inhaling them as I went. They had already scorched their way through Tarinah's protective barriers and seared the inner lining of my lungs. I could hear the roars of a thousand grey and black dragons alike, and the astonished cries of military men and women as they watched me fall. But yet I knew that none of this could harm me. So I lowered my arms away from the top of my head, and turned my legs in midair.

I landed flat on Honore's writhing back and steadied myself. His body felt like the twisting form of a huge snake between my thighs. Scales rose out of the ridges between his glowing plates, and I tried to grab hold of one. But every scale I tried to grasp vanished, and another rose somewhere else in its place.

The God Dragon tossed his head back and came towards me

in a loop, trying to knock me off course. I ducked and let his head pass me by, keeping my body flattened against the shifting scaly texture of his body. The way he moved seemed to tear at the fabric of my clothing, yet still I held on.

Then, as I watched the head sail over me, the faces forever changing, I saw both confusion and hate in their expressions. I started by singing a simple song that I knew would calm the spirits of frightened dragons. Dragonsongs were composed more of harmonies than melodies, not something catchy that the musical mind easily recalls, but more like the vocal version of wind chimes tinkling in the wind.

The God Dragon turned its head back towards me again. At this point, I wasn't focused on what was going on beneath or around us. I wasn't even focused on my own mind and which deity was resident inside it. Every essence of my being was focused on Honore and finding a way through to his mind.

The God Dragon's aim was truer this time. He had angled his head in such a way that he'd readily knock me off with his muzzle as soon as he collided with my body. If I didn't find a way to stop him, I was dead.

But I had it all under control. As Honore's head hurtled closer, I felt the notes of the song shift. At the same time, my heart was pounding in my chest and my palms felt clammy, though my fists remained unclenched. The acrid stench of the secicao burned ever deeper in my lungs. The way that the God Dragon twisted and writhed would have easily thrown me off if I weren't a dragonseer under the protection of the Gods Themselves and fully in control of my body, mind, and soul.

His head of ever-shifting faces was another matter entirely. As I sang, I watched it career towards me. In my own mind, I noticed thoughts brimming to the surface, fearful thoughts of how I couldn't survive this, and how I was about to get knocked off my perch. Yet, I couldn't let such worries affect me, and I certainly didn't change the quality of my notes.

Before I knew it, I had beaten him.

The tension first eased away under my legs, and at the last moment Honore turned his head upwards. He sailed right over me and missed me by inches. He shifted his serpentine body once more until he was travelling straight ahead; his shadow passed over Tarinah's dragon carrier below us, and I felt his pain as another few grey dragons attacked, their claws raking off his skin.

My heart went out to Honore, to be attacked by his own descendants like this. I wanted to communicate to the greys and tell them he could be our ally. But doing so would have involved cutting off my own song and surrendering my chance to find a way into Honore's mind.

One grey veered off course to attack me directly. I caught the stench of its sulphurous breath, then I saw the sharp talons reach out to rake me in two. Then, all of a sudden, the dragon wasn't in front of me but several metres to my left. I had also become part of Honore's twisting form, and I was shifting about in space just like he was.

Agents of Finesia had the ability to adjust their form from human to dragon and back again. It was a gift granted to immortals, and therefore Honore had something similar. Except he was much more powerful even than Finesia, able to transform his body and anything immediately touching it into whatever he imagined, so long as he himself took a dragon form.

As result, he and I were now one.

The God Dragon opened his mind up to me. The channel was open only for me and him to communicate, but through the power of the songs I could also hear other things happening in his head. Above it all, I could hear the incessant nattering of Finesia, sweet-talking him into doing her will. I'd learned a long time ago not to listen to the words, as they held a power of their own and could easily mesmerise me into submitting to her cause. To register them would also alert her to my presence. At the moment she didn't seem to have realised that I'd found a way inside Honore's head.

"Who are you, mortal, to enter the domain of the immortal dragons?" Honore asked in the collective unconscious.

"A protector," I replied, *"come to keep you from the immortal goddess who wishes you harm."*

A normal creature of this world would have become confused at this point. But as I had access to Honore's thoughts, he also had access to mine. We didn't merely share words, but also intentions.

"You speak of Finase's wife," Honore said. *"She was human-born, a companion to the human god amongst immortals."*

"And yet she's become more powerful than any force upon this earth," I said. *"She is no longer human but herself took the form of a dragon when she drank the sap of the Tree Immortal."*

Honore grunted, and his body shook slightly, rocking me off course. Another grey dragon lunged in to attack me, this time fire beginning to burn at the back of his throat. But as soon I felt the heat of the approaching grey, I found myself in another position entirely, looking only at the horizon.

Honore was protecting me, but if I said the wrong thing I'd lose my grip on him. He only needed to think of me as an enemy, and then he'd throw me off into the abyss, and I no longer had immortality to protect me.

He had paused as if to think for a minute. *"How do you know of this?"* he asked. *"You have no connection to any mortals. Yes, I feel you once had mortal blood, but you've had that stripped away from you."*

"And did you not have it also stripped away from you?" I stopped myself before I said any more. I wanted to recruit him as an ally of the Gods Themselves, so it didn't seem wise to remind him of who had taken his power away.

"And now, the woman you mentioned has revived me in my ancient form – when I was banished to the fires of this world, she was a human immortal. Now she claims to be human and dragon both, an overseer to them all."

"That's a lie," I said, and I felt Honore spasm beneath me. I

swallowed my fear before I continued: *"Finesia has brought you back only so that she can destroy you and take your power for herself. Once she's done that, none of the mortal dragons will stand a chance."*

"Of what power do you speak? How is she able to do such a thing?"

I didn't have to explain – Honore only needed to watch the memories as I channelled them into my mind. He saw how Cini II, under Alsie Fioreletta's direction, had ordered the blood removed from Cralanein's body. He saw how many dragons had died at the Pinnatu Crater and at Ginlast and during the dragonheats. All of this, he realised, had been done in Finesia's name.

I felt the hate surging into his throat. My bond to him had become like my bond to Velos, but stronger. I sought out my target on the horizon, the largest of the black dragons, Indira. She was hovering in the distance in a cluster with the other black dragons, wisely staying away from the God Dragon in this battle. Where they had him, there was no need for them to attack.

I pointed at the horizon. *"There,"* I said. *"That is Indira, one of the lieutenants responsible for so many of those deaths. She is our enemy."*

Honore didn't need to respond; he felt it in his heart, the most potent of truths revealed to him. Indira had to die. There was no other way.

His lithe body turned sharply, and he left Tarinah and the flock of black dragons behind. The air beat against me, so strongly that it caused me to clench my jaw and grind my teeth. I turned my head away from the wind so I wouldn't suffocate, then I felt the blood rushing to my head as we gathered speed.

I felt myself slipping, and I would have fallen had a fin not appeared right in front of me. I grasped onto it, not letting myself get thrown off.

"Now," Honore said. *"The deed is done."*

At the same time, I could hear Finesia screaming at us. She had only just noticed what was happening – Indira had kept such distance that she clearly hadn't seen me jump off Velos' back and onto Honore's.

But even Finesia couldn't stop what happened next. I saw Indira's head jerk towards us, and I saw terror in those green, glowing reptilian eyes. It was all she could do before Honore plunged straight into her chest.

It felt like hitting cold water from a high cliff dive, but it only took a moment to break the surface tension of what had held Indira's black dragon form together. One moment it was there, then she was just a plume of black smoke. Her human form fell out of it, male in fact, the inert and naked form of Travast Indorm. He plummeted towards the ground, immortal no more.

Then what must have been a thousand claws appeared beneath Honore's spectral body, belonging to his feet and legs that had just materialised out of nothing. There followed a flurry of light and claws, attacking every single black dragon in the sky as he twisted and warped from location to location.

As with Indira, human bodies of all shapes and sizes fell from the ashen clouds that had taken the place of the black dragons. Any colour had been drained away from them, their skins now as pallid as that of aging corpses.

They all dropped towards the expanse of the Cini-Sanito rivers below, the roiling waters seeming to open up as if ready to bury them for good.

"It is done," Honore said. *"Your battle is won."*

I released a breath that I must have been holding for an awfully long time. Yet my respite didn't last, because Finesia found her way back into our channel.

"Your battle is far from won," she said. *"Dragonseer Wells, you are a fool to think you are in control this situation. Meanwhile, Honore, you forget your deal. I have the young dragon queen heir, and she is the only chance that dragonkind, as you and the God Themselves want it fashioned, will live on."*

Her words held a lot of power, because both Honore and I

had forgotten. Finesia held Gerhaun's dragonet, the future of dragonkind.

A sharp stab of pain flared through my head, and with it Honore's voice boomed out. It sounded as if a thousand dragons had decided to roar their anger from the sky.

"*You are not my ally!*" he cried.

I don't know if he was addressing Finesia or me, but it didn't matter, because with those words he cut me off, out of his mind. His body jerked violently to the side, and before I knew it, I was falling through a cold sky with no one to protect me, not even the Gods Themselves.

PART IV

We eventually learned that we were our own worst enemies, and we could no longer remain stagnant. No matter how much had happened and how uncertain the future lay before us, we could not refuse to grow.

– Pontopa Wells, Dragonseer

11

WHEN I WAS VERY YOUNG, I used to believe dragons were the enemy. Virtually everyone under King Cini III's rule in the Towese Empire had believed this. We were taught by the media that the greys attacked the king's secicao harvesting operations in the Southlands, ravaging soldier and automaton alike. We were told they were beasts of ultimate carnage, which would show no mercy to any living thing. We were instructed to report any that we saw in the local vicinity to the authorities for immediate destruction.

Of course, as a little girl I was too young to read the papers, but my father did, as did the neighbours. Dragons were nightmares to be feared, always to be spoken ill of in polite society, pure predators with no place in the global ecosystem other than as pests to be eliminated.

Back then, my parents had never told me that my first biological mother had ridden dragons, let alone that she was a dragonseer. As far as I'd known, Mamo was my real mother and I had no other.

I didn't blame them for it, though. They'd only wanted to protect me, and they'd had every right to do so. In retrospect, I don't think my parents had ever really formed a negative opinion of dragons. Rather, in public, they spoke of them in the way they were expected to by society.

I guess they didn't want me to think of dragons as the heroes in our stories, as that would cause me to be ostracised from a young age. Still, that didn't stop the dragons entering my dreams, and in those I ever envisioned them in a negative light. Sukina later told me that their true image had always been there, in the collective unconscious. An ingrained part of me knew from my very core that they were our allies, here not to destroy but to protect the planet from us humans, who only wished to do it ill.

When I was seven years old, Velos had entered my life. I remembered being surprised when he presented himself, just a small blue dragon with scales that shimmered in the morning sun, on my doorstep. I was even more surprised when my parents allowed me to keep him as a pet. But they told me that I'd have to look after him, to nurture him from a small mesh of claws and scales into the great beast he would eventually become.

I like to believe sometimes that it was I who brought him up through those times, but really it was he who brought me up. He was a third parent, who matured much faster than I did. The local villagers initially feared him, but the whole country of Tow – including the king – eventually came to love him. He could create a unique blend of secicao by roasting the beans using his fiery breath. Alas, neither he nor I knew at the time that by supporting the secicao he was ultimately serving a cause that his grey dragon brethren fought daily to curtail.

It was Velos who taught me to truly love dragons, even if for many years he was the only one I knew. I guess it was the reason that Honore had let me into his mind during the battle for the Cini-Sanito river that day, though it was probably the human part of me that had caused him to throw me off his back.

In a way, I understood that as well. I wasn't – or at least what I represented as a human wasn't – an ally. Humans and dragons had been at war since the age of myths. Yet, as a descendant of the Ambassadors, I did have some dragon blood in me.

Memories of my past rushed through my mind as I focused on the darkness behind my closely-sealed eyes. I'd dreamed lucid dreams that I couldn't recall, though I knew they came from deeper than my very core. Someone had been talking to me in the collective unconscious from beyond the grave, maybe Sukina, maybe Gerhaun, or maybe a distant ancestor I had never known.

I awoke, cold, my clothes soaked through. For a while I lay on the hard ground, shivering and feeling terribly alone. My ears were ringing and I felt an absence where my connection to Velos should have been. I figured that, once Finesia had again taken control of Honore's mind, she would have commanded him to murder Velos. She would have seen it as revenge for the death of Indira, one of Finesia's favourite servants.

I didn't dare open my eyes, because I didn't want to see death, whatever it looked like. I smelled sulphur and secicao, and my lungs burned, yet I seemed able to breathe it. Did this mean Finesia had won?

The ringing subsided a little in my ears, and sensation first returned to the muscles in my back. I was lying on something hard at an awkward angle, so that the edge of it dug into the small of my back. My body rocked from side to side, but otherwise everything was incredibly still. No bird sounds, no dragons roaring, no thundering of shrapnel-flak cannons or whizzing of Hummingbirds. The battle was clearly long gone.

I opened my eyes to a sea of stars swimming above me within an inky blue sea. Admittedly, it wasn't the stars that swam but the blurriness of my still-adjusting vision that made them seem to do so. I blinked some of the sleep out of my eyes, then sat up to see that I was on a rowing boat. A violent throbbing pain spun around my head as I pressed my palms to my eyelids. I looked for a sign of the one who had rescued me, but I was alone on this boat. Then came the smell of burning peat. It wasn't light enough to see the three clouds of black smoke that appeared before me, but I knew them to be there.

Soon enough, my apparent rescuers – the anthropologist, the biologist and the historian – came into view. It was as if they'd been there all along.

"It was you?" I asked them. "Did you save me from my fall?"

As one they smiled, still always seeming to be a part of a whole. But now I understood that they were connected by a different substance, above anything known to immortals. Something greater than the collective unconscious, or perhaps the distilled essence of the stuff.

The anthropologist spoke first, as seemed their custom with such things.

"You saved yourself," he said. "You directed yourself towards the water from the sky, and we simply did the fishing."

"Surely I would have died, hitting the water from that height," I said.

"Not in that form ..."

"But I was as good as dead," I said. "Somehow what happened up there ... was it me communicating with Honore or was it you?"

The anthropologist looked at the biologist, prompting him to answer the question. I guessed they might have had actual names, but none of the myths wrote of what they were. It was as if once we'd learned of their abandonment of us, we hadn't wanted to imagine them anymore. But they had not abandoned us, they'd instead been brought down here in immortal form. Yet I still didn't know how.

"We were as much in your mind as you were in his," the biologist said. "Really, our minds are all made of the same fabric, both immortals and mortals. Once you realise that, you will begin to understand."

I furrowed my brows, not really understanding at all. I put my fingers in the water and ran my hand through it. It felt warmer than I'd expected.

I decided to change the course of the conversation. Or rather, my mind was directed to change the subject, and still I didn't understand if such direction came from me or the three immortals before me. If I could turn back the threads of time, I would have first asked them what had happened to the dragons and my friends, but instead I found myself focusing on issues that were also as old as time.

"So you've now revealed yourselves," I said. "You are the Gods Themselves. Why didn't you tell me from the start?"

"We were in hiding," said the historian.

"We have been for generations," said the anthropologist.

"Thousands and thousands of years," said the biologist.

"But what, after all, is time but a series of fleeting moments?" said the historian.

Then they all spoke together as one: "It seems only flashes of light and long spells of darkness when you look back upon it with your memories."

I took a deep breath. Something about their words seemed soothing to me, even if they didn't seem to say very much. Perhaps it was the softness in their voices or the slowness with which they delivered their pronouncements. But they made me feel as if there was no threat in this world at all.

I squinted; my eyes had now started to adjust to the darkness. Surrounding me everywhere, I could make out the faint green glow of secicao gas and I felt its acidic roughness tearing at my lungs.

The anthropologist smiled. "You wonder how you are not dead, how you can still breathe here."

"Immortality is a hard boon to take away," said the biologist.

"Finesia can make you feel very sick," said the historian, "but she hasn't the power to strip it away from you completely. Even her power to grant immortality is somewhat limited."

Then they once again spoke together at once, their gazes drifting off into the distance behind me. "Though if we do nothing, that all soon might change."

I took a deep breath of the secicao, realising they were right. I could breathe it the way I could breathe oxygen. As I took more of it in, I felt it writhing through my body. A hot and sticky pulse pounded in my veins, creating a dull pain in every muscle.

But at the same time, I remembered the ability Finesia had given to me and then stripped away from me at the Tree Immortal – the ability to transform into a black dragon. Was it still there?

I felt another question rising in my head, and this time I realised it was one of my own.

"What happened during the Final Battle of the Immortals?" I asked them. "Honore and Finase fought, and Finesia drank the sap of the Tree Immortal. We know all that. But how did you end up here?"

The three elders' mouths twisted up into warm smiles, and green reflections glinted in their eyes. This had been exactly what they'd wanted me to ask, a tale they'd longed to reveal for eons. The puzzle piece from the age of myths that no one had realised they'd been missing.

"That," they said together, "is a story that for generations we've been yearning to tell."

"The Tree Immortal," said the anthropologist.

"Your myths have always lied," said the biologist. "They've said that we created it."

"But really, the tree came first," said the historian. "It was the first immortal being placed upon this world."

Then together: "Older than gods, the roots of this planet. Born of moondust and stardust. From it we were tasked to protect this world, and thus we governed it from our kingdom above the clouds."

I placed my hand upon my chin. "So you're telling me that the tree is like a person. One with agency and will?"

"No," said the anthropologist. "Not a person."

"You must not think of it like that," said the biologist.

"Trying to give it any construct of a rational mind means

you'll fail to comprehend," said the historian. "It simply is an entity that exists."

"Just like the planet is," said the anthropologist.

"A fusion of soul and matter," said the biologist.

"There is no dichotomy," said the historian. "It's neither good nor evil, neither kind nor harsh. It's all of those things and none of them."

And again as one: "It simply is."

I took another deep breath. This time the secicao burned less inside me, and my muscles had a will of their own. "A force of nature," I said.

"Exactly. Difficult to control."

"But possible to harness."

"And for a while, the way to do so was only known by the three of us – creations that the Tree had fashioned to govern the planet."

I nodded. Just as I had connected to Honore, I had started to feel a connection to the three immortals. "But your creations. Honore and his dragons, and Finase, Finesia and the immortal humans. They learned how to harness the Tree's power."

"And in doing so," the three elders said together, "they discovered a conduit to the higher realm. They didn't just aim to gain immortality, but they wanted to take the seat of the gods for themselves. To be completely able to govern anything that happened on the planet. A thirst for power – that has been the weakness of so many for so long. Alas, it will never change."

I looked upon each of their faces. Their eyes seemed sunken, the wrinkles in their faces deep, and their expressions depicting years of torment. I nodded back to them, because I could see a vision coming to my mind.

Thus, I closed my eyes and I dreamed the truth behind the myths.

I saw the creation myth as I'd always known it, the agelong battle between immortal humans and dragons. The land was barren parched earth, a dry ochre cracked desert. The men and women were giants with massive swords, as big as dragons, with the ability to launch themselves up in great leaps so they could cut dragons down from the sky. The dragons themselves had the same form as Finesia's dragons, black scales with a dark opalescence, akin to the swirling rainbows within a puddle of oil.

As the sky blazed with steel and fire, one immortal woman kept away from the battle, watching and waiting for the rest to end each other. She was clothed in shining wraps of golden cloth, and beneath it all her skin glowed like the setting sun. It was the goddess Finesia, looking as perfect as ever. She took a step into the fray, but she didn't join the battle. Rather she was focused on something else entirely.

Soon she stood alone beneath the great boughs of the Tree Immortal, her eyes dancing with lust and glee. She produced a dagger from her skirts and plunged it into the tree's continuously shifting bark. This she then removed so that she could put her mouth to the revealed hole.

The juice went down her throat in spasmodic waves, and as she drank she grew in size and the tree shrank. Time sped up, and before long she was larger than any of the giants had been, larger than any mountain I'd known upon this earth. A colossus that could crush the hills beneath her feet and shape the world.

She'd lost her clothes, displaying the perfect curves of her form. The features on her face were shaped like smooth boulders worn throughout the ages by a rough sea. Except there was no sea in this place, only rock and acidic soil.

The Tree Immortal was soon no more, and in its place three old men descended from the heavens. They fluttered like feathers upon a light breeze, and Finesia saw them fall. She let out a deep laugh that boomed like thunder.

Finesia looked out upon the fallen bodies of her human comrades, and those of the dragons scattered across the land.

Then she turned her eyes back towards the Gods Themselves who must have looked like miniature toy soldiers to her. She spoke in dulcet tones, using a voice I'd heard so many times inside my head. An enchanting, mesmerising voice that trickled from the ears to the mind like the sweetest nectar.

"So, it is done. The Tree Immortal is no more, and the Gods Themselves are grounded in their rightful place."

The three elders lifted themselves off the ground and stared up at the giant goddess. They spoke in bellowing voices that belied their size.

"Your reign is over," they announced. "This planet must now be left alone."

Finesia laughed again, though even this was filtered through a soft and hypnotising lilt.

"So that's how it is," she said. "And it shall be known throughout history that the Gods Themselves abandoned this planet and left it for dead."

Together, the elders still spoke in unison: "There cannot be a history if there is no one left to experience it."

Finesia lifted her massive head and scoffed, and said, "Then make someone that I can share the world with. Put them on this continent, so I will never be alone, and then I can tell them how it really was."

So that was what the Gods Themselves did. Each in turn reached down to the barren soil. Where the biologist first touched it, it became a coarse puddle of mud. He shaped this in his hands to become a simple species of bracken which quickly spread across the land. I could smell the earthy scent of it, even though I had no form within my vision. Other plants, and insects, and birds, and tiny rodents and all kinds of other creatures emerged from this new verdant land.

"This is life," the biologist said, looking up at Finesia. "And it shall forever thrive upon this planet. More immortal in substance than anything you've seen in your time. Each individual creature shall die, but their lifeforce shall forever remain, birthing generation upon generation until it's the planet's turn to die."

He sank into the mud he had formed, to be seen by Finesia no more.

It was then the anthropologist's turn to act. His touch turned the ground beneath him to a much thinner pool of mud, and he picked up some of the sediment from the bottom. This passed between his fingers like dredged up silt, but he had enough of the stuff that he could mould it into a thick ball. He further fashioned it into a man and a white dragon, placing them as two figurines on the ground, which quickly grew to their normal size. He created another two figures, this time female. The woman was only slightly smaller than the man, but also more slender. The female dragon was five times the size of the other dragon, and golden like the dragon queens I'd always known.

"I have created a society," the anthropologist said, "both of men and of dragons. Their goal is to govern what my brother has created. To preserve the lifeforce of the planet and ensure that for as long as they can, nothing can do it harm."

Again, the anthropologist sank into the mud, disappearing into the bowels of the earth. With him, the bodies of the fallen immortals – man and dragons alike – also sank into the swamps formed beneath them. Their bodies returned to the earth from which they'd been ultimately formed.

That left only the historian, and Finesia lowered her head towards him with an expression of scorn. "And what shall be your contribution to this planet?" she said.

The historian put his hand to his chin and paused for a moment as if to think. Then he reached down to the ground and picked up some muddy water from the ground. With a flurry of hands, he quickly shaped it into a nearly opaque bubble which he held gently between his hands. From this he fashioned eight women, the same size as the human woman the anthropologist had created.

Except there was something different about them – their hair was painted in more lustrous tones, and their skin seemed to shine with a certain radiance. They looked almost like goddesses, perfection in every single one of their features, as radiant as Finesia herself. A sneer of jealousy turned the corner of Finesia's lip when she saw them.

The historian spoke up to her with a slight lisp.

"These are the Ambassadors," he said. "Even men and dragons need their governors, and so they are here to watch over it all. Their blood is a mixture of humans' and dragons'. Pure of heart, pure of spirit, they shall command humans and dragons both. You wanted history, and they shall help fashion it. They shall command the stories forever told throughout time."

Finesia's massive brow furrowed from on high. "And what about me?" she asked. "All of this is for the planet, but what shall I gain, she who drank of the Tree Immortal and rightfully gained her prize?"

The historian shook his head. "You and your kind wouldn't stop until everything was destroyed. And so your peers destroyed each other in combat and only you remain. You knew what you were doing when you pulled us down from the heavens. You knew that things would have to change."

Unexpectedly, tears had begun to brim on Finesia's lower eyelids. They shone like crystalline pools, but the liquid beneath them darkened, soon taking on the lustre of crude oil. "I did what I had to do," Finesia said. "I only wanted to survive."

"You wanted immortality," the historian said, "and we made a mistake in gifting it to you from the very start."

"And so you have granted it to this abstract thing, this life-force. Saying it is the only thing that can survive forever."

"No," the historian said. "From now on, *nothing* can survive forever. Everything must ultimately die – even the planet cannot last."

"Then what even is the point?" Finesia asked. "Why carry on if there's always going to be an end to it all?"

"That is for life to discover, and yourself as well, if you please. Because in time even your legacy will wither away. It's now time for the age of the immortals to step aside and be replaced by a new age."

He swept out an arm to indicate everything spread out before him: butterflies dancing amidst sharp and dewy blades of grass; heady pollen drifting from flower to flower and tree to tree; in the distance, a fox chasing a rabbit over a hilltop; the shadow of a dragon passing over them as they disappeared from view; and the first trails of smoke emerging from an even more distant village.

Finesia's eyebrows had furrowed even deeper. Her tears continued to blacken, and her skin now had taken on a greenish hue, the colour of secicao. Her eyes glowed with an even brighter green fury, and her knuckles whitened at the tips of her giant fists.

"I shall never die, and nor shall this planet," she said. "This world is my legacy. I have earned it, and everything here is mine to control."

"Then your desire for the unachievable shall become your undoing."

"*No!*" Finesia screamed out the rebuke at the top of her voice. "You shall be undone by those who refuse to abide by your unjust rules."

"I regret you have chosen to wither and die," the historian said, "because those upon this planet will soon refuse to believe in you. And once every ounce of their belief has dissipated, so will your very form."

"I will always have believers," Finesia said. "And I shall eventually regain control, even when my form has eventually withered."

"Not without belief, you shan't," the historian warned. "There's nothing on this planet that will choose to support you."

"Oh, but there is ..."

Finesia opened her palm, which contained a handful of seeds. They looked tiny in her hands but must have been massive in comparison to anything beneath her. She clenched her fist once again, this time incredibly tightly. When she opened it, the seed had been ground up into much smaller pieces.

"That is—" the historian said, shock apparent in his wide eyes.

"The seeds of the Tree Immortal. Except I shall call them something else, now. You may have your lifeforce on other lands, but this land shall be known as the Southlands, and it shall be the place from where I will establish my dominion."

She lowered her mouth to the seeds and whistled out a slow breath through pursed lips. From her perspective, it might have seemed only a breeze, but I could see from the way it buffeted the plants and trees below her that she'd created a gale. The first seeds of the Tree Immortal fell, and then Finesia cast one last disdainful look at the historian, before she raised her foot to stamp him into the ground. But she wasn't fast enough, because he disappeared just as his brothers had, sinking beneath the muddy waters from which he'd fashioned the ambassadors, and leaving Finesia alone.

Time again spun forward of its own accord.

The twisting roots of secicao arose from out of the ground where the seeds had fallen. As it came, yellow gas ploughed outwards, which soon thickened into a sickening brown. The other flora beneath them withered to blackness, and then became ashes that were scattered on the wind and lost to the clouds. The Southlands soon became the barren secicao wasteland that I'd always known.

As for Finesia, I watched her slowly wandering to the east, still in her giant form. She entered the seas that the Gods Themselves had placed, which seemed shallow compared to her giant form. She wailed as she walked, and her lonely tears filled up the seas, eventually transforming them into oceans.

She shrank as she went, because as the Gods Themselves had

warned, belief in her was indeed waning. She soon had to swim and a tiny husk of herself eventually found land on an island in the Saye Archipelago. But by that point her muscles had withered so greatly that she couldn't pick herself up out of the sand.

Then her body was no more, and out of her ashes a tree grew. It looked just like the Tree Immortal, but I knew now that it was not the same as the original one. There it waited, until secicao had obtained enough power and she could be reborn anew. Within the original seeds of the Tree Immortal that she'd shaped to her will, lay the power to influence humans and dragons to fight again and in so doing to incite her rebirth.

I felt my body returning to me, and I willed myself to open my eyes. Moonlight shone from overhead, reflecting off the brass edges of the boat. It shimmered over the river's surface and gave the night a soft glow.

The Gods Themselves were no longer here; I was alone on the boat. But I could still hear their voice in my head – because they and I knew there was still one question left unanswered. What had happened to Honore, Finase and the other immortals?

They answered it in the collective unconscious inside my mind.

"As for the bodies of the immortals," they said in unison, *"we brought them down into the magma of the earth, where they could live in harmony. Their spirits continued to stir within the molten fires, and from there came the first source of the collective unconscious and from their belief within it we managed to stay alive, keeping close to the lava and always listening to the whispers coming from inside of it."*

Their voice faded to nothingness, and I took a breath of air that was surprisingly fresh. The elders had left me, but during their departure, they had created a temporary bubble in the collective unconscious to push the secicao gas away. But still I was alone on this boat, which didn't even seem to have oars for me to row with.

"What do I do now?" I asked out loud, hoping for guidance from the Gods Themselves.

I didn't need them to answer though, because as I looked down, I noticed two items upon the bench in front of me. The first was a flare and the second a small tinderbox. I then felt something stir in the collective unconscious. My dragon Velos was nearby, somewhere in the sky overhead.

I took the matchbox and lit the flare, which blazed out into the sky with a bright red smoke. Its reflection glinted off the form of Velos' armour above.

12

My blue dragon roared out into the night when he noticed me sitting alone on the boat below. At this point the temporary bubble of the collective unconscious had vanished, and I was breathing the acidic secicao gas once again. The Gods Themselves had said that Finesia couldn't take my immortality away, but that didn't mean I couldn't be killed by a well-aimed shot to my throat.

Velos swooped down towards the river and levelled out just to one side of me. The flare still burned red in my hand, and so it was easy to make out Lieutenant Talato's stocky form on his back. She wore a gas mask, and from behind the glass I saw her eyes widen when she noticed me sitting there by myself breathing in the secicao fumes. Then she made a snap judgment and produced a jar of cyagora from her pocket.

She stepped off Velos' back onto the boat, and stood over me, her wide stance outright threatening. For a moment, I knew she was considering that I might be a foe.

"There's no need for that," I said. "I'm not an agent of Finesia anymore."

Talato's eyebrows lowered into a frown, and she studied my eyes closely for a moment. I'd taught her how to know when

Finesia had taken over someone's mind – there was always a green glint evident in the eyes.

But soon enough the enmity left her expression, to be replaced by the kindness of the loyal woman I'd always known. She nodded, and I didn't waste a moment before asking what had happened during the battle.

The news she gave me tore my heart in two.

Alas, I'd convinced Honore to destroy Indira's forces, and so one of her strongest agents was no more. But once I'd fallen from Honore's back, the God Dragon had killed Tarinah just as he'd originally planned.

Fortunately, Honore had left the humans and other dragons alone, and they were currently sailing upriver back to Slaro to regroup under the protective bubble Faso had created using his generator. General Sako and Admiral Sandao had presumed me dead, but Talato had still asked permission to look for me, to at least retrieve my body.

I understood completely why. She'd wanted to know that I hadn't been reborn as a black dragon whom she might have to fight one day. She'd seen enough of us lost to Finesia.

"Ma'am," Talato said. "We'd thought you'd died. How did you—" she pointed to her gas mask, "—how are you able to breathe the secicao?"

"Finesia, it seemed, didn't strip me of all my powers," I replied.

"But we saw you get thrown from that huge serpent dragon's back. From the height you fell, you couldn't have survived if you hit the water."

"That's what I'm saying. I'm still immortal."

Talato's jaw dropped, and she paused to take time to process the information. Then she merely shrugged.

"I guess I've seen stranger things." She sat down on the bench opposite me where the flare had been. "You know, a couple of years ago I wouldn't have believed this was possible even if you'd told me. But that was before ..." Her voice trailed off.

"Candiornio," I finished for her.

She nodded. "Yes, Candiornio. Ma'am, I wonder sometimes. I guess he's there serving in Finesia's army somewhere, but do you think that if I met him again, there'd be a way to save him? I mean, you found a way back to your own mind, so maybe he could too."

My fists tightened, remembering. "I thought the same of Wiggea," I said. "But ultimately he'd lost his mind to her."

"To Finesia?"

"Yes, to Finesia. She's in all of their minds, constantly talking to them. And I don't know if there's any other way to say this, but neither Wiggea nor Candiornio are dragonseers. They have no dragon blood in them like I do, or Hastina and Valpeonia. It's that which ultimately kept us pure."

Talato lowered her head. Velos was now hovering gently over the water, very slowly flapping his wings to keep himself on the same level. I was still soaked through and so the breeze he sent down chilled me to my skin. But his presence here, despite that, was a comfort to me. In a way, I guess he was kin – after all, as I'd said, I did have dragon blood in me.

Talato's bushy eyebrows remained knotted, and though she would never say it, I could tell she still had a hard time believing this stuff. I guess no one wanted to be told that the lover they'd lost wasn't part of the elite who could resist a goddess' will.

"Then what if Finesia went away?" she asked. "What if we found a way to defeat her? Maybe we could save Candiornio then?"

I considered for a moment about what the Gods Themselves had shown me – that Finesia had long ago planned to use belief to gain power. "Perhaps if we could defeat Finesia, there would be a way back for him. I don't know. That's what I hope anyway – that's what I've always hoped."

"Then that's what we have to do," Talato said. "Defeat Finesia."

"Yes," I said. "I guess it is."

But it was one thing to say it, another to actually do it. I just wished the Gods Themselves had revealed how the wellies we were meant to achieve it, because somehow I felt we hadn't made any progress at all.

I'D STORED a soft woollen blanket in the compartment beneath my seat on Velos' armour, and as we flew back to Slaro Palace I made good use of it to keep warm. It was thick, comforting, and soaked away most of the river water from my fall. I thought I'd be able to catch up with Talato, but it wasn't long before I heard her soft snores coming from behind me.

We passed the fleet, stationed just before the canals at the edge of Slaro. Only a skeleton crew was aboard, the sailors looking out for threats from above. The rest must have been sent back to the city barracks. On call, perhaps, in case Alsie or another of Finesia's minions attacked again.

It seemed that the city of Slaro was fast asleep as we passed over it. The protective bubble that surrounded it was smaller than it had been while Cralanein lived. Faso had placed the generator near the landing pad on which Velos touched down.

Faso's invention buzzed away incessantly like a swarm of hornets. The device was a mass of pulsating pipes, all leading to a large cylindrical tank. Moonlight shone down from above, suffusing the empty palace grounds and the towers that jutted out of the earth at obtuse angles with a soft glow.

My stomach was rumbling. I may have still been immortal, but that hadn't stopped me getting hungry. Velos thumped down against the ground, jolting us a little. Talato grunted, and jumped up in her seat. I looked back at her, smiling.

"Rise and shine, sleepyhead," I said.

Talato lifted her head and yawned. She scanned the ground in front of her, grinning. The grounds were much more desolate than usual. From their high posts, flags with the royal insignia on them – two yellow sabres and a dragon on a red background – stirred with the breeze in the darkness.

"Looks like I'm not the only one who needed some shut eye," she said.

"Looks like it."

Together we dismounted from Velos, and two valets rushed in from their guard post to help us. They wore the pale blue uniforms and neck ties typical of Valpeonia's guard.

One of them saluted when he noticed me. "Dragonseer Wells, is it you? We'd heard you'd perished."

"Do you I look dead to you?" I asked with a cocky grin.

"No, but—" he looked to his peer, "—we should probably wake the Masked Regent—"

I raised my hand, cutting him off. "Not yet," I said. "Everyone needs their sleep, and right now I doubt there's any threat."

The two valets saluted again, looked once more at each other and back at me. Then after realising there wasn't much more they could do, they returned to their posts.

I yawned, appreciating that I hadn't had any sleep myself for quite some time. I considered just retiring to my quarters and catching up on the rest I was sure I deserved, but my stomach groused at me again.

"Are you hungry?" I asked Talato.

"Starving," she said.

I turned away from the city towards the palace gates. "The Regent's Pancake House should still be open."

Talato's jaw dropped. "But the price of it, Ma'am. I can't afford—"

I chuckled. "I'm paying. Come on."

I waltzed off towards the gates before she could protest further.

THE PANCAKE HOUSE smelled of wood smoke and fried batter, a smell I much preferred to the first time I'd visited it. Back then, it'd had the eggy stench of secicao branches burning in the ovens, which had given the pancakes their trademark signature. I'd first visited it when I was a teenager, Papo having had such a good harvest in his vineyard that autumn that he'd been able to afford a treat for the entire family. It had been a hearty lunch that had prepared its blue-collar clientele for a long afternoon of industry. Back then, it had been known as Slaro's Secicao Pancakes.

But my biological mother, Valpeonia, had banned secicao when she'd become regent to the Towese throne. It had thus changed its name to cater to the demands of the new ruler and realign itself with the spirit of the day.

The place was surprisingly busy when Talato and I entered. Waiters and waitresses in black and white tuxedos darted from table to table in an effort to keep up with the sheer onslaught of orders. The floor they navigated roared with conversation, as did the open kitchens with half-a-dozen aproned chefs, stained in cinnamon hues, spinning themselves between the frying pans as if they had three hands. These pans were placed on long iron grills with charcoal underneath them. It was that and the sizzling batter that gave this place its characteristic aroma.

The hostess at the door looked back into the restaurant then at Talato, and she opened her mouth as if prepared to turn us away. But then her gaze fell on me, and she swallowed her words.

"Dragonseer Wells," she said. "We've not seen you since—"

I nodded with a smile. "Table for two," I said. "Anywhere will do, we're not fussy. We're even happy to sit on the floor."

The hostess gave me a sheepish smile. "That won't be necessary. I'll just—" She looked down at her clipboard. "Give me a minute. There's a table for you right over there."

We followed her into the restaurant, and she placed us next

to a pair of young men sitting opposite each other at a table for four. They wore expensive velvet linen, and they didn't look so happy to share their table. But again, they noticed me, whispered to each other in soft tones, then shuffled aside to give us as much room as they could manage.

Talato and I studied the menus we were offered, and both decided on the same. The new house recommendation – standard pancakes with six 'surprise' varieties of melted cheese. Our food was swiftly out of the kitchen, and the smell of the things on my plate caused my stomach to complain even more.

Talato looked up at me after she'd taken her first mouthful of food, seeming as if she'd not eaten anything like it for months. I guessed if she'd been serving on Sandao's ships then she'd spent them eating tinned sardines.

"You know, it doesn't feel right to eat so well in times of war," she said.

"Nonsense," I said. "We've got to have some good times along with the bad. It's the only way to get through. Don't tell me you don't believe in comfort, Talato?"

"I do, it's just ... with Candiornio gone ..." Her gaze drifted away. She was clearly having trouble letting go. "Never mind. You're right, I should just enjoy."

She lowered her head back to her plate to take another forkful. We enjoyed a few moments of silence and quiet contemplation as we both tucked into our food. Each mouthful of cheese seemed to melt for a second time on my tongue, the flavours rich and the batter so light that it didn't get in the way of my enjoyment.

Time flowed by, and for a while I hoped that this meal would last forever. I'd also not taken the time to eat like this for a very long while.

"There you are, Pontopa," said a voice from beside me.

I turned to see Faso sitting at a nearby table with a toothy grin, and Taka sitting opposite him. Two tables had cleared between us and them, which I guessed was why he'd only just noticed us. Faso wore his signature pinstripe suit and Taka was dressed in rich green and red velvet, much like the two men next to me. He was about to become king, after all, but no one here seemed to be paying him any heed. Instead, they seemed to just want to let him and his father get on with minding their own business. I considered that perhaps not as many read the papers nowadays – after all, who wants to be perpetually reminded about the most recent doom and gloom? – and so they wouldn't recognise his face.

Faso punched Taka on the shoulder. "Didn't you hear what I said, Taka? Your Auntie Pontopa's back."

He dragged his fork away from his mouth, taking strings of cheese with it. Then he looked up at his father, blinked his tired eyes as if in disbelief, then finally turned his head.

His eyes were red with huge circles under them. The fifteen-year-old had been crying, I could see that much.

"Auntie Pontopa?" he asked. "I heard you were … but you're alive."

"I am," I said with a nod. "Looks like I'm going to be much harder to kill than we all thought."

"But what happened out there? Grandfather said that you rode that serpent God Dragon thing and then you just disappeared."

"A story for another time, I guess. You're up late." I glanced up at the clock on the wall – it was well past midnight.

"And I'm sixteen," he said. "Not a child anymore, for sure."

"Sixteen?"

"Yes, sixteen," Faso said. "Don't tell me you've forgotten Taka's birthday again, Auntie Pontopa? You're continuing to make a habit of it."

I felt the blood rushing to my cheeks and Faso looked smug as he watched me. The number of times I'd chided him for forgetting Taka's birthday, and here I was now getting my comeuppance. But in fairness, he was Taka's father and I wasn't even a blood relative.

"I'm sorry," I said, turning back to Taka. "What with everything going on ..."

"Don't worry about it," Taka said, and grinned. "I'm just happy to have birthday pancakes."

"Too right you are," Faso said happily.

"You see, that's why Papo's here really," Taka said. "He only decided to celebrate my birthday this year so he would have an excuse to come here."

I shrugged, happy to see the two getting along. "You need it sometimes, both of you," I said. "But Faso, where's Winda?"

"Someone had to look after the generators," Faso said. "You know, we're creating more of them to ship to Spezzio and some of the other cities. We've lost Tarinah and Yol, and that's a great sadness. But we need to learn to survive without them, should the unthinkable happen."

Taka grimaced when Faso mentioned the deaths of the dragon queens. "I thought we said you weren't going to talk about work tonight, Papo?"

"Well, she did ask," Faso said, and he pointed at me with his fork.

"I did," I agreed. "But I didn't ask you to boast about it."

"That's just the way he is," Taka said. "You'll never change that."

"Watch it," Faso said. "That's enough cheek from you, young man."

"Okay. I just have one more work question, then we can forget about business. Where are Valpeonia, Hastina and General Sako right now?"

"Sleeping," Taka said through a mouthful of food. "They're all exhausted. The last several days have taken their toll."

There came a tap on my shoulder. Both the patrons sitting next to us had stood up and they had their plates, cutlery and wine glasses in their hands.

"Perhaps you would like to sit together," the one closest to me said. "It's better than screaming across the room."

I opened my mouth to reply but Faso interposed. "That's a mighty good idea," he said. "Come on Taka. And then we can share your first legal bottle of wine."

He and Taka stood up, and they both walked towards us, plates and cutlery in hand.

"Two bottles," Taka said. "One for us, one for them. And you should pay for it."

Faso's jaw dropped. "I should pay for it? Hang on, you're the King of Tow, with complete authority over what you do with the nation's coffers. I, meanwhile, am merely an inventor in your employ."

"Yes," Taka said. "But the treasury is supposed to be for the needs of the people, and these are trying times."

He sounded so serious about it, as if the country really couldn't afford a couple of bottles of wine. Had we really stooped that low?

"Am I not the people?" Faso asked.

"You are – but you're also my father. And it's my birthday." He grinned.

"Fine," Faso said. "But I'm going to request a raise tomorrow."

The night rolled on, Faso a lot less annoying than usual now that he'd been banned from talking about work. We drank tall glasses of a fruity and heady wine. It went to Taka's head quickly, but mind you, after a couple of glasses mine was spinning too, being immortal and all that notwithstanding.

Eventually the night came to an end, and we agreed to retire to our quarters. The four of us didn't say too much as we walked through the cool shroud of night, continually protected by Cralanein's blood running through Faso's invention. Then, once we'd reached the corridors of the palace, we dispersed towards our own rooms.

I reached my bed alone, and crawled under the thick woven blanket. My head was spinning even more as it hit the pillow, but I found myself free of anxiety.

It's strange how alcohol can sometimes sober your mind and lift you out of your worries. I found myself thinking about what the Gods Themselves had revealed to me on the boat, specifically of how Finesia planned to use the power of belief to become stronger.

That was her plan, and it was what it had been for generations. It didn't matter that Faso had found a way to replace the barriers of the collective unconscious. Finesia wasn't doing it to kill us; it was more a symbol, a show of her power that would make both dragons and humans alike gain belief in her, even if that belief was rooted in fear.

Then, once she'd gained enough strength, she would battle Honore and defeat him. At the same time the Gods Themselves had been revealed, and she could finally hunt them down. After that there would be nothing that could ever stand in the way of her immortal rule.

But that wasn't all I realised. Clear as day, I knew we had little time left to defeat her. We had to find out exactly where she was hiding, march into her lair, and save Gerhaun's dragonet before Finesia had a chance to destroy the rest of the dragon queens.

Thus the decision was made – we couldn't just sit around waiting in our protective barriers, constantly anxious over when Finesia would strike next. Instead, I'd meet with Valpeonia tomorrow and tell her exactly what we needed to do.

But before that I needed to sleep, and I did so until the late hours of the morning. All that time, no one dared knock on my door.

13

SUNLIGHT STREAMED into the throne room through the tall gothic windows that surrounded the high dais. Since I'd last been to the palace, the passageway that had once led down to Cralanein's former chamber had been sealed up with steel planks and rivets.

At some point I hoped she'd have a funeral down there. But for now, I guessed those caverns could become a possible breach point for Finesia's forces. If we were going to see the enemy, we would be better seeing them coming from the air, from the watchtowers above Slaro's inner city walls.

Taka was King of Tow, now. He sat on the main throne wearing rich crimson silks and a purple cloak trimmed with gold embroidery. Valpeonia sat on the throne to his left and Hastina stood guard nearby.

As I approached, both women turned to regard me, and for a second I thought I might have seen green glints in their eyes. But when I reached them, those glints had gone. I guessed I'd probably imagined it – I still needed to catch up on sleep after all.

Valpeonia, Hastina and Taka had already been filled in on the ordeal above the Cini-Sanito river. They knew about Indira's arrival, then the sudden appearance of Honore, how I had ridden on his back and convinced him to attack our enemies, and how Finesia had ultimately regained control and used him to murder Tarinah while I was flung into the churning river waters below.

Indira had in fact been Hastina's mother, but the red-haired dragonseer showed no sign of regret or grief over her death. She'd never displayed any trace of sadness for having killed her husband, Rastano Wiggea, either, and I'd known for a long time that she'd kill any one of us in this room before we turned to Finesia's side.

The three had no way of knowing yet what I had learned from the Gods Themselves. I kept it as brief as I could as I recounted everything they had shown me, and what I had discovered last night. As I related my tale, Hastina kept constantly on guard, scanning the entrances and windows as if expecting another attack. Taka and Valpeonia kept their heads lowered, listening intently.

To my surprise, once I'd finished it wasn't my biological mother but Taka who first spoke.

"So what you're saying," he said, "is that we have no choice but to attack. But what if there is another way? We surely can't just send our troops off to the slaughter."

"If we continue," I said, "Finesia will ultimately slaughter them all. The only force in this world who can destroy her is Honore, and he's not going to do so while the dragonet is in jeopardy."

"Because she's the only fertile dragon queen we have left." Taka put his hand to his chin.

"Exactly," I said, "and so we have to work out where Finesia's base is and sneak in and retrieve the dragonet. After that, Honore is sure to attack Finesia. Presuming she hasn't gained enough power first."

"You make it sound so easy," Hastina said, her hands on her hips.

"With any luck it will be. I'm keeping Finesia out of my head, and so she has no way of knowing about our plans. But what's clear is that we have to move fast."

"I'm ready if everyone else is," Hastina said.

I nodded, but Taka and Valpeonia showed no sign of consent. Instead, they looked a little confused.

"We need to send out our scouts immediately," I continued, hoping a little extra information might persuade them. "Hastina and I can accompany scouting parties of our best dragonelite. They should be small covert operations, gathering as much intel on the lay of the land as they can."

"So where do you propose we search?" Valpeonia asked.

"East," I said. "We've always seen attacks coming from the east, so the Sovereign States would be a good starting point."

"I'm not sure," Taka said. "It sounds pretty risky to me."

Valpeonia glanced at him. "Personally," she said, "I think this is the best option we have. What are your concerns, my liege?"

The way she spoke his title showed me something had certainly changed in the palace. Valpeonia had stepped aside as ruler, to become somewhat more of an advisor. That was the other thing about him turning sixteen – he'd now become of an age to reign. This was the first decision he'd have to make as king.

The problem was the fate of the world rested on its outcome. But then I guessed the fate of the world had rested on the outcome of every decision made in this court for some time.

Taka sucked in a breath. "We've lost dragon queens, and our automaton forces are crippled. We dragonseers are needed to command the grey dragons, and to resolve any disorder created by their losses."

"And if we just stay here and do nothing," I countered, "then we're all eventually going to die. We can't stop Finesia killing the dragon queens unless we strike right at her heart."

"But you're suggesting flying blindly into enemy territory," Taka said, "trying to find a base in a region that's larger than the

Southlands. There's no way we'd have the time or resources to support such an operation."

It was Hastina's turn to bite back. "It's a lot more than just playing hide and seek," she said, then gave Taka a faint curtsey. "My liege, we'll be looking out for flight patterns in the sky, watching the black dragons from afar using our best scanning technology. If you watch the same crow for a day you can discover its nest, and it's just the same for those dragons."

"And who's to say Finesia won't find you first? None of you have any chance of defeating Alsie Fioreletta if you happen to encounter her – and if you stray across Honore's path, I don't think he'll give you a second chance either. I'm sorry, I just cannot endorse such an action. You cannot have the empire's support in this."

I exchanged a glance with Hastina, whose right hand twitched as her eyes turned towards her shoulder, behind which I could see the head of her spear. She was definitely ready to rebel against him here if I was. But then, when I looked at Valpeonia, I could tell that she would support Taka a hundred per cent of the way. Even if she didn't agree with him, she'd been appointed regent so that she could raise Taka to an age where he would make the decisions for himself, and he was doing exactly that.

I took a deep breath. Taka had been stripped of his ability, just like me. Hastina and Valpeonia could still turn into black dragons however, and if it came to a fight between them, I honestly wasn't sure who would win.

There came a click-clack of footsteps on the stone floor, and Faso entered the room. He strode over to us, waving a shiny looking piece of paper in front of him. It was a photograph, but he was flapping it so fast I couldn't see what was on it.

"Maybe it would help," he said, "if I could tell you exactly where the base is."

Taka, or should I say King Taka I, turned a sour look upon his father. "Faso Gordoni. How in the dragonheats did you catch wind of this conversation?"

"That's Papo to you," he said.

"Not while I'm in the court it isn't. Remember who you're talking to. Now answer my question."

Faso had his hands on his hips. "Now just a minute, young man—"

Valpeonia raised a hand to silence him, then she placed it on Taka's shoulder. She whispered something in his ear. I frowned; why hadn't she asked it in the collective unconscious? Something certainly had changed.

Taka turned back to Faso and levelled his gaze. "All right, I can call you Papo, but please remember where you are right now."

Faso composed himself. "Fine."

"Good," Taka said. "Now explain yourself."

"Well." Faso glanced down at the photo. "Here I have—"

Taka cut him off. "First, tell us how you know what we were talking about. We can't have security risks in our palace."

Faso gave him a sideways grin, then pointed to a spherical lens cast into the stone between two of the gothic windows. It was encased in an entrapment of brass and had a spherical rod sticking up from the top of it – an aerial.

"That's how I know, you see. Remember when Regent Valpeonia asked for surveillance after Alsie Fioreletta's attack? Well, surveillance you got. It's a simple invention, but still one of our finest."

I felt my breath catch in my throat; Valpeonia's lips curled downwards, and Hastina's expression also curdled. She reached behind her neck to grasp the haft of her spear, but she didn't draw it yet.

"Please don't tell me that you've been listening in on this entire conversation," Taka said. "Do you realise that this could be construed as treason?"

"But Taka, this surveillance device was authorised before you reached ruling age. I just thought—"

"You thought that you could go ahead and just install things without our permission," Taka said.

"As I explained, I didn't install it without permission—"

"But you went ahead and used it to spy on us without our consent. Did Regent Valpeonia know that you intended to use it in such a way?"

"I didn't intend. I just thought—"

"That's enough, Papo; don't dig your own grave. And think about the consequences. What happens if this backfires? What happens if Finesia finds a way to also use this device to listen in?"

"That's impossible," Faso said. "It doesn't use secicao, nor the Gordoni Rays that you use to communicate with your telepathy hocus pocus. It's just circuits and radio waves, and we've used incredibly sophisticated encryption techniques."

Taka rolled his eyes, clearly unimpressed. "Switch it off," he said.

"What?" Now Faso looked at me, clearly hoping for some support. But I was on Taka's side here – Faso had annoyed me enough times in the past, doing things like this without anyone's permission.

"You heard me," Taka said. "And that's an order."

Faso grunted. "Fine," he said again.

Faso's six-legged ferret automaton appeared from the flared sleeve of his suit and scrambled down his side and onto the floor. Ratter moved with a speed faster than I'd ever seen it move before, which was surprising given it had no telltale glow of secicao running through its circuits. Clearly Faso had been busy with many more inventions apart from the generator.

The automaton scurried up the wall between the windows and jumped onto the spherical surveillance device. It opened its mouth, displaying a fine row of short teeth. Coming out of its throat was a rod used for shooting darts and other projectiles. A spark jumped from this to just beneath the aerial. The aerial retracted with a whirring sound, and the brass casing grew as it rotated, soon irising over the entire lens.

"Good enough," Faso said. Ratter scurried back towards him, his brass paws clacking against the floor.

"Yes," Taka said with a nod towards the photo in Faso's hand. "Now what have you got there? More unauthorised technology, I presume."

Faso's grin hadn't left his face. "It's remarkable how such technology advances during times of war, don't you think? If it weren't for the dragonheats and the subsequent battles, we'd still all be clashing swords with each other."

My nose crinkled as a whiff of secicao came through the windows. Faso's generator wasn't perfect, it seemed. It still let some of the gas through.

Meanwhile, Faso had paused as if for effect. I felt the corners of my mouth twisting; though Faso had his charms, there were many things I disliked about him, and this tendency to drag on conversations was one of them.

"Just get on with it, will you, Faso," I said.

He glanced back at me, and smirked again.

"You heard her," Valpeonia said. "You're already aware that we have little time to spare."

Faso clenched his jaw, then he pointed up at the ceiling. I'd never looked at it much, but in the dome above the archway was a painting of the stars.

"We sent a much more powerful version of my surveillance tech up there – and before you ask – yes, it operates without secicao."

Valpeonia, Hastina and I leaned towards Faso, while Taka stroked his chin. Curiosity had kindled in his eyes.

"Just like our moon," Faso continued, "this automaton satellite is now in orbit around our planet. It's providing information to my scientists as we speak, and they are working round the clock with our automatons to develop aerial views that the satellite sends back to us. A remarkable piece of technology, don't you think?"

"And you launched this without our permission?" Taka asked.

Faso tugged at his collar. "Well, we can't be passing every single piece of technology we conceive up here for approval. We'd never get anything done!"

"This sounds pretty major to me," Taka said.

"I guess it turned out that way. At first when I went through the schematics with Winda, I doubted it would ever work. But now in fact, I hate to say it, I think this might be my most outstanding invention yet."

The pet ferret automaton scurried up out of Faso's sleeve and sat on his shoulder to glare at the inventor with its red crystalline eyes. But Faso ignored Ratter and waved the piece of paper again.

"Your invention?" I asked. "Or Winda's?"

"Mine, of course," Faso said. "I'm the inventor, Winda's merely the engineer."

I grimaced but said nothing. The man was unbelievable sometimes, and I often felt sorry for Faso's wife – and in all honesty I wondered how she put up with him.

"So it's like a photograph?" I asked. "But taken from space."

"It's exactly that," Faso said.

He held up the photo with both hands for us all to see, but it just seemed to show a whole load of spiral white masses over a black background. There was nothing that looked like a city from the air, as I'd seen from above on Velos' back so many times.

"And how does this help us?" Hastina asked, her hand still gripping the haft of her spear.

"Yes, there's nothing but clouds," I said.

"Ah," Faso said, "but that's where some pre-knowledge of meteorology comes in. It's simple stuff, really, when you think about it. Think about tornadoes and cyclones for a moment. In both cases, weather swirls around its source."

I nodded and a Faso-like smirk crept onto my face. I saw

exactly where he was going with this. "So what you're saying is—"

Faso didn't let me finish. "—all we need do is look for the largest swirling mass." He took a metal pointer from his breast pocket and put it to a point on the map. "Here."

I squinted. The map was only a cross section of the map of the planet, so I couldn't see exactly where it was.

"Where is *here* exactly?" Taka asked.

"Exactly where it all started," Faso said. "At least for Sukina …"

Fear curdled in my throat. There was only one place Faso could be speaking of – a city that used to harbour hundreds of thousands of people.

"Ginlast," I said.

"Ginlast," Faso echoed with a nod.

Taka shot up from his throne. "How certain can you be that this is Finesia's base?"

"This isn't a one-off occurrence. We've been observing this pattern for weeks, and unlike cyclones and tornadoes, which move along random paths, the weather here always rotates around the same place."

Dragonheats. Weeks of surveillance, and he'd not given a single one of us any hint. I was beginning to wonder if Faso lacked trust in the four of us – in a way, I wouldn't blame him. Any one of us could be under Finesia's control without him knowing.

"So does that mean you're certain?"

"Absolutely, one hundred per cent," Faso said, his head held high and his cheeks red with pure smugness.

Taka turned to Valpeonia for approval, and she gave him a cursory nod. "So Ginlast it is," he said. "Guards! Call for General Sako and Admiral Sandao at once."

As soon as General Sako and Admiral Sandao entered the throne room and heard the recent developments, they agreed that we had to organise an immediate attack. But this wasn't to be a stealth operation as I'd first suggested, but rather we were going in guns blazing, utilising as many of our forces as we could.

Due to Faso's engineering team's diligent efforts, we had hundreds of war, Mammoth, Ogre and Roc automatons at our disposal, not to mention our tens of thousands of much smaller Hummingbirds – and an additional twenty thousand enlisted soldiers and marines.

Alas, our fleets were useless. There was too much solid earth between Slaro and Ginlast, with no sizeable inland waterway between the two. Our ships would have had to sail around the south and then to the east of the Northern Continent to reach Finesia's lair, and then there'd still be yards of ice to break through. We had neither the time nor the icebreakers – those ships that had once belonged to the merchant traders now lay at the bottom of the Saye Ocean, sunk by Finesia's own.

We also didn't have the aid of the dragon queens and the grey dragons under their control; we now only had two thousand of Cralanein's grey dragons stationed at Slaro. Yol's and Tarinah's surviving greys had already flown east, to join Castlonth's base at Cargorest in the country of Clam. This was the easternmost city we had under our control, part of the Sovereign States and not far from their border with Tow.

Castlonth, in fact, was the now the oldest of the dragon queens, which made her their leader. We agreed that Hastina and I should fly east to try and rally her to our cause. That was if Honore, under Finesia's control, didn't reach her first. In the meantime, General Sako would bring the army and the automatons east on massive steam trains. Castlonth was an ally, and even if she didn't agree to accompany us on our mission, she ought to at least grant us safe passage. We were going to go into Finesia's base with or without her.

Meanwhile, Sandao's fleet would remain in Slaro with

skeleton crews, just enough soldiers and automatons to quell any potential unrest once the civilians learned of the departure of our forces. Taka and Valpeonia also planned to stay behind to help keep the peace.

Thus the decision was made and Hastina and I strode out of the throne room. Our dragons were waiting on the landing pad ready to carry us east, and all I needed to do was say goodbye to my parents.

HASTINA DIDN'T SEEM ALL that thrilled when I left her outside the throne room, telling her I needed to say my good-byes. She scowled as if to remind me that it was I who had first expressed our intense need to hurry. But nevertheless I left her there, feeling a little guilty that perhaps I was betraying my role as a dragonseer. After all, if we won, I would probably see them again – and if we didn't, then what did it matter? None of us would be alive for very long to regret it.

I kept trying to tell myself that I couldn't think this way; that I'd surely come back and be reunited with them. But despite all the years of mental training I'd had as a dragonseer, I still couldn't help feeling that this might be the last time I'd ever see them. I couldn't die knowing that I had left without at least saying goodbye.

I took a deep breath, tasting the stale air. Though Faso's engine to generate a protective barrier of the collective uncon-scious was clearly working, the air wasn't as fresh as it had been when Cralanein had been alive. Secicao, and I guess that meant Finesia, seemed to be finding devious ways to break through the ancient mantle that the dragon queens had always offered us. Her power was clearly growing, and if we didn't act now, she'd eventually become too powerful for any of us to hope to defeat.

I stopped a couple of guards on patrol as I went through the corridors, one male and one female, and asked them with expressed urgency where my parents might be. They looked at each other, their brows furrowed as if wondering whether they should divulge their location.

"Just tell me, will you?" I said, faking a smile. "I've been through a lot, and believe me, I have a thick skin."

"It's just," the female guard said, "I'm so sorry, Ma'am. They discovered the pavilion and decided it would be a nice place to have a cup of tea."

"The pavilion?" I asked, and then I realised why they might have been afraid to tell me.

"Believe me, we wondered if we should tell them of its history," the male guard said, "but then we thought they're probably right. I mean it is a beautiful place, after all, don't you think?"

The female guard cast him an acerbic look and hit him on the shoulder.

"It's okay," I said, taking a deep breath.

The King's Pavilion, as it had been called when I'd first encountered it, had been where I'd taken my first dose of the addictive drug, Exalmpora. King Cini III had forced it upon Sukina and me at the time, knowing it would make us highly suggestible, which was good for him as he'd wanted us to officially agree to marry the Lamford brothers, namely Francoiso and Charth. But it was all being masterminded behind closed doors by Alsie Fioreletta, as the Exalmpora had eventually turned me into a dragonwoman, causing the chain of events that had ultimately resulted in Finesia's rebirth.

"I guess it's still is a nice place, just as you say," I said with a shrug.

The male guard smiled. "They commandeered it from the guards," he said, and the female guard thumped his shoulder a second time. He rubbed it and scowled at her.

"It's okay," I said, putting my hands out in front of me. "Really it is. No worries at all."

Though admittedly I felt a little nauseous and dizzy as I

walked away from them and navigated a series of corridors, recalling the way via muscle memory alone.

I found my parents sitting at the same table, under the shade of the pagoda, where Sukina and I had drunk with Cini, Francoiso, Charth and Alsie. It hadn't changed at all. It was still made of the heaviest mahogany, with ornate designs of past kings carved into the tabletop. Someone had also kept the surface incredibly polished, and the sun glinted off it as I approached.

Trees of many different varieties grew around it, flowers of all shapes and colours poking out from between the leaves. Somehow they managed to cling to life here, despite not being suited for the environment.

The three elderly adults sitting in the pavilion had a small teapot and three incredibly delicate porcelain teacups in front of them. They had once also been a part of the king's inventory, but fortunately I didn't have to drink Exalmpora out of them. The trio at the table seemed to be enjoying what they thought might be their last moments by indulging in luxuries. There was the familiar and heady scent of South Saye tea in the air.

Papo was the first to lift his head from his cup and the conversation to notice me.

"Flaming wellies!" he said. "It's Pontopa."

He hurried towards me, still sporting a limp from his previous injuries. Before I knew it, he had swiftly embraced me. It didn't matter how much I aged, there was nothing more comforting than a hug from either of my parents. Just as it had been when I was young, I felt that it could protect me from anything, and for a moment I could pretend that they had the power to keep Finesia at bay. I wanted to hold onto this feeling forever.

"The number of times that we've seen you come back from the dead," Papo said, brushing away a strand of my hair. "But I always worry that one day you won't come back. We both do."

I buried my head in his shoulder, trying to hold back a rush of tears. "I wish you could have had an easier daughter."

"Maybe," Papo said. "But then, I wouldn't trade *you* for the world."

He stepped aside to make way for my mother, who also wrapped her arms around me.

"Pontopa, dear," she said, and held me back to study me. "Valpeonia wouldn't let us see you. We'd heard you'd survived, but you needed sleep, and no one close to you was allowed to make contact until you'd been debriefed. I guess they needed to know you were safe. Is it true – did you ride that massive dragon? We could hardly believe it even existed until Faso showed us an image of the thing he captured on photographic paper."

I frowned, wiping the tears from my cheeks. "When did he do that?" I asked, knowing that Faso hadn't been present during the battle.

"You mean when did he take it?" Mamo said. "He didn't, apparently – instead, he'd equipped cameras on all the Hummingbird automatons – said it was to obtain intelligence for the military. We could see you riding the thing. It's just, I thought that Faso might be playing a trick on us. I've heard you can achieve such things with various techniques. Cipao, what do they call it?"

"Compositing," he said.

"That's the word, compositing."

I gritted my teeth. Faso's 'surveillance' clearly extended far beyond the reaches of the throne room. As Taka had pointed out, what would happen if Finesia got hold of one of those Hummingbirds and extracted essential intelligence from it? I shuddered at the thought.

"Are you okay, dear?" Mamo said.

"Yes. It's just … there's something I need to tell you."

Mamo fluttered her eyelashes gently. "You don't need to say it," she said. "I can already see it in your eyes, and a mother does know."

"What?"

"You're flying into danger again, aren't you? And there might not be any coming back this time."

"It's more than that," I said. "We're going right into Finesia's lair. Faso's worked out exactly where it is."

"Flaming wellies," Papo said. "You've got to be kidding."

I looked at him sadly as I shook my head. "There's no other way, Papo."

"But you—"

"Cipao, please," Mamo said, and she loosened her hold on me so I could step back a little. "We've always known it would come to this."

"Yes but … why now?"

"Papo," I said. "There really is no other way."

He stood looking at me for a moment, his eyes sunken. Then he just sighed. "I guess you're right; we've always known from the day that Doctor Forsolano transferred you from Valpeonia's womb into your mother's. You always were such a stubborn one."

I pulled my mother back towards me, shuddering in her comfortable embrace, though my words were meant for both of them. "I just wanted to say – thank you. All this time, for not giving up on me. Even when I was a traitor to the king, and became an agent of Finesia. You never let go of me and you were always there when I needed you."

"That's what parents are for," Mamo said, and though I couldn't see her face I sensed her smile.

"And *surrogate* parents," Cipao put in, with a grin of his own.

"Papo, you will always be my real father. I couldn't have asked for anyone better."

Valpeonia, in fact, had never told me who my biological father was. Whenever I tried mentioning it, she always changed the topic to something else.

"That's good to hear," Papo said. He stepped forward and wrapped his arms around Mamo and me to join in the hug.

We held onto each other for a long moment. Tears were shed by my mother and me, and Papo probably shed a few of his own, though I didn't see them. I broke the embrace first and took a step back.

"I really should be going," I said. "I don't want to leave Hastina waiting too long."

"Oh no," Papo said with a chuckle. "That would the worst way to die."

"Cipao," Mamo said.

"I'm just saying. She doesn't quite have the charm that the boy, Faso Gordoni, has."

"He's not a boy," I said, then simply shook my head. Papo was just teasing me after all, though I had told him many times that I'd never be interested in that man. And he also knew Faso was now married to Winda.

Mamo and Papo both laughed together, and I joined in for a moment. Then Mamo said, "We love you so much, you know, and we're awfully proud of you. No matter what happens or has happened, nothing can change that. You do know that, don't you?"

"Of course," I said. "And I love you both too, and I really mean it. I couldn't have asked for better parents."

I turned to see Doctor Forsolano loitering in the distance, a warm smile on his face. He nodded at me in acknowledgment. "I don't have to tell you to be careful out there," he said. "And to look after your health."

"I'll do my best, doctor," I said, with a salute.

"And do you have everything you need?" He looked down at the bulge in my jacket pocket where he knew I stored the cyagora.

"I'm fine – but thank you."

And that was the last any of us said to each other. Before I went, I held onto each of my parents' hands, and I didn't let go until the rest of my body pulled me away, towards uncertain danger and the ordeal that I knew lay in wait.

PART V

Finesia may have had thousands of immortal black dragons at her disposal, but she didn't have our soldiers, nor did she have our will to fight for our survival no matter what the stakes.

– General Orgati Sako

14

HASTINA and I had about four hours of travel before we reached our destination. We left with a simple meal of oatcakes and bacon in our bellies, which Hastina had retrieved from the kitchens while I said goodbye to my parents. She was quite right in pointing out that we shouldn't be flying into such affairs on an empty stomach. Admittedly, my tummy wasn't protesting one bit.

We took off from the palace, sucking in as much fresh air as we could until we'd left the protective barrier that surrounded Slaro. Neither of us bothered wearing gas masks once we'd left it; I'd already learned from the three elders that I could breathe the stuff, even if it did make me nauseous. Hastina had been able to breathe it for years.

For a while, Hastina and I passed the journey in silence, broken only by the occasional growl from Velos or Bellroot. The two dragons had never quite seen eye to eye. Though I could never understand what they said to each other in their grunts and grumbles, I could sense Velos' emotions whenever Bellroot was around. Perhaps they shared the same kind of friction I often felt between Hastina and me.

Admittedly, Hastina had never been the most talkative sort,

and my heart was still filled with a sense of nostalgia after the conversation with my parents. In many ways, I wished I could have been a child who'd never experienced danger, who had lived a simple life, got married, had children that my parents could love until they died. But as Mamo had said, they'd known what they were getting into when Mamo had offered to have me transferred into her womb.

Eventually, after probably a good hour of passing over the dull and thick layer of secicao clouds, Hastina decided to break the silence.

"You know," she said, her voice coming from the speaker system at the base of Velos' armour. "I don't say this often, but this time, I want to apologise."

I turned towards her in surprise. She didn't turn to look back at me, but instead kept her steely eyes focused dead ahead.

"I don't think I've ever heard you say that," I said.

"Fine, maybe I shouldn't have said it then."

"No, no. It's okay. But tell me, what are you apologising for?"

"It's just the way I looked at you when you said that you had to say goodbye to your parents. You probably thought I was angry or annoyed, and I didn't mean to be so cruel."

"You weren't cruel."

"Maybe not cruel then, because I was just jealous. I don't have people who love me like you do, people to say goodbye to."

I took a deep breath, even if the secicao around me tasted absolutely disgusting. As the story went, Hastina had left Wiggea after he'd left her for dead in Oahastin when she'd been mauled by wolves. But she hadn't died – she'd drunk Exalmpora and become a dragonwoman. Fortunately, the dragon queen Bassalhan had saved her from Finesia's wiles and trained her to be a dragonseer.

Much later, Finesia had taken control of my mind and compelled me to murder Bassalhan in my black dragon form. Though we hadn't talked about it for a long time, I still had the impression that she'd never truly forgiven me for it. But then, if I were her, I wouldn't have forgiven me either.

"What about Valpeonia?" I asked.

Hastina snorted. "You mean your mother?"

"She's not my mother."

"Oh sorry, I forgot. It's complicated."

"It's not like that – it's just that I won't consider any parents as mine, other than the ones I've known since birth."

"I know ..." Hastina said, her voice trailing off. "But that's just what I was saying. I don't have anyone like that; Valpeonia is hardly an ideal parent figure."

I nodded, knowing exactly what she meant. The woman was a great leader, and a powerful and well-respected figure in our society. But when it came to personal issues, she was cold as a glacier. "I'm sorry too."

This time Hastina did turn to me. "For what?"

"Sometimes, I forget these things. It's just too easy to assume."

"Perhaps. But you forget I did once have a mother – you killed her when you decided to ride on the God Dragon's back, or so the rumours say."

My breath caught in my throat. Really, I didn't know what to say. "I'm so sorry," I said.

I couldn't tell if she was genuinely upset, and a selfish part of me wanted to remind her that she had killed Wiggea, a man I'd once had feelings for. But then it was she who had been married to him.

Hastina clenched her fists at her sides. Her voice soured as she spoke. "I guess ... just a little part of me, though I know it's irrational, wishes that you'd left her for me."

"I can understand that in a way," I said. Though I didn't quite endorse it, I did understand the desire for revenge.

"Just forget it," Hastina said, turning back to focus on the horizon.

And for the rest of the journey, it seemed like we had.

Though I did hear a slight low crooning from Velos to Bellroot, and then back from Bellroot to Velos. I felt a little acceptance rising in Velos' chest and I guessed he'd realised Bellroot wasn't so bad after all.

CARGOREST, which used to be called Carkh, had gained its new name upon King Cini II's conquest of the city during the dragonheat wars. The tyrant monarch had already set up factories all over the Sovereign States, their goal to produce automatons to aid in his fight against the dragons to the south. It wasn't long until Cini had enlisted Cargorest not just as the capital of its home country of Clam, but the capital of the entire Sovereign States – an area covering thousands of square miles. It served as the last port of call for any cargo produced by the factories, carried in through steam trains so wide that they trundled along four rail tracks.

These fourfold tracks were what I first saw as we emerged from the secicao clouds, leaving the eggy and acidic stench of them behind. Given Hastina and I were both immortal, we didn't wear masks to protect our lungs. Despite the ugliness of the brown gas pushing at the reaches of Castlonth's protective bubble, the tracks still made for a bleak yet impressive sight, not so much for their beauty but because of their stark aspect.

Cast iron shipping containers lay stacked along the length of the tracks, and signal houses stood at regular intervals. There were areas of the track that must have been over a hundred yards wide. At the centre of this network lay Cargorest station, the city's hub. There must have been a good two dozen tracks leading into it from every different direction.

The roomy red brick station house towered above it all. Despite its size, it wasn't much to look at. The bricks had been stained a more yellowish-brown by the smog that used to linger in the air here before Valpeonia had banned the use of secicao across the empire. Great holes had been knocked out of sections of the wall, apparently a memento of the dragonheat wars that had never been repaired. In the intact areas, windows spanned the façade at regular intervals, with dirty glass and crumbling sills.

The building used to be massive warehouse able to house hundreds of Roc and Mammoth automatons alone. Now it served primarily as the dragon queen Castlonth's home base. Grey dragons circled around it, keeping an eye out for any threat that might emerge from the clouds. They were unusually on edge about something, so I sang out in the collective unconscious to try and calm them, but I could only detect static in their minds. They seemed suspicious even of me, though I had no idea why. I tried to announce our arrival to Castlonth, but there was no way through to her in the collective unconscious.

"Hastina," I said over the speaker system that Faso had installed in both Velos' and Bellroot's armour, "I can't reach Castlonth."

"Me neither. She's blocking us out."

"Then we need to talk to her in person."

"Agreed, but we need to hurry."

Dragonheats, Hastina had felt it too – something really wasn't right here. I pushed down on Velos' steering fin and sang a quick song to encourage him to speed towards our target.

I turned quickly to glance at Hastina, flying on Bellroot at Velos' side, and I once again thought I saw a green glint in her eye. Again, I dismissed it as the aftereffects of my encounter with the Gods Themselves. Hastina seemed perfectly in control of her sensibilities.

As we flew lower still, I caught wind of the wooden shacks and houses that had been built around this station, stretching out for miles between the network of tracks. Before Cini II's occupation of the Sovereign States, this had been quite an opulent city, with sprawling terraces covered in ivy and minarets of gold. But the king had demolished all of it to instead create this industrial powerhouse. He'd built it for function instead of beauty, and so everything looked rigid and controlled, with not a treasure in sight.

The roof of the central structure had been cleared of crates and mechanical cranes, to serve as a dragon landing pad. Velos and Bellroot touched down on this and thus we dismounted. A few of Castlonth's human guards, dressed in sandstone-red uniforms, eyed us suspiciously on the way to the staircase, but in the end they said nothing.

Now Cralanein was dead, we couldn't announce our arrival to Castlonth from Slaro itself via the medium of the collective unconscious. Admittedly we could have sent a Hummingbird across, but that would have taken time. Right now, we had the element of surprise in our favour, and we didn't want to waste it. Particularly given we had no idea when or where Finesia would order Honore to strike next.

We found our way through a maze of wide corridors, filled with thin layers of construction dust. I sneezed once or twice as we filed down the stairs, and soon our feet – and I guess our sense of the collective unconscious – led us straight to the massive warehouse room in which Castlonth lay upon the floor.

She had her eyes closed and her head lying flat on the ground. She looked so helpless there that it made me immediately think of Cralanein. My breath caught in my throat, and then I remembered that the bubble of the collective unconscious was still holding strong around the abandoned station, which meant she wasn't dying.

I stepped forward, and she opened her eyes. They glowed with their characteristic golden colour, but there seemed to be an unusual greenness swirling beneath it. I looked at Hastina, who assessed Castlonth with a narrow glare. I once again caught that green glint in her eyes. My heart skipped a beat, and a shiver tickled the hairs on my forearm.

Something wasn't right here, but I hadn't a clue what was going on.

Castlonth's voice came out thin and reedy – which surprised me. For as long as I'd known the dragon queens, they'd neglected to speak to humans using their physical voices, instead asking dragonseers to translate what they said in the collective unconscious. Gerhaun and perhaps Yol had been exceptions to this, but not the other dragon queens, who generally didn't like humans. After the dragonheats and the murder of so many greys in the Southlands, I didn't blame them one bit.

"So this is all Tow could send," she said. "Two dragonseers with only your dragons to escort you? After the message I sent to alert Cralanein's greys, I would have thought you'd at least bring some of your dragonelite."

"We needed to fly ahead," I said. "Finesia has been attacking the dragon queens through the mythological dragon Honore." I didn't pause to test whether she believed me. "No doubt you have heard from the other queens how Cralanein, Yol, and Tarinah have met their ends."

Castlonth moved her head as if trying to lift it. But as soon as she did, her eyes flashed green. I watched her, my hands wanting to reach behind my back for my rifle but my brain knowing it wasn't smart to outright anger a dragon queen. Castlonth snorted, and then the yellow glow returned to her eyes, pushing the green away.

"The rest of the dragon queens are dead too," she said. "And if I can't keep control, I too soon will be." Besides me, Hastina already had her spear drawn. I reached out and I lowered her weapon. She didn't resist but shot me a look that said if I touched it again, she'd drive it right through me.

I turned back to Castlonth. "What happened?" I asked.

The dragon queen paused for a long moment. The colour of her eyes kept oscillating from yellow to green, and her massive reptilian brows wobbled as if she were trying to keep control. "Finesia," she said, then as if talking to someone else, "you shall not do to me what you did to the others."

"Finesia?" I asked. "What is she up to? What did she do?"

"She's gaining power, becoming too strong. Now let me focus. I must keep her out."

There came a smell from beside me like burning crude oil. My eyes widened in horror, as I saw black smoke start to rise from beneath Hastina's feet.

"Hastina?" I asked.

She turned to me, a wicked grin on one side of her face. Her eyes glowed green for a moment, and I could see that she had let Finesia in. I produced a jar of cyagora from my pocket, but Hastina spun her spear around and knocked it out of my hand. Castlonth continued to groan and murmur as she also wrestled to keep Finesia from taking control of her mind.

Fear curdled in my throat. I realised what was happening, but it was too late. She'd gained enough power of belief through murdering the other dragon queens, and now she had decided to strike right at Castlonth's heart. And if what Castlonth had said was true, if she'd found a way to kill three dragon queens at once, that would have caused a huge spike of fear in the dragon and human population. There was no better time to strike. But still I hadn't yet discovered how they'd died.

Hastina still hadn't transformed into a black dragon, but her features were twisting and writhing on her face, black scales growing out of the edges. Meanwhile, she spoke in Finesia's voice.

"Aeons upon this planet, and I have no patience for your struggle, dragon queen Castlonth. If you shall not end your life as the others did, then I shall have one your *faithful* allies murder you herself."

I knew it wasn't Hastina talking through her own lips anymore. It was Finesia.

"Hastina, no!" I cried. "Block her out. Don't let her take control."

She turned to me and sneered. "I shall deal with you later, *Dragonseer*."

I reached behind my back for my Pattersoni rifle and drew it, cocked it, raised it and aimed at the quickly transforming black dragon. Castlonth looked up at the creature with tired eyes. I fired, and the bullet clipped off the top of Hastina's wing where it would do no damage, just as the emerging black dragon swiped her jagged tail around. She swept me off my feet and I landed with a hard thud on my behind.

"Hastina," I said again, but it was too late.

Fully transformed into a black dragon, Hastina was now charging at Castlonth. She barrelled forward on her two powerful hind legs, and I knew that no mortal force could stop her. Neither could I.

"So it's true," Castlonth said, and I saw resignation in her eyes.

Hastina extended her claws, and I closed my eyes, unable to watch.

This was it, the end of an era – the last of the adult dragon queens was about to die. As soon as Finesia learned of her death, she wouldn't hesitate to end the life of Gerhaun's dragonet. Then Honore would have no reason to protect the dragons. Finesia's source of belief would then become so strong in the minds of the people, so that Faso's generators would no doubt stop working. Either that, or Finesia would send Honore to wipe out the cities before destroying him with her own sharp claws.

I kept my eyes sealed shut. I had no hope left; I believed with all my heart that this was the end. As my belief dwindled, I felt Finesia reaching out from the corners of my mind. Within moments, she would take control of my own soul, and when she did, I already knew she would never give it back again. That was assuming that she even wanted to let me live.

"*Let me in, dear,*" she said. "*Embrace your destiny.*"

My mind opened up to finally let her in, once and for all.

But she was quickly washed away by a shimmer in the collective unconscious. Something else had emerged nearby, and the pounding panic in my heart quickly subsided. There came the smell of burning charcoal, and I heard the reassuring voice of three elderly men speaking together as one.

"We cannot allow this," they said in unison. Their voices carried far more power than they'd had when I'd first met them inside the Pinnatu Volcano.

I opened my eyes to see the three elders blocking Hastina's path, except to my surprise they were no longer in human form. Instead, they had taken the form of three large and spectral green dragons, looking down on Hastina with fiery eyes. Smoke billowed out of their nostrils that took on a slight glow as it rose into the air in front of them.

Hastina barrelled into the biologist in the centre, and it was like she'd charged into a stone wall. There came the sound of cracking bones, and she rebounded, tumbling over the floor. She bared her teeth at them, hissing and roaring.

"You," she said, again in Finesia's voice. "So you have revealed yourselves. But your powers are weak."

"But enough to stop one of your own in the act of murder. You may have converted her to your cause, but you shall not have the final queen."

"I can always send more," Finesia said. "You cannot defeat all of us."

"Then do so," the Gods Themselves said. "Abandon your base and see what happens next."

"You speak of Honore, but he is mine! What did you do to him?"

"He has merely agreed to leave this war alone for the time being," said the elders. "When a resolution has been found, he will decide what to do next. But he knows it's not in his best interest to act either way."

It didn't take me long to realise exactly what they meant by this – Honore's best plan right now was one of inaction. Attacking us or another dragon queen would merely further the annihilation of the mortal dragon line. But Finesia was growing in strength at the moment, and there was no guarantee Honore could defeat her in battle. The implications were alarming. If she was strong enough to defeat Honore, then what hope did we have?

"It is only a matter of time until I control everything," Finesia said through Hastina's voice. "It is futile to struggle against me."

"Then we shall learn what time has to say about that," said the Gods Themselves. "Now as for you, Dragonseer Wiggea. You may now return to yourself."

Each of them put their hands out in front of them, and their palms emitted a brilliant glow. This turned into six narrow beams that spread out into a blanket of white that enveloped Hastina.

The black dragon hissed at the immortals. "No, you shall not have her."

Before the Gods Themselves had had a chance to complete their magic, she spread her wings and flew out through a hole in the wall.

15

I WATCHED Hastina flying away from the westering sun, my heart filled with regret. I couldn't yet see it, but I could smell the secicao gas pushing through Castlonth's protective barrier. Though Castlonth had survived her encounter with Finesia, the shock had clearly weakened her.

For a moment, nothing passed between me, the Gods Themselves, and the dragon queen. I only felt a spike of pain in the collective unconscious, and then a roar shook the building. This hadn't come from anyone present in the room, but from Bellroot bellowing aloud at Hastina's treachery.

I then felt compassion rising in Velos, who no doubt was trying to calm the citrine dragon down. Just as Castlonth and Gerhaun's dragonet were the two last known dragon queens, Bellroot and Velos were the last known fertile male dragons. Overexposure to secicao in the Southlands had long ago made all the greys infertile. So, in a way, their lives were almost as precious as the dragon queens'.

Soon enough, Hastina's silhouette shrank to just a pinprick on the horizon. I turned back to the Gods Themselves, who had once again taken on their human forms. They were crouched around Castlonth, examining her. The dragon queen's eyes were tightly shut, and though she didn't snore it was evident from the rise and fall of her chest that she was fast asleep.

I approached them, and the anthropologist spoke first, as was customary with such exchanges.

"The last of the adult dragon queens," he said.

"A new era is about to emerge," said the biologist.

"The dragonet must survive," said the historian.

Then they rose in one choreographed motion and swivelled around on their heels to face me.

"That's why we're here," I said. "Hastina and I planned to scout ahead and try to get Castlonth and the other dragon queens to help us. We hoped to enlist the help of their grey dragons in an all-out assault on Finesia's base."

"She has already allowed you to take them," said the anthropologist. "And you already know that all the grey dragons in Tow have no living queen."

"What's happened?" I asked.

"We went to try and protect them," said the biologist. "We tried to stop Finesia taking their souls, but they were already too far gone."

"Once she was in their heads," said the historian, "they simply lost the will to live. A simple mental flick of the switch was enough for them to will their hearts to stop beating. That was all it took."

I furrowed my brow. "Then Finesia has gained in power," I said.

"That is why we cannot let Honore near Finesia," said the anthropologist.

"If we do, she will surely kill him," said the biologist.

"But still, if she grows strong enough, she'll be able to get inside Honore's mind, to do with him as she pleases," said the historian.

I looked back out at the opening through which Hastina had flown. The brown clouds were roiling violently in the distance. Green lightning sparked at the edge of the protective barrier.

"Hastina, she—"

"She has embarked upon her own path," the anthropologist said with a lowered head. He spoke in a soft tone, as if measuring his words. "You cannot focus on her for now."

The biologist also lowered his head and spoke in an equally quiet manner. "Because when Castlonth dies, and Finesia murders the queen dragonet, the truth of the situation will be far too much for the world's population to bear."

"Finesia will then have access to the minds of every living thing on this planet," said the historian. "Even we three will be unable to resist her charms."

That made a lot of sense. Finesia had said as much through Hastina before she'd whisked her away. *It is only a matter of time before I gain control.*

As if they'd registered my realisation, the Gods Themselves again spoke as one: "Castlonth only has a few days left in this world. She was the only dragon queen to have resisted Finesia's will, but she'd already seen her own death approaching, and now Finesia knows exactly when she will die."

I shook my head. My chest felt as though my heart had just done a deep dive through my stomach. If Finesia knew Castlonth was about to die, then there'd be no point attacking her. As soon as the goddess knew she had enough power to defeat Honore, Gerhaun's dragonet was as good as dead.

I took a few steps forward and put my hand on Castlonth's head. She flinched when I touched her, but she didn't awaken.

I closed my eyes so I could have a glimpse into her dreams. She was there, sitting in front of the goddess Finesia in her gigantic black dragon form. Finesia looked as if she wanted to speak to Castlonth, but the black dragon's muzzle was sealed shut with thick threads of dream magic.

The dragon queen wasn't asleep, I realised – instead, she was focusing every essence of her being on keeping Finesia at bay. She was tiring as she did so, and she couldn't sustain this for very long.

"There's nothing we can do," I said. "We've lost."

"No, we haven't," said the anthropologist.

"There's always hope," said the biologist, "even in darkest times."

"And we still have power," said the historian. "Power which we wish to bestow upon you."

I blinked in astonishment. "Power?"

"Yes," they said in unison, their lips moving in perfect sync as if part of a choir. "Castlonth still has time, and your allies are on the way. Now close your eyes and meditate, and we will grant you all we have left to give."

I took a deep breath, then decided I really had nothing left to lose. These old men had been full of mystery since the day I'd first met them, but they'd never done anything to cause me any harm.

The wooden floorboards were hard and splintered. I ignored this as I sat down with my legs folded beneath me. The skin of the three old men in front of me began to glow, sending a soft warmth through the room. They became so bright that closing my eyes seemed the most natural thing in the world.

A sensation of calmness washed over every muscle in my body. I felt like I'd stepped under a cool waterfall on a scorching day.

"Ambassador," said the God Themselves together. "We had put eight of you upon this planet, but now we must pass the power of the immortals over to one of you. Dragonseer Wells, as you are known in this world, we grant you the power of the spectral form. Use it wisely, as we hope that this gift will save the world.

"Meanwhile, always remember that fear is the greatest weapon an enemy can wield against you. But that is only if you let them. Now, open your mind."

Their voices seemed to drift off into the void, and I felt a sense of stillness all around me. Through the darkness behind my eyelids, I saw the network of the collective unconscious. It glimmered from thousands of different threads – an ancient structure like a mycelium through which flowed the essence of everything.

I concentrated on this for what must have been hours, though it felt like only minutes inside my mind. As I did so, I noticed patterns within the forms of the collective unconscious, and through observation I absorbed knowledge untouched by anything since the very age of the immortals. As my brain expanded, so did my spirit, and soon I became an embodiment of the collective unconscious itself.

When I came to, the Gods Themselves had imbued my mind with the essence that made them whole. I dared to open my eyes. Now there was only Castlonth, lying in front of me, her eyelids flickering as she tried to keep Finesia away in her sleep. The Gods Themselves were no longer there. I could only hear their voice inside my head.

"This is the end of the line for us," they said. *"But not for life in this world. We have seen it struggle, and we leave this world in pure contentment, as we know that we've created something beautiful. When the time comes, you will know how to make use of this power. Now save this world, Pontopa Wells. Save this world."*

Then they were gone, and a rift opened up in the collective unconscious that I also felt in my chest. It surged through everything, and even the secicao clouds stopped moving for a moment.

In the end, the myths had come true – the Gods Themselves had abandoned us, leaving us to fend for ourselves. But at the same time I felt invigorated, and my heart brimmed with hope.

Of course, I had no idea yet how to unleash this power that the old men had gifted me with, or what I could actually do with it. But I had full faith that I would know how to use it when the time came. Strangely, with the Gods Themselves' passing, I had more faith in them than I'd ever had before.

My thoughts were interrupted by a chug-chug-chugging sound coming from the west. This was followed by the shrill whistle from the funnel of a steam train, and I knew that my allies had finally arrived.

As the allied steam train rolled closer, the Cargorest Station building shook with such a force that it seemed a thousand Mammoth automatons were marching nearby. I took one look at Castlonth and decided to leave her sleeping there. After all, if Finesia knew she only had a few days to live, she didn't need to send anyone to end her life.

I turned to leave, but then the dragon queen opened one yellow eye and said, "You can take the greys, Dragonseer Wells. I won't be needing them anymore."

Then as if she felt she shouldn't have spoken, she immediately shut it again and her eyelids went back to flickering as she fought the battle inside her mind.

I rushed out of the room, through the corridors and up the staircases to the roof. There, I found Velos and Bellroot curled around each other, seemingly taking a nap. It appeared that the loss of Hastina to Finesia had caused them to bond.

Perhaps that had been the reason for their conflict in the first place. Velos, I knew, had never trusted Hastina – but then I guessed Bellroot would always have defended her, both dragons equally loyal to their dragonseers.

There came a shrill whistle from the tracks, then I caught sight of something huge and lumbering approaching from the west. My mouth opened in surprise when I noticed the size of the thing. Clearly, Faso's scientists had been busily at work during the last several days or so, as I'd never seen the likes of any such train before.

It didn't travel on two lines of tracks, but six of them side by side, and as it moved it seemed to sway gently. Every three carriages had a funnel with black sooty smoke emitting from it. I inhaled, remembering the scent of my childhood when everyone used to burn wood and coal instead of secicao. Somehow, the smell reminded me of when we would toast marshmallows over our fireplaces, and my mouth watered longingly for the sweet and gooey taste of them again.

As the train rolled even closer, I got a sense for how massive it truly was. Each carriage seemed to have its own function: the first was the engine, black and shiny, and the second was a gun coach with six Gatling turrets at the top of it, each manned by one of Valpeonia's – or should I say Taka's – pale-coated soldiers; the two carriages behind that seemed to be dragon carriers, with hatches at the top to let the dragons fly out of them. I sensed at least twenty dragons to a carriage, and I could feel them in there waiting for orders.

Further carriages had windows installed, and so I assumed them to be full of troops, and others still had no windows, but hatches on the sides – some small, some man-sized, some as big as Mammoths. No doubt these would flip down to release automatons from inside. The train was so long that I couldn't see the end of it through the clouds. Clearly, my allies had brought a mighty army indeed.

A man and a woman were standing at the side of the train, leaning over a railing. The man was waving at me, while the woman peered upwards. As the train came to a stop, I recognised them as Faso and Winda. He had the characteristic smug look on his face, and admittedly Winda looked mighty pleased with herself, too.

Honestly, I don't think I'd ever been so happy to see them as I was that day. I rushed down a fire escape staircase at the back of the building to greet them, my soles clanging against the rusted metal on my way down.

BY THE TIME I reached the platform, Faso and Winda were already off the train. General Sako stood beside them with his hands on his hips as he stared up at the station building and the dragons looking down over the rim of the roof.

"I've only heard about this place in stories," he said. "The legendary Cargorest train station. I told Sukina we'd come and visit it one day when the war was over."

"Sukina would have liked that," I said.

General Sako chuckled. "Blunders and dragonheats, she wouldn't have. She'd have hated this place for its industry and its contribution to the war effort."

I shrugged. "I guess Cadigan might have been better, then."

"When it had prairies and wolves, yes," General Sako said.

He took a cigar from his pocket and lit it, while Faso took a step forward. The inventor looked at over his shoulder at Winda as if to check whether he had permission.

"Well," he said, indicating the train. "What do you think?"

I cocked my head. "It's certainly something," I said.

"It certainly is." Faso was literally beaming at the compliment.

General Sako coughed on his cigar smoke and his face fell. "Dragonseer Wells, I'm not sure how to deliver this, but we bring bad news."

I nodded, knowing exactly what he was about to say. I opened my mouth to speak, but Faso cut in instead. "Hold on, General," he said.

"What?"

"We need to check that she's safe. Remember what we agreed? Protocol?"

The general huffed and shrugged his shoulders while still looking at me. I returned a curious, and admittedly slightly irritated, frown.

The inventor then pursed his lips and Ratter appeared from his flared sleeve. The ferret automaton ran up his arm and perched himself on his shoulder, and then it gave me that freaky stare with its red crystalline eyes. These soon changed colour, flashing from green to amber to red repeatedly. Something whirred, starling me, and an aerial rose out of the nape of the automaton's neck.

Faso reached into his suit pocket and produced a boxy device. It had a screen on it with a green line running across it. He studied this for a moment, then said, "Well I never. It looks like there are no Gordoni Rays here at all."

The inventor had named these rays after himself, after apparently having discovered the medium that dragon queens and dragonseers used to talk to each other telepathically. He'd used this discovery as the basis for a shield he'd installed in my helmet that I'd used at the time to block Finesia out.

"What the wellies are you talking about, Faso?" I asked. "Because there's no way I've lost my connection to the collective unconscious."

Faso looked back at Winda over his shoulder, ignoring me. "I just wanted to double check I remembered correctly. The last few measurements we took of her, we found a steady fall in Gordoni Rays, am I correct?"

Winda nodded, looking at me sheepishly. I knew from her look that Faso had shared something that he shouldn't have.

"Winda?" Faso said.

"Yes," she said. "Though they have really fallen since we came here."

My hands were clenched by my sides. I hated the way that he did things like this. "Faso, you'd better start talking now," I said. "Because I'm sure you don't want a repeat of that black eye incident."

Faso looked down at my fists and took a step back, holding his hands out in front of him. He stammered out a few words, not really saying much of value. His wife, Winda, stepped forward to speak in his place.

"We must apologise for all the secrecy about this, Dragonseer Wells," she said. "But since we learned about Finesia's ability to control anything that has imbibed or consumed secicao, we had to take matters into our own hands."

I crossed my arms, tapping my foot. "Go on ..."

"You see," Winda continued, "around the same time, we made a discovery in our labs. These Gordoni Rays weren't in fact caused by communication in the collective unconscious at all, but rather were a result of the chemicals inside secicao themselves. You, Hastina, King Taka, Regent Valpeonia and the dragon queens produced stronger signals than anyone else, and tests that we've run on samples of your blood have shown that you had higher levels of secicao than any other human alive."

I could feel my blood boiling, heat rushing to my cheeks. "Where in the dragonheats did you get my blood samples from?" I asked.

"We forced Doctor Forsolano to produce them via miliary edict," Winda said, looking sheepish. "General Sako authorised it."

I turned to the general. "You did *what*? So it's not just Faso – all of you have been operating behind our backs?"

General Sako's moustache twitched. Faso took another step back, but Winda held her ground, her grey eyes fixed resolutely on mine.

"Please understand," she said, "we had no choice in the matter. We've seen all four of you dragonseers turn into black dragons. Recently, the Gordoni Rays produced by secicao have become stronger, and we highly suspect that this is how Finesia can access your minds. We have had to be careful not to divulge any of our plans. Now that you seem free of Gordoni Rays, we can trust you. Or at least we hope we can."

"Just give me a moment," I said.

I took a few deep breaths and relaxed my hands at my sides. After everything that had happened, I guessed I was a little on edge about things.

"Okay, I understand," I said. "So now it makes sense why you went behind Taka's back to install that surveillance equipment."

"Yes," Faso said, stepping forward and glancing at my hands

as he did so. "I suspected with the change of his mood that he might have had Finesia telling him what to do that day. Strange how Regent Valpeonia backed him, don't you think?"

"I'm not sure," I said.

"But how did you manage to get rid of all that radiation inside of you?" Faso asked, and he seemed to be suspecting a trick. "It just happened so fast."

I cocked my head, considering how to explain it all. Faso seemed to have accepted the whole telepathy thing now that he had a scientific explanation for it, but I wasn't sure how he'd react to information about The Gods Themselves, let alone how they had suddenly departed and bestowed upon me their divine gift.

"I don't know," I said. "Something happened here. I saw things, and then something changed inside me. I let go of something I'd been holding onto for so long."

"And what the wellies happened to Hastina," General Sako interposed.

I shook my head. "She's gone. We've lost her to Finesia."

"Blunder and dragonheats," General Sako said, his nose crinkling. "See, that's why we've employed Faso and Winda and their team to work undercover. We never knew—"

"You don't have to explain," I interrupted. "I fully understand."

Really, the number of moments I'd been through when I didn't even trust myself. I could understand their reasoning completely.

"Good," Faso said. "Because I wasn't sure how you'd react to this, but we've found a way to make secicao safe again."

I raised my eyebrows. "Go on."

Faso turned to Winda. "Maybe I should allow you to explain, given that it was your discovery."

Winda's cheeks went a bright shade of red, and her cheeks dimpled. "Thank you, Faso." She turned to me. "Well, there's a chemical, you see, which had a type of radioactivity. As I'm sure

Faso explained at some point, it emits these Gordoni Rays instead of gamma rays, or alpha or beta particles."

My eyes started to glaze over, as they always did when someone went technical on me, and it didn't matter whether it was Faso or not. "So there's something in the secicao itself that was bad?" I asked.

"That's one way of putting it, yes," Winda said with a nod. "Well, we found the perfect way to purify the chemical – the blood of a dragon queen."

The hairs went up along the back of my neck. I wasn't sure I liked where this was going, but I supressed my feelings, knowing that whatever they'd done to Cralanein's blood, they'd done in the name of science.

Winda had paused for a moment to study my eyes. She was much more sensitive to my reactions than Faso was. "You're okay with this?" she asked.

"Just get on with it," I said.

"Well, it turns out that all dragons have within them the ability to purify secicao and remove this chemical that produces the Gordoni Rays. A dragon queen's blood has the ability in a concentrated form, which is what allows them to push the barrier of the collective unconscious away from themselves. By passing secicao through the silver blood, we cleanse it so to speak, producing a new version of secicao that is just as powerful, but without the risk."

"I see," I said, a hand on my chin. Most of that admittedly had gone way over my head, but I understood the gist of it. "And this has been thoroughly tested? You know it to be safe?"

"Well, we can't be sure just what Finesia is a capable of," Winda said with a shrug. "But we do know that there's a high correlation between devices and creatures emitting Gordoni Rays, and her ability to control them."

"Darling," Faso said, "don't put yourself down. Of course it's going to work. But you've not explained why the dragon queens still emit Gordoni Rays if their blood cleanses the secicao they eat. Why, in other words, is that chemical still present in their physiology?"

I hadn't even thought about that, but I nodded along, pretending that I had.

"I didn't think it was necessary," Winda said.

"But—"

I raised my hand to shut Faso up. "Winda's right, it's not necessary. I've heard enough and I trust you. So I guess we've got supplies of this on the train?"

Faso nodded, looking slightly unnerved, though he didn't express it out loud. "We've managed to supply gallons and gallons of this stuff since gaining access to Cralanein's blood," he said. "We've also made a second generator, which is onboard this train and has enough dragon queen blood in it to generate a protective barrier for the length of the journey. But ..." Faso lowered his head and folded his hands beneath his waist. "I was wondering if we could secure some of Castlonth's blood to help us?"

I shuddered at the very thought. I hadn't yet told them how close to death Castlonth was; she needed all her blood right now so she could at least survive another day.

"Don't even think about it," I said.

"But—"

"A no's a no. If we run out, the troops will just have to wear gas masks."

"I think that's alright," General Sako said. "It's how we've all been fighting all along. Also, fortunately for us, Finesia's base is on the tracks between Cargorest and Ginlast. It means we have everything we need to take the battle straight to her."

He certainly seemed pumped up about it. Mind you, I guessed this was all he had now since he'd lost his daughter so many years ago to Finesia's schemes.

"I guess we'll all be fighting for Sukina," I said. "She'd have wanted us to be brave."

"That she would," General Sako said. "Anyway, I'll brief you about our plans on the way. Come on board the train."

He turned and climbed up into the carriage behind the engine cabin. I felt just as pumped as he seemed to be as I followed him aboard.

Just before we left, I sang a song to Velos and Bellroot to instruct them to board the train as well. I added some notes to instruct Castlonth's greys to follow us, although I felt sad about the need to do so. Alas, they had no choice but to leave the dragon queen to die alone.

16

THE TRAIN DEPARTED with a hiss and a shriek seconds after I had boarded, which was good, because I didn't want to hang around any longer to wait for Castlonth to die.

As I walked the length of the train's freight cars – some of them packed with cargo, others with soldiers – I got the sense that everyone was just as eager to get on with the battle as I was. We all needed closure, I guessed. We'd been stuck in limbo for so long, and we definitely felt that now was the time to learn whether or not we'd survive.

The men and women I passed didn't express any real exuberance. Rather, everyone's faces looked long and tired. In the vacant expression in their eyes, I didn't see the faith I wanted to see. It seemed no one on this train, apart from Faso and Winda, truly believed that we could win.

We had a long journey ahead of us before the battle, of course, and so I had a little time to spare. All the while, General Sako and a few of his officers were busy preparing the strategy carriage for our briefing, although Faso and Winda had decided to retire to their cabin for a short time.

I chose instead to go for a walk through the train, passing grey dragons and automatons in their carriages on the way. Now that I was inside the train, I could still smell the secicao coming off the automatons and brass tanks that I found scattered around. The stuff had a similar odour to it, but it didn't induce nausea in the way that the old secicao had.

The train was so long that it probably took around ten minutes to reach the canteen car at its centre. The smell of cooked food hit my nostrils immediately, and my stomach reminded me how hungry I was shortly thereafter.

The carriage was as spacious as some of the smaller restaurants I knew in Slaro, though there were no waiters buzzing around the floor being a waste of space here. There were a good few dozen soldiers though, sitting at the square and evenly spaced tables. I spotted Lieutenant Talato sitting at a table by herself at the back of the coach, and so I grabbed a bowl of soup from the counter – tomato and basil with some smoky strips of pork and a solid portion of rice added to it – and I went to join my old wartime friend.

She had a bowl of soup in front of her, but no steam was rising off from it. As she gazed out of the window wistfully, she rotated her spoon in a slow circular motion.

"Dragonseer Wells," she said as I sat down, though she hardly turned her head from the window.

"Talato."

She sucked a breath through her teeth. "I heard about Dragonseer Wiggea. I'm glad you made it though."

Well, it seemed that news travelled fast on this train. "Who told you?"

"Winda," Talato said. "She was in here earlier, telling me how her inventor husband can be kind of sweet sometimes."

"Can he now?"

Then she turned to me and gave me a lopsided grin. "You don't think?"

"I think—" I paused to measure my words, "—that Faso has a unique personality."

I took a sip of soup from the bowl. It tasted good – exactly what I needed at that moment.

"Well, at least he's here," Talato said, her gaze returning to the window.

The generators were on, and so we could see the twisting secicao plants curling towards the tracks as the train sliced through their thorny branches. Green lightning flashed overhead, where the bubble seared through the clouds. I guessed if I were seeing this from above, it wouldn't have looked like a bubble, but more like a symmetrical wedge cutting its way through the pollution.

Talato sighed. "I'm sorry – I just can't get my mind off Candiornio sometimes. But you're probably right, he won't be coming back whether we defeat Finesia or not."

I thought back to our conversation on the boat. Was that really what I had said? Somehow, though, I felt differently now.

"You know, I've been thinking," I said. "I've learned a lot since we last talked. And I think, when we find a way to defeat Finesia, that Candiornio will return to himself. I think all the black dragons will. I don't think we've lost them for good."

"That's what you want to believe, isn't it?" Talato said, studying me through narrowed eyes.

Really, it was disturbing to see her like this. Talato had always been the strong one, the person you could rely on to stick it through, no matter the peril. But now, like I had almost done before, she seemed to have given up.

"It's more than just belief," I said. "Something has changed within me since Cargorest Station. I just can't explain it, or if I did you wouldn't believe me. But somehow, I know this. Just have faith, Talato."

But she shook her head. "You'll have to excuse me," she said. "I guess I'm just not in the mood."

In a way, I felt bad for even having initiated a conversation with her, so I just ate my soup in silence and watched the bleakness of the landscape out the window.

After a while, I found my spirits sinking as well in much the same manner as Talato's. I couldn't help thinking about all the plants and animals that used to thrive in the fields we were passing through when it had once been verdant countryside. It was no wonder Talato was feeling so grim.

LITERALLY JUST AS I'd finished my soup, one of General Sako's lieutenants came and requested that Talato and I join the briefing.

According to the officer, some Hummingbird scouts had detected a bit of black dragon activity about an hour away. The briefing room was only a couple of coaches down from the canteen, but still we hurried as fast as we could. Thus the officer had only just wrenched open the two steel doors to the carriage before we flurried into the room.

General Sako stood at the front of the carriage with a white roller screen set up. Faso's ferret automaton Ratter sat on a table around a yard from this with an optical lens sticking out of his mouth, projecting an image onto the screen of the aerial photo that Faso had shown me before in the palace. But on closer examination I noticed that the whirling pattern was larger than it had been before, and certain features had been sharpened so that we could get a sense of what was within it.

All the seats were full, apart from a couple of the front row right next to Faso and Winda. Talato and I went to sit on these, and then General Sako proceeded to flick through a series of images, detailing possible approach vectors, breach points, areas where the satellite had picked up increased black dragon activity, and places where he thought it best to focus our assault.

We'd be flying into a storm, he pointed out, with gale-force winds at almost hurricane strength. Any dragon riders who hadn't harnessed themselves properly to their dragons would be likely swept from their mounts.

The narrow area at the eye of the storm had remained at exactly the same location since the satellite had started its surveillance. Therefore it was the most likely location for Finesia's base of operations, and also where we would be able to retrieve Gerhaun's dragonet, if she was still alive.

"We employed the aid of some of Slaro's best cartographers," General Sako said. "And they pointed out that there's a massive limestone cave system right beneath this spot. It's most likely that Finesia's operating from inside of it."

Which admittedly wasn't good for us. Caves tended to have plenty of hidden places from where Finesia could easily spring an ambush. Although the general did make a point when he explained that this also meant we could fortify positions of our own, so that it would be easier to spot anything coming from the air.

The general continued to show sketches drawn by explorers, and maps that they'd taken from Slaro library's cartographic archives. Then came the big surprise, something that all of them had neglected to tell me at the train station, though I guessed we'd not had much time to talk.

The generator that Faso had on this train wasn't a generator at all – it was in fact a bomb, which they hoped to detonate once we had reached Finesia's key location.

"Our engineers," the general said with a nod to Faso and Winda, "have run some tests using Cralanein's blood on some black dragon autopsies. It seems that a successful blow will at least stun any of Finesia's minions in the room, and perhaps even render Finesia insensible herself."

I kept my jaw clenched and my lips pursed as General Sako said this. If I had been in a better mood, I might have found it darkly funny in a dry sort of way. After all, a massive exploding dragon-blood bomb had to be the most ridiculous thing I'd ever heard of. But this was Cralanein's blood that King Cini had exploited to make Exalmpora. Now we were planning to use it to defeat Finesia. I just hoped it would work.

There were a few murmurs from the troops, and clearly I wasn't the only one who was feeling a bit apprehensive. But General Sako ignored it, and instead proceeded to mark up some routes with a red marker on a map of the cave system.

"Right?" he asked once he had finished. "Does anyone have any questions?"

Klaxons sounded as if to answer his call, and the light in the room went from a warm white to a harsh flashing red. A solider entered the room and stood to attention.

"What's happening out there, private?" General Sako asked.

"Sir, Hummingbirds have sighted black dragons ahead. They're ten minutes from us."

General Sako harrumphed. "Everyone, take defensive stations," he said. "Gordoni, it's time to test out your new technology."

And the hair prickled on the back of my neck, because I'd already realised that these weren't normal black dragons. Instead, I sensed Alsie Fioreletta looming in the collective unconscious and lying in wait.

VELOS AND BELLROOT had stationed themselves in a dragon-carrier compartment, several coaches away from the briefing room. I'd already instructed Talato to fly Bellroot – she was after all the only soldier experienced in operating dragon armour.

Back in the briefing room, she'd given me a wary look. The last time she'd flown Bellroot had been at the Battle for the Tree Immortal, when Candiornio had been knocked off Velos' back.

"Talato, just pull yourself together," I said. "No one else can fly him."

She nodded. "Affirmative, ma'am." And we rushed off towards the doors between the carriages.

Faso's dragon automaton was in the carriage before ours, and he stopped us so he could reach into a crate beside the automaton and hand me a hip flask. It had a simple design with a brushed metal finish.

"This secicao is safe," he said. "Throw out anything you might have used before."

I gave him a curt nod and unscrewed the cap to take a sniff. It still had the addictive allure that secicao had always had, but the aroma was cleaner than before.

"Thank you," I said.

"Any time."

Talato and I didn't wait around, but rushed into the next carriage where Velos and Bellroot waited. A private had already swung the upper doors in front of them open, and so both dragons, and the other eighteen greys in the carriage, were ready to fly.

I took hold of my helmet and sprinted up Velos' tail, feeling a sense of elation to be flying that I hadn't felt for a long time. I'd already harnessed myself into the front seat before Talato had climbed the ladder to the top of Bellroot's armour and started fiddling with her helmet. I pulled back on Velos' steering fin, launching him into the sky.

I could see the dragon automaton ahead of me, Faso at the front and Winda on the Gatling turret at the back. I flipped a switch on the control panel in front of me to set Velos' back turret to automatic mode. Talato then launched Bellroot from behind us.

"Don't forget your gas masks," Faso said over the speaker system.

I turned to see that Talato had already put hers on underneath her helmet. "I don't need one," I said.

"Wellies, I don't think I'll ever understand how that works," Faso said.

I smiled. "Everything okay over there, Talato?" I asked.

"Affirmative, Ma'am," she said, but still there was no energy in her voice.

We hit the secicao clouds, and I took a swig from my hip flask. All of a sudden, the world was ghosted into speckled green, allowing me to see heat signatures through the clouds. In the distance, I made out the forms of the black dragons approaching, still miles away.

Through the augmented powers of the secicao, time seemed to be moving much slower than it usually would. But still the black dragons were moving swiftly enough to make it difficult to track their numbers. I figured there must have been hundreds of them, perhaps approaching a thousand. But then a huge flock of greys joined me, and over my shoulder I could see the aerial automatons – Rocs and Hummingbirds – launching from the carriages towards the front of the train.

Soon after, I heard Alsie starting to form a thought in the collective unconscious. I decided to get in the first word: *"Alsie Fioreletta. It is now time for our final battle, and fate itself shall determine who will win."*

I was paraphrasing the words she'd presented many times to me before the Battle for the Tree Immortal. There, I had fought her in a secicao-induced vision beneath the Tree. She had always claimed that it would be our final battle. She had defeated me then, in the vision driving a dagger through my chest which had turned out to be a wooden stake in the real world, pinning me to the inside of the Tree Immortal. But to Finesia and Alsie's dismay, we had escaped, and I wasn't going to let her defeat me again.

There was a long pause before I heard Alsie's response. *"You know, out of all of Finesia's Fallen, she thought you would be the easiest to bring back to her side. She's impressed by how well you've managed to resist her thus far, so much so in fact that she has asked me to offer you a place by her side."*

'All of Finesia's Fallen' meant there were others. I wondered who. Hastina? Valpeonia? Taka?

"She is just alarmed that she can't find a way through to me

anymore. And she will never find a way through to me again, because I have finally gained the courage to resist her."

"*Then you have gained the courage to die,*" Alsie said.

And she was right, of course – one of us two was going to die today. There would be no prisoners taken in the battle to come.

By the time we'd reached Alsie's company of black dragons, the automatons had already left their carriages and caught up with us to increase our numbers. The spherical Hummingbirds whirred around the more massive Rocs in vast numbers, ready to swarm anything that proved a threat to the larger automatons. Meanwhile, the Rocs opened their great mechanical beaks to let out their loud, shrill screeches.

King Cini's scientists had originally designed them this way to drive fear into the hearts of his enemies, but now we were fighting an enemy without any fear at all. Finesia's black dragons didn't believe they could die, and they were closing in at an alarming speed, their targets the grey dragons who had swarmed in to protect me. If I didn't do something quickly, Alsie's forces would massacre them, knocking out of the sky before we'd even had a chance to fire our first shot.

"What are they doing?" Faso exclaimed over the speaker system. "We need to send the automatons in first."

I didn't need to be reminded twice. I took a deep breath, unconcerned about the acidic secicao gas burning the inside of my lungs – I knew I was immortal now. Then I sang a dragon-song; the harmonies came first, familiar ones that I'd known since childhood and learned from my own dreams. But as I focused on the notes, I connected to a deeper part of me. Memories of Sukina and Gerhaun, and all the other allies who had helped me on the way, powered a new succession of notes I'd never known before. Then I saw the three elders in my mind's eye, and I knew I was drawing power from the Gods Themselves.

The notes had an ancient melody to them that was as old as time itself. They seemed to push the clouds away, and I felt the emotions of the dragons then, every single grey around me, and Velos and Bellroot, as if they were all one. I could sense the dragons were feeling the same kind of despondency as Talato was, and which I'd seen on the faces of the other soldiers as I'd passed them in the train's carriages.

The greys had all lost their dragon queens, or in Castlonth's case, knew they were about to lose her. Unlike the black dragons, they were flying into this battle believing they were about to die.

The Pontopa Wells I'd known before this moment would have been dismayed to see the black dragons lurching towards my allied dragons with such precision. Instead, I kept my breath slow and my heartbeat remained steady.

I simply focused on the song. The Gods Themselves had imbued me with the power to lift the spirits of the greys. As the notes tumbled effortlessly from my lips, it felt like I was recalling a tune I used to sing every day but which I hadn't performed in a while.

In extremely graceful motion, as if part of a choreographed whole, the greys spun away from the black dragons and retreated to allow the rocs to charge forwards. The great mechanical beasts of the sky lifted their wings to reveal the missile launchers underneath, and then launched their ordnance at the black dragons. There were a good forty Rocs on the battlefield. Faso had retrofitted them with twenty-five missiles on each of their wings, making for a thousand missiles in total.

These screeched across the sky, twisting and turning as Faso's vulnerable-point tracking technology kicked in. A cannonade of booms filled the sky ahead of us, followed by the loud metallic rattling of the smaller bits of shrapnel as they exploded and collided their way through the air.

Then there were cries of pain from the black dragons in front of us. Because I was augmented by the new variety of secicao, I saw it happening in slow motion. Bodies went limp in the sky, and the great scaly beasts we'd once thought immortal plummeted to the earth. I turned to Talato, to see her jaw clenched, and I realised that Candiornio could have been among those we'd just brought down. But she said nothing.

Instead, I heard Alsie complaining in my mind, and she no longer sounded the confident and controlling woman that I'd met so many times. Her voice was laced with fear, her power waning.

"What is this?" she asked. *"These automatons aren't meant to work. You need secicao to do this."*

"No, we do not," I said. *"You see, despite the way Finesia has tried to scare us, we've had our scientists working tirelessly around the clock. That's what mortals do, you see. We find a way to fight against the odds."*

"But it's futile," Alsie said. *"You cannot beat Finesia. She has already won."*

"No, she hasn't," I replied. *"Not while our boots tread the earth and our wings beat the sky. Now take a back seat and experience the defeat you deserve."*

Instead of giving me a pointless reply, I caught sight of her in the distance turn towards me, and then I felt her presence in the collective unconscious, focusing. I knew what would come next. A powerful screech resounded in the medium, which usually had the power to render me and the dragons around me insensible. Yet I this time, I managed to brace against the screech as it pierced through the collective unconscious. I used my will to stop it affecting my mind, and I kept my notes laced with courage so that it didn't touch one brain cell of the dragons under my command.

Once Alsie's attack had passed, I turned the notes around to instruct the greys to attack. But there was more in the song than that – I still had the power of the Gods Themselves thrumming through me, and with this I felt at one with the whole world. Every single sense of mine was in tune with the environment. I could hear every dragon's heartbeat inside my mind and feel their fluctuating emotions. That included the black dragons, and as courage surged through the greys, I also felt fear entering the hearts of the black dragons.

Yet through my dragonsong, I found a way to the black dragons too. Information about them flooded into my mind. I knew their names, their former identities, and what status they believed they had under Finesia's thrall.

I could also hear Finesia's voice inside their heads, constantly nagging at them, telling them they were worthless. Arguing that they needed to focus on destroying us. Insisting that if they survived today then they would be able to enjoy their immortal lives forever. Always talking, but never explaining why.

But my song washed over all of that, and for the first time the black dragons became aware of what Finesia had actually done to them and the world at large. Realisation dawned on them as they started to hear their own voices again. They didn't need to listen to her anymore, because they now had wills of their own.

The grey dragons and the black dragons banded together. They formed a wide circle around Alsie, hovering and watching.

"*What is this?*" Alsie said in the collective unconscious, and she wasn't talking to me now but to every single dragon on the battlefield. "*You cannot defeat Finesia. If you turn on her, she will hunt you down in the thousands. Not one of you, not thousands of you, have the power to best her.*"

"*When belief in her is strong, that might be true,*" I replied to Alsie. "*But all we need do is take away that belief, and secicao dwindles, Finesia dies, and we'll live again. Now what do you want to do, Alsie Fioreletta? Will you join us? Or do you choose to die?"*

I felt Alsie focusing again, and there was a sudden change in her position. It was like the lightning before the thunder, and I saw the screech coming in the collective unconscious. Once again I adjusted the notes of my song, putting an extra flair into them so they would also protect the black dragons.

"I guess your decision is made," I said, once Alsie's screech was over.

I felt regret in my heart, but I knew the troops and the dragons both needed to see this. For a long time, and long before Finesia's rebirth, Alsie Fioreletta had been the world's most powerful enemy. Indestructible and undefeatable, she had created the initial culture of fear that had allowed Finesia to grow in strength. Simply put, she needed to be brought down.

My voice gained the sharpness of a spear tip, and my song was laced with anger. There was no hate in my soul, but at the same time I felt everyone's need for vengeance. Therefore I let the grey dragons stand back as I gave the black ones permission to attack.

Hundreds of roars filled the sky, and green lightning flashed from all directions. I felt something pushing into the collective unconscious. It was Finesia, trying to regain control, but I couldn't let her. Alsie tried another screech, but it lacked power. No one here feared her anymore.

I closed my eyes so I could watch the battle in the collective unconscious as I remained completely in tune with my inner self. The sky was filled with grunts and roars, and Alsie showed no resistance. It didn't matter which of the black dragons delivered the killing blow, because in spirit every single one of them felt that they had done the deed.

When I opened my eyes, Alsie was falling through the secicao clouds, her hulking dragon form reduced to limpness, soon to be lost to the brown and roiling dark.

I DON'T THINK anyone who witnessed Alsie Fioreletta's demise truly understood what had happened that day, including myself. But everyone understood the significance. We'd defeated Finesia's second-in-command, a victory which we'd all desperately needed for a very long time.

I had considered inviting the black dragons to join our ranks, but then I realised I had no guarantee that Finesia wouldn't find a way back into their minds and get them to turn on us. I had no clue if I could reproduce what I just had done, should that happen. It all seemed like part of a dream, and the Pontopa who had defeated Alsie was someone I could never reach. So then, I willed the black dragons to fly south, as far away from this continent as they possibly could. I hoped that I'd never have to encounter them in this form ever again.

On the way back, the storms in the secicao clouds seemed to have died down a little, as if they were mourning Alsie. It even seemed to stink less than usual, though I wasn't sure if it was just an illusion created by my jubilant spirits. Naturally, we hadn't even gone a mile before Faso started asking what had happened over the speaker system.

"I've never seen anything like it," he said. "What did you do to get the dragons to turn on each other? There must be some scientific explanation, because I just can't believe in magic."

"There is a scientific explanation," I said. "I'll keep it short for you: If I remove the fear, then I can restore the belief."

"That's not science. That's philosophical mumbo jumbo."

"Call it whatever you like. In the meantime, whilst the iron is hot, I want to speak to the troops when we get back to the train. Is there any way of doing that?"

"Announcements are made in the surveillance room," Faso said. "Why, what do you want to say?"

"You'll find out when everyone else does," I said, and I left it at that.

THE SURVEILLANCE ROOM was just two carriages away from the front of the train, situated on the upper level of the series of cabins where the officers slept. Boxy glass displays of green light displayed the goings on in every single carriage of the train. The room stank of oil, and it had an incessant humming sound that rattled the ears.

Faso explained how you needed to navigate a series of switches in order to flick between them, but as usual his explanation went way over my head. I found myself blinking at him, my jaw low until he shook his head and said, "Fine, just leave it like this."

He put me in front of a microphone that was almost as big as my head and indicated for me to speak into it.

"When do I go live?" I asked.

"Whenever you're ready."

I took a deep breath and prepared myself to speak. When I'd boarded this train, I'd endured the dwindling spirits of the soldiers, but it had gone on long enough. Now was my opportunity to turn things around.

"Blunders and dragonheats," General Sako said from the doorway. "What's going on in here, then?"

"Pontopa wants to make a speech," Faso said.

"Does she now? Dragonseer Wells, we have formalities about these things. Request forms to be signed, encryption engineers to book. This is war time, after all."

I spun round on my swivel chair and looked the old man straight in the eyes.

"There's no time," I said. "We'll reach the heart of the enemy soon, and everyone needs to know that they're not just marching off willy-nilly into a suicide mission."

"Sure they're not," he said, shaking his head. His moustache twitched.

He looked as if I'd caught him at his own game, as if he'd

served the last couple of years as a general in disguise and had been waiting for the mask to be finally yanked off.

"Didn't you hear what happened out there?" I asked. "We beat Alsie Fioreletta. We managed to turn the black dragons against her, and we won."

"*You* beat Alsie Fioreletta," General Sako corrected. "But she's one thing, and Finesia's another. We're talking about an ancient goddess here."

"An ancient goddess who thrives on the power of belief. That is what I want everyone to understand. Our goal isn't to run in guns blazing. It's to fight back against the fear we have of her, and then her power will dwindle."

"And what do you plan to do then?" General Sako asked.

I shrugged. "Honore – the God Dragon. He will come to our aid."

"Can you be sure of that?"

"No," I said. "But I have faith."

General Sako's cheeks puffed as air blew out from between his pursed lips. "I guess we've got nothing more to lose. We could do with a bit of bravado within our ranks, if it means we might live a little longer."

He lingered near the door as he watched me lean into the microphone.

"I guess that means you're ready," Faso said.

I nodded, and he flicked a switch on the control panel. I heard static, and then a red light turned on above the screens.

"That means you're live," Faso said. "And an announcement bell has already rung in every carriage."

I took a deep breath, then I said what I'd intended to say all this time. It was just like singing the dragonsongs: I delivered words intended to incite courage, and I spoke from a much deeper part of myself than I'd known for the last several years.

I spoke of how courageous all these men and women had been to come here today on this train, not so much because of their will to fight but because they were incredibly uncertain of the outcome. I pointed out that beyond what we'd seen on the satellite images, we had no idea what we'd encounter in Finesia's domain, or what traps she might have set for us. We had no idea, in truth, if we could win.

I watched on the screens in front of me as men and woman lifted their heads. Even some of the dragons in their carriers turned their eyes towards the cameras.

"But despite that," I continued, "we still have to believe that we can win. Many of you were out there today and you witnessed Alsie Fioreletta's defeat. I'm sure many of you were also present when I rode the God Dragon above the Cini-Sanito river. But I'm guessing none of you truly understand what happened.

"I'll tell you now: The hold that Finesia has on this world, the magic that she seems to wield, can be whittled down to a simple set of rules. Yes, she exists, none of us I'm sure can doubt that now. And yes, she is powerful, but only so far as we let her be."

On every single screen now, I saw not one pair of eyes that wasn't glued to the camera. I could feel something growing in the collective unconscious as well. A spirit of togetherness that I had never felt before.

"You see, Finesia is – and has been for generations – drawing on the power of belief. She first started influencing us through cups of secicao. We believed secicao to be good. We believed that we would change the world. Yet Finesia lived within the substance of the stuff as it seeped through our blood and coursed through the electrical circuits in our brains. She was always watching, always waiting for the opportune moment to strike.

"Then, when we saw secicao turn on us and destroy the world, we didn't believe we could defeat it. We didn't believe we could defeat Finesia, either.

"The rules, as I say, are simple. The more we don't believe we can win, the more powerful she becomes. But the inverse is also true – the more we believe, the more she weakens.

"I've come to understand something over the last few days. I've heard dragonseers like me referred to as mystics, and that our connection to the collective unconscious is something that no one except us can fully comprehend. But you too can have such a connection. It's not as supernatural as you would think. You only need to believe in yourself, and believe in our civilisation, and believe that we have the ability to persevere, no matter what the odds."

I paused to take a long breath as I watched the screens. Eyes were wide, heads leaning closer. In just one single speech I'd lifted the hearts of an army, and I now had them exactly where I wanted them.

"The final battle is looming closer," I continued, "and the stakes as you know are high. For now, let's just share a moment. Close your eyes and open your mind, because I have a song for us all."

And then I sang. I didn't sing just for the men and women but also for the dragons, and it came from the same place inside my soul that I had called upon when I'd defeated Alsie.

At first, I sang alone, tendrils reaching out into the collective unconscious as they soothed all remaining fears about the uncertain abyss looming ahead of us. The tune had more of a melody than usual dragonsongs – this was needed for the humans to latch onto it.

After a short while, I heard General Sako humming the notes under his breath, and then Faso joined in with a whistle. He leaned forward and smiled at me as he flicked another switch on the control panel, and then I could hear from the screens what was going on in the other carriages too.

Next, I saw Bellroot and Velos sitting close to each other, opening their mouths. They crooned out the song from the top of their throats, though admittedly I heard it more in the collective unconscious than the limited speaker set in front of me. The greys in the carrier around them soon joined in, followed by greys in other carriages.

I saw Talato sitting in that same spot in the canteen where I had spoken to her earlier. At a table nearby sat Winda, who also joined in the song. Individual by individual, other soldiers joined in too.

Our song resonated through the collective unconscious, and within it I felt the amalgamated souls of many dragon queens and dragonseers stir. It reinforced the bubble outside the carriage, pushing it out even further. I looked out the window to see that the storm on the horizon had subsided. But most importantly, I could feel the lifting of the morale of soldiers and dragons alike.

I let the song carry on until its end, before I pulled it back. Then I let us share a moment of silence as we all revelled in what we had achieved.

"We shall sing this song again once we enter Finesia's domain," I said. "It shall reinforce our belief, the most powerful weapon against Finesia that we have."

I cut off my speech on that note, knowing that I had given our troops the courage to fight on. I had put so much of my soul into my delivery that I felt quite exhausted. General Sako therefore ordered the ensign standing guard outside the room to usher me to a cabin – a bare bones room with a window, a small table beneath it, and a bed with a pillow and sheet.

I probably got a good six hours, before I was roused by a knock on the metal door. I opened it to see Lieutenant Talato standing there apologetically.

"General Sako asked me to come and wake you, Ma'am," she said. "Because it looks like we've arrived."

PART VI

No matter how much I've tried, things happened that day that I can't use science to explain, and this is how I came to believe in magic.

– "Sir" Faso Gordoni

18

AFTER TALATO HAD DELIVERED the summons from the General to me, I leaned out of my cabin window to gaze in rapture at the maelstrom rising above us. It was still light outside, though still as gloomy as it always was under the veil of the secicao clouds. If I could have seen through them, I might have caught an early glimpse of sunset. But instead, they served as a sombre backdrop to this menacing tower of wind, emphasising it even more.

The phenomenon was like no natural force upon this world. It couldn't be held up by physics alone, there must have been magic in it too. If there was ever an apt display of Finesia's power, then this was it. It wasn't simply a natural occurrence, but rather a demonstration of her strength and an act designed to solidify her culture of fear.

"Ma'am," Talato said from the doorway. "General Sako also said if you were to delay, that I should remind you of the urgency of the situation."

I removed my head from the window and turned.

"Fair enough," I said, and I followed her through the corridors and out towards the control room.

As I walked the length of the train, I sensed the spirit of the troops and dragons waning in the collective unconscious, and so I chanted same dragonsong that I'd sung over the announcement system earlier that day. It enabled the humans to connect to the collective unconscious just like the dragons did, so I could feel everyone's spirits lifting once again.

"I liked what you did with that," Talato said after I'd finished. "I hadn't realised what power you held in your dragon-songs until that announcement. It was beautiful."

I looked at her, surprised. "Thank you," I said.

"I guess I also wanted to say I'm sorry," Talato continued. "You tried to communicate with me in words what I needed to know before, but I didn't want to listen. But the song forced me to hear what you were trying to say."

"And what did you learn?"

"Well, I started thinking about Candiornio and how he'd want me to behave – the version of him that isn't under the influence of Finesia, that is – if he's still alive. If you could call it living."

Talato paused a moment, a wary look on her brow as if she were wondering if she had permission to speak. I guessed I'd never heard her express something in so many words before and with so much passion.

"Anyway," she continued, "Candiornio wouldn't want me to dwell on his memory. He'd want me to live and fight on, and not give up. That's what you effectively told us in your speech. We cannot give up."

"I guess that's one way of putting it," I said.

Suddenly, the train bucked. It let out a screeching noise and started to slow down. We were almost at the briefing room now, but I checked out of the window in the corridor anyway to see what was happening. The front of the train had now reached the whirlwind and was ploughing through it. I saw sparks flickering out of the front wheels. I couldn't see the tracks through the twisting secicao branches, but from the noise it was making I could tell that this train was now running off its tracks.

I swallowed a hard lump of air, reminding myself that Faso and his team probably knew what they were doing. Even with my dragonsong, one of our dragons wouldn't have a chance to fly through this thing. But I doubted it had the strength to lift a train this big into the air. Dragonheats, our train was literally a fortress on wheels.

The officer at the door saluted me as I entered the strategy room, and then climbed the staircase to the uppermost deck. The control room was inside, with officers peering out of periscopes, turning dials, and tapping commands into what looked like glorified typewriters. General Sako was whirling between the desks, shouting out commands as he went.

He turned and saw me approach. "Dragonseer Wells, what time do you call this?"

"Time to enter Finesia's base, I guess," I said. "Isn't that why you called me here?"

He huffed out a breath and examined his pocket watch. "Time to get to the dragon carriage," he said, and then he turned to Talato. "Lieutenant, why did you bring her here?"

"I thought that's what you wanted, sir?"

"No, I said I wanted her on Velos, and you on Bellroot. Faso and Winda are already there. I said that, didn't I? I'm sure I did."

From the knot in Talato's eyebrows, I could tell that he hadn't quite said as much to her. But she didn't point it out.

"Affirmative, sir," she said instead, and together we virtually sprinted out of the room.

JUST AS GENERAL SAKO had stated, Faso and Winda were in the dragon carriage. I'd expected them to be tinkering with the dragon armour and checking that everything was in good condition.

But they'd already lifted Velos and Bellroot up onto some kind of scaffolding, to allow them to mount the cannons onto their underbellies. These massive electromagnetic guns had allowed our dragons to shoot Mammoths and Rocs down in a single shot before this. I doubted, however, that they'd do much against Finesia. Not even when we'd depleted her of her powers by stripping away the belief in her.

What I hadn't expected, however, was to see two chains leading from the base of each cannon to a device that was all too familiar to me. When I saw what it was, fury began to rise from the base of my chest.

They had chained both dragons to the generator – the bomb containing some of Cralanein's blood – that we were meant to detonate as close to Finesia as possible. The chains were connected to what looked like two quick release mechanisms attached to brass half-pipes that had been welded on to the generator.

"What the wellies do you think you're doing?" I asked.

Winda looked up as Faso backed away. I tried to chase after him, but she stood in front of me, her arms crossed and her legs wide. "We're doing only what we were ordered to do, Pontopa."

"Ordered by whom? You're not telling me that this was General Sako's idea?"

Winda turned back to Faso, a nervous smile on her lips.

"No, it was my idea," Faso said. "But we got General Sako's approval, and given he's the boss around here, that makes it an order, doesn't it?"

"Have you forgotten that I, as a dragonseer, outrank General Sako?"

"Yes, but—" Faso started.

"Yes, but, you've stopped trusting us. I know all that. But when were you going to tell me about this particular detail?"

"We've not exactly had much time," Winda said. "Look, we're sorry, but things have been moving too fast. You have to understand, Velos and Bellroot have the best chance of getting close to Finesia with you on board, and they're also the only dragons strong enough to carry the bomb, because of their dragon armour.”

“And not the dragon automaton? I thought it was the most powerful automaton you’ve ever invented, Faso?”

“Yes, but it was designed for speed and stealth and not for carrying a great weight,” he replied.

“So we’ll be carrying this thing, and when Finesia attacks us, then what?”

“Well, I’m hoping you can do that singing thingy to get the black dragons to turn on Finesia, like you did with Alsie.”

“I don’t know if I can do that again,” I said. “Dragonheats – you’re impossible sometimes, Faso.”

I just wanted to thump the man. It would have taken just a few seconds for him to tell me what he was planning. But that, I guessed, had never been Faso’s way. Again, I had to remind myself that he was only there to help, and by the look on both dragons’ faces when they turned to look at me, I could tell they were on Faso’s and Winda’s side.

There was one thing that wouldn’t help in this upcoming fight and that was my temper. I had to remain calm.

Klaxons sounded from the speakers around the carriage, and the light went from soft white to a harsh red. Ratter jumped out of Faso’s flared sleeve and scrambled up onto the man’s shoulder. The hatch on the ferret automaton’s back opened, and out of it came a display screen.

Faso peered at it for a moment, then turned back to me and said, “Well, it looks like we’re close enough to the eye of the storm that you can brave the elements out there. There’s a big red button on each of your and Talato’s control panels. Press it when you’re ready to deploy the bomb and press it a second time to detonate it.”

“A big red button,” I said. “Couldn’t you have thought of anything better, Faso? I mean, what happens if one of us presses it accidentally?”

Faso’s eyes went narrow. “You won’t,” he said, and then

turned on his heel. "Now if you'll excuse us, Winda and I need to man the dragon automaton."

I nodded. I guessed I'd have to save that punch until later, when we survived this battle, and I had every hope that we would. "Good luck. We'll be fine."

Faso patted me on the shoulder, and Winda also gave me a brief nod before both of them rushed out of the carriage. A couple of soldiers in pale blue uniforms were already on top of their grey dragons, bareback. They turned, called out to us and saluted.

I saluted back, then I sprinted up Velos' tail and scrambled over the dragon armour to get to my seat. Much to my surprise, Talato did the same and she was more agile than I'd ever seen her. I hadn't actually noticed it before, but it seemed that she'd lost a little weight.

Outside, the thud-thud-thud of Gatling fire started up, and I heard the screeches of the black dragons. Either the gunfire was coming from the train, or some of our Mammoth automatons had already deployed.

A voice came from the speakers above us, the klaxons lowering in volume for a moment. It was General Sako on the other end.

"Dragonseer Wells, Lieutenant Talato, give me a signal when you're ready."

I raised my fingers in an okay sign. Talato, who was already watching me from Bellroot's seat, did the same.

"I guess that's that then," General Sako said over the announcement system. "Lowering the bay doors."

As they had before, the coach doors slid open towards the roof, revealing the dull brown landscape beyond. Talato and I both took a swig from our secicao flasks, and then we launched our dragons out onto the battlefield, where Finesia's black dragons were already out in force.

19

THE WALL of the maelstrom looked even more solid on the inside than it had on the outside. If the black dragons had had the power of independent thought, they might have seen it as a prison from which they couldn't escape. The stench of secicao hung thick in the air, as acrid and nauseous as I'd ever known.

That was all I managed to learn about my surroundings before the first black dragon lunged in on the attack.

Because I had previously augmented on secicao, I saw everything in speckled green and in slow motion. I focused on the dragon's claws, a song rising through my lips to keep the allies around me in check. Then I twisted the notes to knock the black dragon off kilter a bit.

The beast missed Velos by inches, and my blue dragon opened his mouth and let out a deafening roar that rocked his body from head to toe. I swung Velos quickly around. Beneath us the chain holding the bomb that was dangling between Velos and Bellroot creaked, hampering Velos' mobility. But still we turned enough to face the black dragon again, who had turned into position much faster. Then he spoke to me inside my mind.

"Finesia told me that you've come a long way since our last

meeting," he said, with an old and cackling voice, and one I'd recognise anywhere.

"Colas," I said.

"Dragonseer Wells," Colas replied. *"You have grown up, it seems. Though you do realise, I'm sure, that you wouldn't have come so far if it weren't for our exploits with Exalmpora."*

"No," I said. *"I survived despite that."*

"And enlisted the power of the Gods Themselves, it seems. Tell me, where are they now? Are they too afraid to face Finesia in battle?"

I didn't wish to tell Colas about how the elders had sacrificed themselves. The less Finesia knew, the less chance she would murder the queen dragonet. *"Just shut up and fight,"* I said. *"On even terms."*

"On even terms? You've fallen from Finesia's graces, and you no longer have the power to transform into a black dragon. You have nothing in Finesia's domain, and so I will destroy you now."

In the corner of my eye, I noticed a grey with one of our soldiers on its back being pursued by a black dragon. Both human and dragon seemed unaware of their pursuer, and if I didn't do something they'd be dead in moments.

"You're wrong," I said. *"I have this."*

I pursed my lips and sang the dragonsong that had been gifted to me by the Gods Themselves. For a moment I felt it, and I hoped that the others did too. But the song only created a shimmer in the collective unconscious and then died down.

The black dragon pounced on its quarry, pinning human to dragon with its massive claws. It drove them down into the secicao clouds, the grey letting out loud shrieks and squeals, but to no avail.

I turned back to Colas, my heart hammering in my chest.

"You forget that you're in Finesia's domain now," the old man said in the collective unconscious. *"Your tricks won't work here."*

I looked over at Talato, who was staring down at the device dangling between Bellroot and Velos.

"*Oh, what's that I see? You do realise that normal ordnance won't work against an immortal goddess?*"

"*I'm telling you nothing further,*" I said.

"*Too bad, I was hoping to have some entertainment before you die. It's just a shame that Finesia told us all not to spare you. I guess this is just the way of things.*"

Colas flapped his wings twice and then charged forward a second time. My senses were still augmented by the new form of secicao, and I watched him cautiously, trying to work out which way was best to dive.

I almost left it too late, but I pushed down on Velos' steering fin at the last moment, and then his Gatling guns powered into action. They sputtered out bullets after Colas, but they just ricocheted off the immortal dragon's oil-coloured scales.

"*That was just a warm-up,*" Colas said, ignoring the onslaught of bullets coming at him. "*Oh, I could do this all day, or at least until Finesia's dragons eliminate every one of your comrades.*"

I didn't grace him with a response. Rather, I drew my Pattersoni rifle from my back and looked down the sights.

"*Do you really think you can beat me with that measly little thing?*"

I said nothing. Instead, I tried singing the song of the Gods Themselves again, hoping that it would at least weaken Finesia's mantle of belief. At the same time, I focused on the rifle – the coldness of the trigger against my finger, the weight of the heavy handle, and the straight line between me and the black dragon's throat. All it would take was a steady hand, and the courage not to turn away this time.

"Incoming," said a voice from below, startling me.

It was Faso's voice, coming from the speaker system. Next thing I knew, the dragon automaton charged up out of the clouds, Faso and Winda on board. The automaton headed straight towards Colas, as Winda plugged a second stream of Gatling fire at him from another direction. They swerved away to avoid impact, just as Colas turned his body to assess the new threat.

"What the wellies?" I replied to Faso. "I had him in my sights."

"You had one shot, and our Gatling guns have thousands," Faso replied.

"None of which seemed to have hit the mark," I said, watching Colas turn back towards me.

I focused again on the song and adjusted my aim. But before I even had time to look back through the scopes, Colas took a third opportunity to charge.

"*This time, I will end you*," he said. "*And Finesia will be so proud.*"

An involuntarily spasm went down my spine, and my aim wavered off course. I moved the scope back into position, and found my mark. But Colas was too close, almost upon me. I had no opportunity to steer Velos this time.

Instead, I fired. The rifle cracked. The shot went wide.

Dragonheats, I'd missed. All I could see was Colas' claws, and the memory flashed in my head of Colas shooting me in the stomach on his airship above the Pinnatu Crater. I felt a sudden vestigial pain right at the base of my gut.

There came another crack of a rifle, and the scales imploded around Colas' throat. His body went limp and barrelled right into me and Velos, but there was no life left in it anymore.

With a roar, Velos turned his body to shake the dead black dragon away from him. Colas' lifeless form tumbled idly to the ground.

I took a moment to survey the battlefield. The Roc automatons in the air and the Mammoth automatons on the ground had now set up a perimeter, sheltering the greys from our enemies. I couldn't see any greys in the secicao thorns below, but I could feel a good hundred of them writhing on the ground, dying alongside the soldiers who had been mounted upon them.

I sang a song in the collective unconscious to thank them for their service and for being so brave. Then, I tried the song that I'd learned from the Gods Themselves once again.

Now that the black dragons were no longer together in a mass, the song seemed to be working. I felt the courage in the troops and dragons on the battlefield restoring itself. Everyone was ready to fight once again.

20

OUR FORCES PUSHED SLOWLY FORWARDS while those of Finesia retreated at the same pace. All the while, we coordinated our movements with General Sako through the speaker systems on Velos' and Bellroot's armour, as well as on the dragon automaton. We couldn't yet see the entrance to the cave system, but we knew from our satellite reconnaissance and Slaro's cartographic records that it was close.

A wall of Mammoths and Rocs continued to protect us from the enemy. The black dragons seemed to have realised, or rather their puppeteer Finesia had realised, that if they got too close the automatons would release their vulnerable-point tracking technology, destroying them en masse.

This provided ample room for the Hummingbirds to whirr around us, recording aerial photographs to submit to the control room on the train. These were sent to rapid response polaroid printers, set to print every twenty seconds or so, allowing the general to watch the action in real time. Meanwhile I had augmented for a second time. So, fully aware of everything going on inside and outside of me, I watched the motion unfold in speckled green.

Admittedly, there wasn't much action to see. I didn't quite

understand it – Finesia had always been so aggressive. Always the first to attack, striking at unprecedented speed in unexpected moments. The black dragons couldn't retreat forever, and I doubted they'd let themselves be cornered. Otherwise, it would just all be too easy for us, and Finesia had never allowed things to be easy.

The maelstrom that surrounded us continued to roar from its walls, sending the putrid stench of secicao in towards us. Resolute, I sang the song taught to me by the Gods Themselves, hoping that it would at least push some of its power away. And I guess it did help a little.

Below us, beneath the giant hooves of our Mammoth automatons and the spindly legs of the war automatons, the mist around the secicao seemed to stir up. From my vantage point, it looked as if we were inside a great cauldron in which Finesia was brewing some ancient and eldritch spell. I had a sickly feeling that we hadn't yet seen every card that she had to play.

But I couldn't let these fears entered my mind. I'd already given the troops a brash speech about how this emotion was the true enemy. I couldn't let anything sap power away from my song. I had to stay strong.

"The entrance," Faso said over the speaker system. "I can see it."

To my left, I watched as he raised his arm and pointed to a dark spot on the horizon, getting closer to us ever so slowly. The entrance to the cave system – our destination.

"Roger that," a female officer replied from the control room. "Confirmed that an entrance is located at bearing two-thirty-three."

"But something's not right here," Talato said. "With all due respect, Ma'am, I don't think Finesia would let us get this close to the caves without a good reason."

"You can say that again," I said. "Can you feel it too, Talato?"

"I don't know what you mean, Ma'am," she said. Then after a pause, "But something doesn't feel right in my gut, yes."

"Oh, here you go with all your collective unconscious mumbo jumbo again," Faso said. "Can't you all just speak in logical reason for once?"

"Faso, is any of what you see here logical?" I asked.

"Well, Gordoni Rays explain a lot of it," he said, "and I've got a new theory that—"

He didn't finish his thought. Instead, his gaze snapped right to where mine, Winda's and Talato's had. The four of us were all hovering on our dragons – two organic and one mechanical – side by side. Indeed, just as we were discussing the matter, Finesia had chosen to reveal what she'd been hiding from us all this time.

Massive columns of black smoke rose up out of the ground in before us, just in front of where the cave mouth lay. They spun and roared like miniature versions of the maelstrom we had entered. Oddly, the black dragons seemed to have abandoned their quest to attack us, and instead were flocking towards the columns. Shrieks filled the sky as they flew into the gigantic towers, but I had no idea what these columns veiled. As the towers gained black dragons, they also seemed to gain substance and mass.

I suddenly heard the goddess' voice inside my head, though I'd been managing to keep her out all this time.

"*You cannot mask me from your thoughts anymore, my Fallen,*" she said. "*Not while you're in my lair, despite holding the power of the Gods Themselves.*"

"*Finesia,*" I said. "*We've already destroyed three of your most valued lackeys, and now these moments shall be your last.*"

"*Oh, such strong words for such a measly mortal. You speak while you fail to acknowledge what is happening before your very eyes. Because while you've been developing your 'technology', I've also worked out ways to become stronger by harnessing the collective unconscious as a medium.*"

"You do not harness the collective unconscious. You twist and deform it in malevolent ways."

"How ironic that you should say that," Finesia said. *"Because the collective unconscious doesn't just bind minds together, but also matter. And here I've found a way to manipulate matter itself to do my will. Just watch and you'll understand."*

While Finesia was speaking in my mind, I'd been studying the cave mouth, trying to ascertain the best way in. But my eyes turned back in horror to the columns, as I realised what was emerging from them.

They weren't formed of clouds at all, but instead were vertical areas of some kind of coalescing magic that, piece by piece, seemed to be ripping the black dragons apart and rebuilding them again. They didn't look like columns at all anymore either, but instead had fattened out and bulged at the bottom to create massive, jagged shapes.

I'd seen Finesia's form once as a black dragon, and she'd been the largest beast I'd ever witnessed – three times as large as a dragon queen, perhaps more. Her shape had seemed to warp perspective and confuse the mind as to how big things should actually be. But these beasts also seemed to alter my perspective. I guessed it was Finesia's culture of fear playing tricks on my mind. It wanted me to see them as bigger than they actually were.

"What are those things?" Faso said over the speaker system.

None of us managed a reply before the beasts – now a good dozen of them – opened their mouths and let out a series of bone-shattering roars.

Then, they charged.

THE SECOND ROAR from the black dragons shook the earth below us and the scales and armour on my dragon. It was so loud that it seemed to have the power to push me off my dragon's back. My cheeks wobbled and I felt the blood pounding in my head.

They were charging forwards, and our Rocs at the edge of our aerial perimeter rotated slightly to track them. The Mammoths who guarded the same position on the ground turned their heads and the Gatling guns on their flanks whirred into action.

The enemy came swiftly into range, the claws of the black dragons flashing in the dim light, as if they were made of some kind of alien metal. The battlefield devolved into a cacophony of mechanical crashes and screeches. The automatons sputtered out their bullets and the Rocs fired missiles from underneath their wings. The bullets hit their target first, ricocheting off the massive black dragons and doing zero damage.

General Sako's voice came full volume over the speaker system. "Blunders and dragonheats," he said. "I've only just seen the polaroids. What the wellies are those things?"

Faso's reply came at an equal volume. "Don't worry," he said. "The VPTT will finish them off, the arrogant swine."

My heart was filled with trepidation as the missiles exploded short of their targets. But this was how they were meant to work, allowing the micro-missiles created by the first explosion to seek the enemy's vulnerable points.

I saw them moving in slow motion, looking like tiny streaks of light in my augmented vision. They converged on the throats of each of the huge beasts, and I held my breath waiting for a result.

We all must have done, because there was a deep silence in our ranks for a good few seconds. I felt the fear spiking in the collective unconscious within our ranks, and I resumed my dragonsong. It had some effect in soothing our numbers, but I could feel the effect was dwindling, particularly as we watched the black dragons emerge from the cannonade unscathed.

"*Your song is useless here,*" Finesia said once again in my mind. "*As are the vast numbers of soldiers, dragons and automa-*

tons you've brought here today. You've simply made my work easier by bringing your entire army to my front door."

I knew it would do no good to reply. She was trying to distract me from my song, trying to buy the best opportunity she could to wipe us out quickly. But I couldn't lose faith or hope. To my left, Faso was watching the gigantic beasts with wide eyes. Meanwhile, Winda fiddled with the settings on the side of their rear-mounted Gatling turret.

On my right, Talato already had her Pattersoni rifle loaded and cocked, and in the narrowed slits of her eyes I could see her assessing which one to fire upon first. I could just imagine what she was thinking: Was Candiornio one of the black dragons that had now turned into those massive beasts? If so, there was surely no way he could have survived.

The grey dragons that had remained behind us now pushed in front to form a protective wall. Below us, like a whole row of organised ants, the war automatons had formed a second perimeter of their own, allowing the Hummingbirds to retreat behind them. The Mammoths continued to sputter out bullets from their cannons while the Rocs just hovered there doing nothing, as if waiting for their own imminent destruction.

"Gordoni?" General Sako shouted. "Why aren't the Rocs launching their second ordnance?"

"I overrode that feature," Faso said. "It's too close now, it would destroy the Rocs."

"Then scratch that override. We need to throw in everything we've got."

"But–"

"Faso Gordoni, that's an order. And if you break it, there'll be a court martial for sure. That's assuming we survive this, which I thoroughly intend to do."

"But—"

"Do it, or I'll order Winda to relieve you of your command."

Faso looked over his shoulder at his wife. I saw the colour

leaving his face as he turned back to his control panel. "Yes, sir," he said, and he punched in some commands.

Just as the gigantic black dragons were about to bear down upon them, the Rocs released a second slew of missiles. They exploded immediately, and I saw the plates tearing off the Rocs as the fire washed over them. The micro-missiles bore into the throats of the black dragon beasts, but again to no avail.

The sound the claws of the beasts made as they ripped the Rocs' remaining plates from their rivets was like chalk scraping across a blackboard but ten times worse. The Rocs fell towards the secicao forest in pieces, and the black dragon beasts bore down upon the Mammoths next. Their Gatling guns continued to fire, but they had nothing on these massive invincible behemoths. For a moment, I worried that we had no chance of defeating them at all.

I scanned around for a solution, trying to concentrate amidst the racket coming from the perimeter. I could taste bile at the back of my throat, and my heart felt like a snare drum in my chest now. I kept singing my song, but with what was happening, even the power of the Gods Themselves didn't seem like it would work for much longer.

I sighted the cave mouth then, unguarded, and saw an opportunity. It gaped at me, wide and inviting, with a pale green light flickering across its red walls and ceiling. The glow emanated from a layer of concentrated greenish-brown mist outside of it, much thicker than the secicao gas that surrounded us within the maelstrom.

If I was stealthy enough, and fast enough, then Talato and I could get in there together, and drop this bomb right at Finesia's feet. If Faso was right it might destroy her, and of course I was hoping that it would. If not, I also had the power of the Gods Themselves within me, and perhaps I could use it to find a way.

There came a voice in my head, sweet and alluring.

"*Come to me, my child,*" Finesia said. "*I invite you to witness*

Alas, it seemed like I didn't have the element of surprise on my side after all. I pushed Finesia's voice from my mind, because I didn't want to let go of my song just yet, even though I knew I had a better chance to keep her out if I could focus entirely on her mind. Fortunately, I still had enough strength to block her out of my own thoughts.

"Keep them distracted," I said over the speaker system, and I addressed it to everyone who could hear me except Talato – General Sako, Faso, and all the officers in the control room on the train. "It's time for me and Talato to face Finesia, alone."

"Blunders and dragonheats, no!" General Sako said. "We need you here."

"Exactly," Faso said. "I don't know how, but your song is pushing the Gordoni Rays away. I can see it on my readings."

I shook my head, my eyes narrowing, and I focused my will on the cave mouth. I could feel something there, a purer presence in the collective unconscious – one that I'd known so long ago with Gerhaun. The young dragon queen was in there, and she was still alive for now. But within her presence, I could also sense a feeling of increasing danger. She seemed to know that she might not survive for much longer. Once Castlonth died, her innocent life would be forfeit too, and that would mean the eventual extinction of all dragons, whether we survived this or not.

"If I stay here, we will all die," I said. "And Finesia won't let anyone else in but me."

General Sako and Faso continued to mutter their protests, while Winda remained resolutely silent on the dragon automaton's back. I turned to Talato, on the other side of me, who studied my eyes, and I knew she was looking for the telltale green glint – the influence of Finesia – inside of them. After a moment, she gave me a nod of approval and that was enough permission for me.

"Keep them distracted," I said, cutting off Faso's and General Sako's voices. "That's an order. Talato, with me."

Thus, with a heavy heart, and Finesia chiming in inside my head, I pushed on Velos' steering fin to turn him towards the cave mouth. Velos roared out a rebuke, clearly not keen to get so close to the enemy. From my right, Bellroot let out an equally defiant roar.

I added notes to my dragon song to remind him that his and Gerhaun's dragonet was still in there, alive somewhere. I could sense her, breathing. Though I didn't know how long we had left before Finesia decided to murder her. Velos let out a growl, then lowered his head and flew onwards without a second complaint.

It was time to enter the very heart of the enemy that we'd feared for all this time. Together, we two individuals, soldiers loyal to our cause who had both lost lovers to Finesia's regime, flew into the dark and beckoning unknown.

21

I COULD SENSE reptilian eyes focusing on me as I flew through the cave system's corridors, coming from the darkest crevasses that let in no light. The black dragons watched from a distance as Talato and I, on the backs of Velos and Bellroot, navigated through the labyrinth.

I had only my sense of the collective unconscious to guide me. After a while I noticed how the heavy layer of clouds that had concealed the cave floor now seemed to all be flowing away from us. The gas had formed rivers, all stemming from the same source – the will of Finesia herself.

"I see you have brought us a gift," Finesia said. *"What is that thing you carry?"*

Dragonheats, she had noticed the bomb through the eyes of the black dragons. I didn't know what we'd been expecting, really. It had been Faso's idea, and we'd all gone along with it. I didn't turn to look down at the device that dangled between Talato and me, unwilling to draw more attention to it.

"A generator," Finesia said. *"Filled with dragon blood. And, now what has it been modified into, a bomb? Oh, how convenient. You forget that I have one of your own here, who knows your secret plans."*

Hastina. The word came unbidden to my mind, but I didn't even let that thought reach Finesia. Even though in here I knew Finesia had increasing control over us, I managed to continue to keep my thoughts my own. I had stopped singing my song now, knowing that it wouldn't reach outside the wards Finesia had built within these caverns.

"You have finally managed to mask yourself from me," Finesia said. *"Perhaps, in another universe, you could have taken my position as supreme ruler. So what, pray tell, do you wish to do with one of these 'generators' of yours? Do you really think that a bubble of the collective unconscious can protect you here?"*

The corridors turned sharply to the right, and we hit a wall of thicker secicao gas. Velos rocked violently against a wave of turbulence. The stench hit me dead on, making me want to throw up. My eyes watered, and my nose became stuffy. The tunnels darkened.

"Very well, I shall let you bring it to me. It shall be an interesting experiment. But you must realise that you will not have any more power in here – this is my domain!"

As we moved, I continued to scan all around me, looking out for signs of the black dragons. I should have been able to see their green glowing eyes, surely. But I could only sense that they were there, hiding behind the darkness and the cover of the swirling brown mist.

It was then that I noticed that the abilities granted to me by the secicao had worn off. I could no longer see through the darkness, and time wasn't slowing down but rather seemed to be accelerating. Also, the secicao gas was thickening so much that I couldn't see anything in the immediate vicinity.

I tried to take another swig from my flask, but the contents no longer affected my senses at all.

"That won't work anymore, my dear," Finesia said. *"Here I have complete control of secicao no matter how much you've attempted to modify it."*

I continued to ignore her and turned to look for Talato, but she had vanished behind the murk. Even Velos' scales seemed to have merged with the darkness, and I could no longer see the top of his head. My dragon growled from beneath me, his body rumbling as he read my emotions.

"I don't like this, Ma'am," Talato said through the speaker system.

"Just keep straight on and don't let Bellroot waver," I said.

"I can, it's just that I hear a voice in my head, and I've never heard it before. She calls herself a goddess and says that this world will soon be hers. Am I going mad, Ma'am?"

Then came Finesia's voice in my own head again. "*I will soon have dominion over everyone. The final catastrophe is only moments away.*"

Dragonheats, what was she talking about? Then I remembered the song and wondered why I had stopped singing it. There was some reason, I was sure, but I couldn't remember it. Something was taking control of my mind.

But I still had some power of thought, and I remembered the wishes of the Gods Themselves. "*When the time comes, you will know to use this power,*" they had said. And Talato, Velos and Bellroot still needed my encouragement.

I let the notes trickle out of my mouth again, pushing Finesia's voice to the back of my mind. As I sang, I also listened to everything around me. I could hear Talato's breathing against her gas mask, the rhythm slowing. I could hear the beat of the dragons' wings, and the patter of bullets being fired in the distance outside.

It soothed my heart, and I felt Velos' courage return a little too. It pushed away the clouds so I could see clearly again, and my night vision returned enough that I could trace the outlines of the black dragons watching from their perches on ledges scattered all along the walls of the caverns.

It also revealed a massive opening right in front of me that flared bright white in my vision as soon as I noticed it. My eyes soon adjusted to it, enough that I could see the forms beyond the light. I first saw the dragonet, golden but with that same ugly patina that I'd witnessed before on Cralanein. A glowing green barrier of same kind of magic surrounded the young dragon queen in the form of a dome. Within it, the creature seemed almost petrified, not moving a single muscle except to breathe. Clearly the magic was sapping the dragonet's strength, and now I'd pinpointed her location, I could feel her pain even more intensely in the collective unconscious.

A cold shiver ran down my spine. To kill a dragon queen was one thing, but to cause so much pain to such a young creature, who hadn't even had time to learn of her own innocence, was an atrocity beyond imagining.

Gerhaun's dragonet looked tiny and ratty next to the massive black dragon who stood beside her. She wasn't much smaller than Alsie had been. And I recognised her as Hastina, her eyes glowing green, her posture refined, patiently waiting.

She was lingering near an even greater form, as if protecting it. I didn't have to focus for very long to see the glint of light off its huge scales. A black dragon, towering up towards the ceiling of the cavern, taller than any creature I'd ever known, including the beasts that my allies were fighting outside.

This was Finesia, and she was curled up there in her black dragon form, her cold steely eyes watching us approach, her back and neck straight and holding her head high, as if she had no fear in this world.

"*So you've finally arrived,*" she said. "*Welcome to my domain.*"

Then I felt the push of her powerful mind in the collective unconscious. Out of it came a screech that sent my head reeling and charged my nerves with static. It was as if all the symptoms of a migraine had hit at once.

I felt it strike Velos' and Bellroot's minds so hard that it surged through their blood and caused their hearts to stop. Next thing I knew, both dragons were sent spiralling to the cavern floor. Then, all of sudden, their eyes shot back open, a bright glow coming from within.

My connection to them had been lost, as Finesia had found a way to enter their minds.

"Ma'am," Talato screamed over the speaker system. "Bellroot is ... I've lost control."

I turned to her, tried to find her eyes behind the glass of her gas mask. The brown gas was pressing hard against it, making it look all clouded up. The effects of secicao had completely left my system by now, and I could see everything in normal colours, though admittedly my vision had become a little hazy.

I didn't answer her report. Instead, I continued to sing my dragonsong, hoping that it could somehow wake the dragons out of their trance. At first, I thought that Finesia would cause them to dive hard towards the ground, killing us all. But instead, both dragons continued to descend at a slow and level pace as we continued to approach Hastina and Finesia's black dragon forms.

It felt strange not to be able to sense Velos' emotions. Then I remembered Velos' helmet. Faso had created a system to block the Gordoni Rays coming out of his head. I flicked a switch on the control panel in front of me to activate it.

But it didn't work – the green glow remained in Velos' eyes, and he continued on his steady path to the ground, as did Bellroot.

"The dragons can't land with the cannons equipped," Talato said. As she spoke, she drew her rifle and aimed down the sights towards Hastina's throat.

The smaller black dragon didn't seem to have moved, her eyes glowing brightly just like Velos' and Bellroot's. "Don't shoot," I said. "That's Hastina."

"That's—" Talato lowered her rifle. "What do we do now, Ma'am?"

"*Yes,*" said Finesia inside my mind. "*What do you do now?*"

I fathomed that we were still a good thirty metres or so above the ground, though it was difficult to judge distance through the thick pungent gases below. It was a bit like gazing into a murky pool of water.

My gaze snapped onto the big red button that Faso had placed there. It had a glass case over it, which I flipped open, then I punched down on it with both my palms.

The chain dangling from Velos creaked and jerked abruptly upwards as it released its load. It came flying towards me, and I ducked away so that it didn't knock me unconscious.

Then the generator was falling. It hit the ground with a thud. There came a roaring explosion, not of heat but rather of sound as the plates of the generator split apart. Silver dragon blood spilled out everywhere. Some of it splashed over Finesia. A speck of it went sailing towards Hastina, and a glob of it landed on Velos' nose. In front of me, the colossal black dragon that was Finesia flinched. I felt a quiver in the collective unconscious, but that was the only effect it seemed to have had on the empress. Soon the rest of the dragon blood was swallowed up by the murk.

"*Is that the worst you've got? Dragon queen blood?*" Finesia said in my head.

"*No,*" I replied in the collective unconscious. Then I spoke softly to Talato, knowing that she would be able to hear everything much louder over her speaker system. "Fire the cannon."

"But Ma'am, we're too close to the ground. It might kill us."

"It's our only chance," I said. "Put everything you have into it."

"Yes, Ma'am," Talato said.

I also did exactly what I'd ordered her to do. I flicked some more switches on the control panel and then turned a dial to fire up the gauss technology inside the massive cylindrical chamber beneath Velos' underbelly. Faso had improved the technology since I'd first used this thing, and it powered up much more rapidly this time.

The tanks on the sides of Velos' armour were now filled up with the safer variety of secicao. It seemed he wouldn't be needing it anymore, so I turned another dial to redirect it into the chamber. The mechanism resisted being turned, and the tanks hissed and growled on both sides as I ramped up the pressure. But still I managed to dial it up to the max.

A green light on the dashboard told me that the cannon was ready to fire, and so I pulled back on a throttle that served as the trigger. A massive beam of white light came from beneath Velos, heading just slightly to the right of Finesia. I had no control of Velos, but maybe it was enough.

I unbuckled myself from my seat harness so I could lean over to the side, secicao gas whipping at my hair and the heat from the beam searing my skin. There came a second loud whining sound from Bellroot's cannon, and the stench of ozone grew thick in the air.

I pulled myself back up and saw that the beam was now hitting Finesia in the chest, but she just sat there, basking in it as if it were warm sunlight. Bellroot's beam pushed straight towards Hastina, who shrieked, spread her wings, and then lifted into the sky, barely dodging it.

All of a sudden, Velos' armour bucked, and then the beam cut off. All it had left on the dark plates on Finesia's chest was some smoke and a slight green glow. Bellroot's beam cut off soon after, and Hastina levelled out her wings and glided back to her former location.

"That's the last of your technology, it seems," Finesia said. *"Now it's time for you to experience the magic that will govern the future in its purest form. But first, an event to mark the occasion – the last of the dragon queens."*

She turned to Hastina, and for the first time I heard her speak out loud. She wanted Talato to hear this too. Unlike in the collective unconscious, her voice was loud and gravelly, with the texture of rocks colliding.

"Acolyte Wiggea, I hope you are prepared for this. Because when it happens, it'll finally be time to sacrifice the young dragon queen."

"No!" I cried out. "Hastina, remember who you are!"

At the same time, the tiny golden dragonet seemed to realise the danger and I saw the panic in her yellow eyes. She opened her mouth to let out a chirp. But whatever green magical barrier surrounded her, it permitted no sound to escape.

Talato once again had her Pattersoni rifle readied and aimed, but I could see beneath the glass of her mask now and her gaze was wavering. "Ma'am," she said. "It's too strong. What is this?"

I could feel it too. My muscles were numb, as if someone had just injected me with a strong dose of general anaesthetic. My eyelids felt heavy, and I could feel a sense of something like gravity upon my shoulders pushing me towards the ground.

"It's the power of belief," Finesia continued to say out loud, her voice booming through the cavern. "My fallen acolyte whom you call Dragonseer Wells did so well in convincing you that you had power over your own faith in yourselves. But ultimately, life has always been fated for death, and none of you believe that you'll survive forever. It just isn't logical."

"I can't ... keep ... awake," Talato said, and in my peripheral vision I saw her slump on Bellroot's back, the seat and harness of the citrine dragon's armour fortunately keeping her safe.

"What a shame," Finesia said. "She's going to miss the main event."

I opened my mouth to say something, but the muscles in my throat had weakened so much now that I couldn't form words. Beneath me I heard a loud metallic crunching sound, and another one came from my side. It took all my strength to turn my head towards Bellroot, as I saw the cannon crumpling under the dragon's weight.

"*Now it's time,*" Finesia said in the collective unconscious, *"for you to witness the death of the dragon queens. Finally, I shall have enough strength to defeat their once loyal protector, Honore."*

I didn't even have time to wonder what she was talking about, because it came suddenly, a shockwave that pulsed through the astral world. It reached out to every single lifeform of the planet, not as a plea for help, but instead a call denoting that it was time for the world to change.

A rift opened in the collective unconscious, and it remained for a long moment as the realisation washed over me. Castlonth's death had come early, and now it was all about to end. Velos crumpled onto the ground, and I looked down in horror as the branches of the secicao plants reached out to anchor him place.

I could do nothing to save him. I could do nothing to save any of them. Instead, I closed my eyes, and entered the darkness' embrace.

<h1 style="text-align:center">22</h1>

"*Isn't it beautiful?*" Finesia said in the collective unconscious. I couldn't see her behind my tightly-shut eyelids, but I still imagined her there, her colossal and terrifying form glaring down at me with her green glowing eyes. The cruellest creature to have ever set foot on this planet. The destroyer of us all.

"*Everything has come full circle.*" she said. "*The world, once governed by immortals, until the Gods Themselves took it away. Now, rule returns to the immortals and it is mine to govern as I please.*"

I could feel nothing but the slowing rhythm of my own heart, my shallowly coursing breath. Branches of secicao rubbed against my elbow and tangled around my waist as they grew upwards. They extended their thorns, which pierced into my skin in thousands of places. Through them they started to leech the lifeforce out of me.

I felt my spirit being sapped away, my hope for the future of humanity and dragonkind. All that was left was an empty space. A place devoid of anything except for my desire to end this as soon as possible.

"*A time for a new era,*" Finesia continued. "*You killed my best agents, Pontopa Wells, and I've been considering how best to repay you."*

The secicao branches continued to creep around me at an alarming pace. They soon covered my chest, and then wrapped around my throat. There, they tightened enough that I could feel the pressure on my most vulnerable point. All Finesia had to do now was will the secicao to squeeze hard enough, and she'd end me within seconds.

At that precise moment, I wanted her to do so. I had nothing left in me. But Finesia hadn't finished with her cruelty yet.

"Honore," Finesia continued, *"I can feel you nearby, waiting. Why don't you come out and face me now? You might as well get our battle over sooner rather than later."*

The secicao continued to grow up my neck, and then the vines duly tangled around my face. They flowed through my hair and tightened around my temples. Soon, I could feel that every centimetre of me, from head to toe, was covered. If I hadn't still had the gift of immortality, I wouldn't have been able to breathe.

"Now open your eyes," Finesia commanded. *"And witness as your loyal ally destroys that which you've fought so hard to protect."*

It hadn't been necessary to command me to do so, as the secicao around my eyes forced the lids open. Light flooded into my vision, green and sickening.

First, I saw Finesia, but she was no longer in her black dragon form. Rather she looked more like the God Dragon that I'd ridden above the Cini-Sanito river. Her black scales had gained a bright green glow and an eerie light pulsed through the gaps between them, and her shape was constantly shifting.

She wasn't just an immortal anymore. She had truly taken on the substance of a god.

"Now, Acolyte Wiggea," Finesia said. *"End it!"*

My gaze shot over to the black dragon that had once been Dragonseer Hastina, as I watched her slowly turn her head towards the young dragonet.

I wanted to try to tell her again that she didn't have to do this. I wanted to remind her of who she was. But I couldn't even find her in the collective unconscious. The chemicals that the secicao thorns were pumping through my veins had rendered me immobilised in both body and mind. I was more helpless than I'd ever been.

A wicked grin stretched across Hastina's glistening reptilian lips. I had to remind myself that they weren't Hastina's lips anymore; they belonged to Finesia now. We all did.

The green glowing dome vanished from around the young dragon queen. The dragonet looked up in surprise, but Hastina was already there, towering over her. One of the black dragon's forelegs was raised, and her long, sharp claws glinted despite the reedy light.

Hastina stopped there in that position, Finesia holding it to cause maximum torment in us. I had expected the young dragon queen to try to flee. To do anything, even if utterly futile, in an attempt to escape her inevitable fate. But instead, she folded her hind legs underneath her and sat down in a meditative stance.

Then, her golden eyes focused on me, and I read within them a plea for help. I felt it in the collective unconscious too.

Yet there was nothing I could do …

The secicao tightened even more around my throat. Finesia applied enough pressure so that I knew, once Hastina had ended the dragonet's life, the goddess would end mine.

… Until there came a shimmer in the collective unconscious …

… Like the most brilliant diamond being forced to the surface of a volcanic spring …

Black Dragon Hastina's claws shivered, and I could see the moment coming when she would bring them down in a graceful arc. More chemicals were emitted by the secicao, and I felt something else coursing through my body. The drug that I'd always taken to slow time, except now I was taking it in its most primal form.

... And there was something waiting for me underneath the surface ...

... It had been waiting here for an awfully long time ...

"*What's the matter?*" Finesia said in my mind. "*Do you want to sing your dragon song? Instil courage in your allies and give them hope that they can beat their destinies? There is no hope for you, my Fallen, there never has been. All that ultimately awaits each one of you is your untimely end.*"

... Calling for me ...

... Waiting for the ultimate moment ...

... Steam rising from the dragon queen's blood ...

... Melding with the secicao on the ground ...

... A chemical cocktail that would change everything ...

... Within it, truth; within that truth, magic ...

Hastina's claws started their graceful descent. The secicao tightened even more around my throat. My muscles felt nothing but numbness; my lungs couldn't move. My heart had virtually ground to stop. There was no hope. Nothing I could do.

... And yet ...

... The parting words of the Gods Themselves came unbidden to my mind ...

... "*We leave this world in pure contentment, as we know that we've created something beautiful. When the time comes, you will know to make use of this power.*" ...

... It was not too late.

Time was evolving in an ever-slowing motion. Hastina's claws had almost reached the dragonet; she had almost killed her, extinguishing the future of dragonkind.

Now I knew what I had to do.

Because in my heart of hearts, I had contained the final gift of the Gods Themselves. They hadn't just taught me a dragon-song. I'd sang them many times during my childhood, throughout my adolescence, up until the present day without really knowing I'd been singing it.

Now the dragon queen blood that was spilled over the

ground was stirring. And now was the time to call upon all their spirits. My lips were covered by the terrible blight that Finesia had created.

But she could never cover up the ultimate lesson that Sukina and Gerhaun and many of my other mentors had tried to teach me, all this time.

And so I did what I had to do.

SINCE THE BEGINNING OF TIME, the collective unconscious had been recording the mental impressions of everything that moved. Every single emotion any lifeform had ever experienced – even an immortal – was contained within its essence. And within that essence itself lay an everlasting void.

The only thing that mattered was my connection to that void. Because it connected me to everything in existence. In realising that, I learned to let go.

In that moment, I shed the skin that was my birthname, Pontopa Wells. I shed every single identity that I'd been marked with throughout my life – child, renegade, entrepreneur, dragonseer, Acolyte, Fallen, traitor, saviour. All of these were just masks that I'd worn to serve a purpose, but what really mattered was deep within.

The song that I'd learned from the Gods Themselves flooded into my mind and dominated every inch of my consciousness. It seeped into my subconscious and then my unconscious beneath that, and as it grew, it spread its tendrils into the collective unconscious. I didn't need a voice to sing with it, because at the end of the day we were all connected. We were all one.

First, I found Velos and Bellroot, trapped within their own minds as Finesia continued to suppress their souls. In that brief instant that defied time, I showed them the way to push past her. Then I found Talato and helped her push Finesia out of her own mind. I could see how exhausted the lieutenant was, and so I let her continue to sleep for now.

Hastina's claws must have been millimetres from the young dragon queen by the time I reached the other dragonseer's mind. Inside it, I found more fear than I'd ever experienced within my own consciousness. For generations, she had built up walls to protect herself from Finesia. They hadn't been enough.

When I offered Hastina a way out, she accepted it gracefully. And for the first time she let me guide her to where she needed to go. After escaping her mental prison, she immediately clenched the muscles of her foreleg and retracted her claws so that she didn't even touch the young dragonet.

My mission wasn't over, however, because there were other black dragons to free. They were watching from the walls of the cavern, and at first I sensed their mal intent. But I didn't let that faze me.

Instead, I touched their minds and opened the doors that had locked away their memories. They had all lost their identities to the goddess, but that didn't mean they couldn't reclaim them.

It took a simple twist of my consciousness – it was easy once I had worked out how. But in doing so, I needed to stare death in the face one last time and understand its place also as a part of the fabric of time and space.

Within seconds, I had released the black dragons from Finesia's thrall, and the goddess had only just begun to realise what was going on.

"*No, you shan't,*" she said in the collective unconscious.

The secicao tightened so suddenly around my throat that it felt like steel wire cutting through it. But I had already read Finesia, and I didn't let the sensation last.

I wove the song through the collective unconscious to work on the secicao itself, because that too had been born of the immaterial fabric that connected us all.

It was enough to loosen the secicao around my throat before it could kill me. Slowly, it started to peel away, and I also loosened the secicao from around my mouth so I could sing through it. Inch by inch, sensation returned to my body, and every part of it became a part of the song.

I directed it then at my ultimate target – the soul of the world itself.

The black dragons that I'd released from Finesia's clutches had now flown out and were hovering before her. There were hundreds of them, and though I couldn't see many of their eyes, I could see in the stiffness of their backs and feel in the collective unconscious their desire to destroy the goddess.

Finesia let out a wicked laugh that shook the walls of the cavern. She was still glowing bright green like Honore, her incandescent form illuminating the walls with a sickly light. This time she spoke out loud.

"None of you can kill me. I've become too strong, and if you betray me now then I will rule this world without you. Even if I have to do it alone for a while, I'll work out how to create creatures of my own."

She was absolutely right, of course, and so I added some notes to my song to direct them to fly outside. There, my allies could probably do with some help, and Finesia hadn't yet faced what she'd willed upon herself. Bellroot joined the black dragons, after I'd freed him from the clutches of the secicao, carrying the still-sleeping Talato to safety.

Only I, Finesia, Velos, Hastina and the young dragon queen remained. But Hastina also knew her place, and she moved her wing to shelter Gerhaun's dragonet. She knew very well what was coming next.

"What is this?" Finesia said out loud. "You can't possibly hope to face me alone."

I didn't answer her, still completely focused on my song. But I now directed it at the ground where the dragon blood from the generator was reacting with the secicao. A silver-coloured smoke had started to rise from it, and out from it the figure whom Finesia had previously summoned had begun to form.

The smoke melded and merged, forming the shapes of the dragons of old, and some who hadn't yet even been formed. It depicted the past, present and future. Dragons as I had always known them had forever been part of our world, and the will of an errant goddess – an imposter – wasn't going to change that.

And so out of the ground came Honore, in his full splendour. He looked like a giant snake emerging from a misty lake, shrouded in a silver cape of gas as he revealed his form. Soon, there was a good hundred feet of mystical dragon serpent hovering in the air before me, his entire body curled into a spiral towards the ground below.

Finesia's form also twisted, her body wreathed in black smoke. She unfurled into an equally impressive form. The difference was that Honore's scales had a tint of silver to them, almost losing their original greenness. Finesia's, on the other hand, edged towards that oily opalescence that I'd seen on the black dragons so many times.

It was she who spoke first in the collective unconscious.

"*You cannot survive this, Honore,*" she said.

"*I don't intend to,*" the ancient king of the immortal dragons replied. It was the first time I'd heard his voice, and it had a soft lilt to it – harmonious, like the dragonsongs.

"*Then you admit defeat? You will sacrifice yourself?*"

"*Both of our existences need to be forfeit,*" Honore replied. "*The time of the immortals is over. It is time for us to step aside to make room for this world's new residents.*"

"*Never!*"

Finesia accompanied her rebuke with that same scream she'd let out before, that had paralysed all of us. Yet somehow it didn't seem to have the power now that it once had.

"*You have no choice,*" Honore said.

"*But this world is mine. It was I who drank of the sap of the Tree Immortal. It was I who claimed destiny and this world as my own.*"

"*And yet you have forgotten who you are.*"

There came another scream from Finesia in the collective unconscious and she charged straight at Honore. Her face seemed to warp into a thousand dragons at once, and then all I saw was the most fearsome gaping jaw I'd ever beheld – sharp teeth, and dripping ichor, and green flames of rage boiling at the back of her throat.

Honore's reaction was far more graceful. The God Dragon turned to face his nemesis, then he opened his mouth equally wide. The features of his face twisted into so many of the dragon queens that I'd known throughout history. I saw Gerhaun, and Bassalhan, Castlonth, Yol, Tarinah, and the other dragon queens who had died. And many other dragons' faces that I'd seen on the tapestries of Fortress Gerhaun. There were other dragons that I'd seen in my dreams, and then I saw human faces as well. There was Wiggea, and Sukina, and Francoiso, and Charth, and others who had shared my life's journey.

In his absence, it seemed Honore had been undergoing a metamorphosis. He'd evolved from a dragon to an embodiment of everything that lived upon this planet. It seemed that he had absorbed the fabric of the collective unconscious and now was directing all its power towards his target – Finesia.

All this had happened in a split second, but it seemed like a million moments. But then the two dragon gods collided, and the cavern filled with bright white light. I caught the stench of secicao burning first, then a strong tang of ozone. Heat seared my face, and my vision blurred.

Soon enough, the secicao that had been wrapped around me crumbled to ash and a sensation of calm washed over me. This was followed by a feeling of being more alive than I'd experienced since childhood.

The light faded, leaving only a thin and almost transparent mist where the two colossal dragons had collided. Just as Honore had promised, the age of immortals had ended, and Finesia was no more.

HASTINA HAD LOST her black dragon form, and instead stood before me fully clothed and grasping her characteristic spear in one hand. She stared at me warily, and then her legs bowed, and her eyes closed as she collapsed, only to be caught by the carpet of secicao below.

There was no brown gas being produced by the plant anymore, and as I surveyed the scene before me, I noticed that it had also lost its thorns. Instead, it looked like a field of pre-flowered heather stretching out before me, lit only by a green glow that seemed to pervade the cavern walls.

I felt the presence of Gerhaun's dragonet in the collective unconscious even before I turned my head to regard her. In response, the little dragon queen chirped out a greeting of recognition and waddled over. She hadn't yet learned to speak my language, which was why we had never given her a name.

Traditionally dragon queens chose their own names. She would grow up in a strange and lonely world, the only female dragon left – at least for a while.

The dragon queen stopped at Velos' snout to regard him, and I could tell she knew that she was looking at her father. Velos was still asleep, but also safe. I could feel his slumbering presence in the collective unconscious. The dragonet nodded her approval, then jumped up onto his snout and climbed towards me, stopping just in front of the control panel on the armour.

She leaned forward slightly, inviting me to touch her snout. When I did, a wave of reassurance surged over me, because I now knew that everything was going to be all right.

I STAYED IN PLACE, meditating on what had happened for about half an hour, my eyes open so that I could watch the changes within the chamber. Gerhaun's dragonet, who still sat on Velos' neck, joined me in my contemplation, and we shared for the first time a type of connection that I'd not experienced since her mother, Gerhaun Forsi, had passed.

I could no longer hear the battle outside the cavern walls, and I had no idea how many, if any, of my allies had survived. But for now, that information was inconsequential.

I could smell the secicao still, but just like the oil that our scientists had modified to make it safe, it had lost its sickly quality. The plant still grew across the cavern floor, but it had changed somehow. I could feel it where it touched the collective unconscious, and it no longer seemed to be trying to modify it. Rather, it had become as natural as any other flora on this planet's surface, content to thrive among the other things.

I only needed to wait for Hastina and Velos to awaken, so the four of us could exit these caverns together, leaving them as a monument for the historians. Time flowed as I listened to the changing sounds within the cave structures.

There had first been a scratching sound against the walls,

while the secicao seemed to be undergoing a metamorphosis. But that had soon passed, to reveal a silence so deep that I could hear Hastina's breathing from the other end of the cavern. And all this time, the dragonet remained opposite me.

Velos awoke first, and he did so with a growl. His head shot up as if he'd emerged from a nightmare, almost knocking the young dragon queen from his neck. But then he seemed to sense his daughter dragonet there and relaxed a little.

Velos slowly turned his head to scan the chamber, and I could feel the anxiety ebb within him as he did so. He gave off another growl, but this was more one of satisfaction. Following that, Hastina awoke.

She jerked upright, clearly as alarmed by her dreams as Velos had been. But when her gaze snapped onto me where I sat on Velos' back, her expression softened. She looked around her, plunged the end of her spear into the ground with a mighty thrust, and laughed.

After a moment, she seemed to remember herself. She looked up at me.

"I know what happened," she said. "Finesia took control. But somehow, you pushed her out. And now – is it true? Have you really beaten her?"

I shook my head. "Not me. We all finally remembered who we were, and then Honore struck the final blow."

"The God Dragon?"

"He too is no more."

Hastina lowered her head. "I'm so sorry," she said. "For everything I did."

I shrugged. "Well, I guess we're finally even."

Hastina grinned from one side of her face. "So that doesn't mean I owe you a drink?"

"I'll think about it," I said. "Meanwhile, hop on. Velos can carry us out of here."

She took her spear off the ground, and stumbled forwards. Walking seemed hard for her, but then she had just had her powers stripped away. As she stumbled forwards, I put my hand to my chest and felt my beating heart. I listened to the rhythm of it for what seemed like a long moment, and I noticed the differences in the slight palpitations.

Once again, I could tell that I was mortal. No longer would I live forever on this planet until something landed a well-aimed blow at my throat. Everything was once again as it was meant to be.

WE EMERGED from the cave system that Finesia had previously been using as a base into fresh air that tasted better than any I'd breathed for a long, long time. We cradled the young dragon queen in the central seat of the armour, and Hastina sat at the back. A quick glance over my shoulder confirmed she was once again sleeping. Honestly, I also felt exhausted, but I wouldn't have missed this moment for the world.

The soldiers and the greys hadn't left us yet, but they were no longer in combat. The maelstrom had dissipated, the cloudless sky had a rich blue hue, and for the first time I saw the roots and branches of secicao offset against it. Without the toxic gas shrouding them, they didn't look too different from bare rhododendrons, stretching out as far as the eye could see.

However, they no longer adorned the caves' vicinity, because the soldiers had taken hold of machetes and were lined up in a long row. General Sako stood behind them all, and he bawled out commands at the top of his voice, telling them when to cut and when to lift the blades.

The greys hovered above them, in a loose circle. I could sense in the collective unconscious that they were also ready to scorch the secicao once the soldiers had cut it to shreds.

It was all part of a ritual, I realised. Not particularly necessary, but it was symbolic. Many times I had heard people discussing plans for how to restore balance to the world. After the secicao had been cleared, lime would be added to the soil to reduce its acidity. Then seeds would be planted so that nature could thrive once again.

Alas, all our automatons had been ripped to shreds by the enemy, because the Mammoth automatons would have been mighty useful in this task. They had, after all, initially been designed to harvest the secicao in its native home in the Southlands, long before it had spread to the other continents.

Now we only seemed to have one automaton present in our number. This was the dragon automaton that hovered above the men as they toiled. Both Winda and Faso had their seats reclined on the armour, but while Winda seemed to be sleeping, Faso was watching the spectacle below with his arms and legs crossed as if he were glad not to have to join in the toil.

Faso, in fact, was the first to notice us emerging from the cave mouth.

He turned his head towards me, did a double take, then I heard his voice over the speaker system, "Blunders and dragonheats, Pontopa. You made it!"

"Isn't 'blunders and dragonheats' General Sako's line?" I asked.

"Not anymore," he said. "I asked, and he said that if we survived this battle then I have permission to use it. And guess what? We did."

"That we did," I replied.

"Yes, but we weren't too sure about you. Why didn't you send news over the speaker system? The good old general was considering sending in a search party."

"So why didn't you?" I asked.

"Well, we just got busy," Faso swept his arm outwards to indicate the troops cutting the secicao below.

"It doesn't matter," I said. "Anyway, do you mind telling me what happened out here?"

I could see Faso's smirk clearly on his face despite being yards away. This was exactly what he'd been wanting to do all along.

"You know," he said, "those massive black dragon beasts never actually got past the automatons in the end. All of a sudden, there was that black gas again, and those behemoths split into the thousands of black dragons that had formed them. They fluttered to the ground like feathers, I tell you. Then there were more plumes of black smoke, and normal humans emerged from the dragon bodies, fully formed and fully clothed. I saw some tribespeople we met beneath the Pinnatu Crater, I saw some of those slaves we encountered at the factory, and I could swear even some of the people I knew when I used to work for Cini at Slaro Palace. I've never seen anything like it."

"And I hope you will never have to again," I said. "So what happened to those people?"

"They went back to the train," Faso said. "We're planning to depart for Slaro soon, and then I guess they'll become the Regent Valpeonia's problem."

"Don't you mean Taka's problem?" I asked with a chuckle.

"Yes," Faso said. "I guess it will be Taka's problem, won't it?"

I let him have a moment for that to sink in. Afterwards, I asked, "By the way, do you know where Lieutenant Talato is? I want to have a word with her."

"She headed back to the train with the refugees," Faso said. "But if I were you, I wouldn't disturb her. It might not be all that pleasant for her."

But I didn't even ask Faso what he meant before I pushed down on Velos' steering fin and directed him towards the train. It wasn't just because I wanted to speak to Talato – I needed to get Hastina and the young dragon queen back so they could have some rest. Plus, I really felt like a hot shower myself.

"Wait, before you go," Faso asked, "did my bomb idea work?"

"Kind of," I said, and I left him alone to ponder what that might mean.

It took a good half hour to reach the train. Admittedly, Velos took his time getting there, beating his wings softly in slow motion as he deeply inhaled the air. He was enjoying flying for what it was again, and admittedly I was enjoying it too.

I could taste the freshness in the cool air, and it didn't matter that my stomach was grumbling over how I hadn't eaten for hours. I just wanted to stay up in the sky and savour the moment forever.

I spent the journey over there contemplating the events that had transpired since Sukina had first come to recruit me from the Five Hamlets. She'd told me I was a dragonseer and at the time I'd had no idea what that even meant. I certainly hadn't expected that it would ultimately lead to the battle I'd just faced, in the caverns that I now planned to leave far behind me.

I saw the train from miles away, now completely uncovered from the secicao clouds. The shiny plates that armoured it reflected the sun in rainbow-coloured patterns. Once I'd have thought such a thing to be a mechanical monstrosity. Now, against such a backdrop even it looked beautiful. It was amazing how, within less than an hour, much of my perspective of the world had changed.

I found Talato standing outside the fourth compartment from the engine carriage, facing away from me. My instinct was to go down and greet her; she deserved a commendation for her former courage and she would be first in line for my medal recommendations.

But then I saw that she had someone in her arms, and they were embracing passionately. It didn't take me long to recognise the object of her affection with his round and ruddy face, still wearing his officer's uniform.

"Blunders and dragonheats," I said – because if Faso had permission to use the phrase, then I would damn well claim it too. "It's Candiornio."

I didn't say it to anyone in particular, and only Velos seemed to have heard. He roared out in approval, and both Candiornio and Talato broke their embrace and peered up at us.

I gave them both a salute and I didn't even look to see if they'd acknowledged us before I careened Velos towards our dragon carrier coach. Faso had suggested, though I hadn't quite understood it, that Talato deserved her privacy. She could have my commendation when she was ready for it, but for now, she needed to some time with her old flame.

As we came in to land in the carriage, I turned back to look at Velos' two passengers. Both the dragonet and Hastina were fast asleep, strapped into their harnesses. And as my eyes fell on Hastina, I couldn't help but feel a pang of jealousy for Talato.

She had recovered her lost amour, but both Hastina and I had once had feelings for Lieutenant Wiggea, and I was certain that he wasn't coming back.

But at the same time, I knew it wasn't good to dwell on the past when I such had a long future ahead of me. So just as Velos touched down on the metal deck plating of the carriage, I told myself that my future would be worthwhile. And I shared my promise with everyone in the vicinity, by singing the dragonsong of hope that I'd learned from the Gods Themselves.

I THINK PRETTY MUCH every soul on the train slept during the majority of the journey back from Ginlast to Slaro Station. I certainly spent most of my time in the cabin that General Sako had afforded me. After a quick bar of packed cereal and dried fruit to raise my blood sugars a little – medic's orders – I retired directly there.

For a while, I tried gazing out the window, amazed at how diverse the landscape looked now I could see it without the secicao clouds. Secicao still covered every single square inch of land, but it couldn't mask the contours of the rolling hills and the varying gradients of colours in the sky.

But soon enough my brain dragged my eyelids shut, and so I lay down and slept until I heard the shriek of the train whistle as we pulled into the capital city.

There was music outside, and a loud fanfare coming from a brass band playing nearby. I propped myself up in bed and peered out of the window to see a parade of men and women dressed in suits of dragons of all kinds of different colours. The main spectacle was one long green dragon, with glowing candles arrayed along its length. Serpent-like, with long but flat teeth made of felt, this was meant to be the incarnation of Honore. News had travelled by Hummingbird already that it was he who had fought Finesia and sacrificed himself to save us all.

Grey dragons followed the parade from above, except for the first time I realised they weren't actually grey. Rather, slight variations of colour had returned to their scales. I saw green, and yellow, and indigo, and blue, and perhaps a thousand different shades of brown.

I later learned from Faso that this was due to the secicao that had been cleansed using the dragon queen blood. Now that the greys had started feeding on it, their colours had begun to return. We would always need secicao to keep the dragons alive, and there was hope that the new strain of the plant would eventually cause fertility to return to the greys.

Over time, Gerhaun and Velos' dragonet would birth many other dragons of all kinds of different colours, not to mention enough golden dragon queens to help repopulate the dragon population. The world would eventually return to the state written of in stories of old.

I was one of the last to leave the train, it seemed. Everyone seemed happy to put this journey behind them. As the parade left us behind, I stumbled out the train door and onto a platform of thousands of soldiers reuniting with the men, women and children they'd left behind.

I didn't need to walk far to find my parents, waiting for me on the platform. I ran to them, and my mother first embraced me in a hug.

"Pontopa," she said. "Please tell me this is the last time we almost think we've lost you."

I shuddered into her shoulder. Tears came unbidden to my eyes, but these were joyful ones, because it was finally over.

"This is it, Mamo," I said. "No more adventures."

"Oh, something tells me that isn't true," my father said from nearby. "There'll soon be something else that puts you up on Velos' back and flying across the world."

I looked up and him and laughed, wiping my eyes.

"Fine," I said. "Let's just say no more adventures that involve Finesia. This world is about to change for the better."

"You can say that again," Papo said. "I read all about it in the—"

"*Tow Observer*," Mamo and I said together, cutting him off.

Papo dropped his jaw in mock surprise. "How the wellies did you know?"

Again, the three of us shared a laugh, and then both Mamo and Papo looked up, their gazes going distant. Their eyes had turned towards Valpeonia, my biological mother, who was approaching, the tail of her black cloak trailing behind her.

"I think congratulations are in order," she said. "The country is proud of what you've achieved, Dragonseer Wells."

There we were, back to her way of speaking. Not 'I am proud', but the country is proud. Some things would never change.

"It wasn't just me," I said. "We all did it together."

"So I've heard," Valpeonia said. "Now come."

She led me over to where the young dragon queen sat looking around at all the people surrounding her. Her golden eyes were wide with astonishment. This was clearly the first time she'd seen a crowd quite like this.

Hastina, Taka, Faso and Winda were all nearby. So too was Ratter, Faso's ferret automaton, who scurried around the young dragonet, examining her using a red-light scope attached to its head.

Faso must have noticed my expression of concern. He wielded that scanning device with a screen that I'd seen him using quite a few times.

"Don't worry," he said. "Ratter's just been scanning the whole place for Gordoni Rays. It's remarkable – he hasn't found anything at all."

"I guess they came from Finesia," I said, "so maybe we need to rename them."

Faso glanced at Winda, who smiled back at him meekly. "Oh no," he said. "They were still my discovery. I'm not surrendering that to anyone, particularly an extinct phenomenon."

"That's all you think Finesia was?" I asked with a raised eyebrow. "A phenomenon?"

"Well—" Faso tugged at his collar, "—there are other explanations."

He looked as though he didn't want to continue this conversation, and was saved by Taka stepping forward. The young king wore a newly fitted crown – of gold lace and encrusted with diamonds, with rich red silks and velvets adorning the rest of his attire.

"Thank you for your service, Dragonseer Wells. The crown commends what you have done for the empire, and we will be eternally grateful."

I couldn't help but laugh. Clearly, he'd been taking lessons from Valpeonia.

"You can call me Auntie Pontopa," I said. "Just like you can call your father Papo sometimes."

Taka lowered his head, and then in his eyes I saw a hint of the boy I'd helped bring up in them. "I'm so glad you're back, Auntie. And there's so much to share with you."

"Just give me the lowdown," I said. "What happened while I was away?"

"Well—" Taka looked to Valpeonia, who gave him a nod,

"—I came to a decision just yesterday. A new law that we'll pass within the next week."

"And what's that?" I asked.

Taka reached down and petted the young dragon queen on the snout. "Regent Valpeonia will remain regent. Not of me, but of the dragonet until she reaches ruling age. Once she does, both she and I will become joint rulers of the kingdom. We are about to enter a new age, just like the age of legends, where both humans and dragons will govern the world together."

It seemed as if the young dragonet understood what Taka was saying, because as soon as he'd finished speaking, she opened her mouth and out of it came her very first roar of approval.

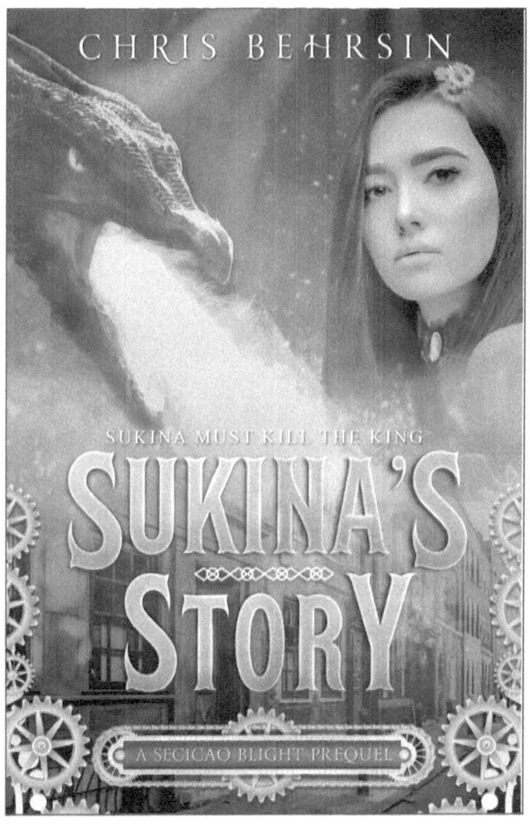

The Sukina's Story novel tells the story of how Sukina came to be a dragonseer, which you can download by signing up to my email list.

I send emails approximately twice a month. You can subscribe at chrisbehrsin.com/sukina/.

ACKNOWLEDGMENTS

THANK YOU to the usual team, including Tarryn Thomas for editing and proofreading, my family, particularly my parents for their continuing support and my dear wife Ola for reading early drafts and providing valuable input.

Also, thank you as always to my ARC team. I really appreciate all the work that you put in helping to promote my novels.

Finally, thank you to every single reader – I appreciate everything that you do to support authors and the world of literature at large.